Carolina Wolf

By Sela Carsen

All it takes is a spark of Grrrrrl power to set the swamp on fire!

Librarian Debra Henry is boring. And she's okay with that. Really. It's not as if the teensy amount of witchcraft that flows in her veins is worth getting excited about. Yet someone—or something—thinks it's worth crawling out of the swamps to attack her. Those "somethings" are werewolves.

When one of them is hurt saving her, the least she can do is take him home and patch him up. Healing him stirs more than her senses. Maddox Moreau awakens the magic that sleeps in her blood. And suddenly, life's not quite so boring.

A wildlife manager at Congaree National Forest by day, Maddox likes being the BWIS—Big Wolf In the Swamp. By night, he lets his wild side out to play lone wolf. At least until he meets the one woman who can share his soul. Perhaps it's best, though, if he holds off on sharing his preference for raw meat.

Rescuing her seals his fate—but only if he can protect her from a rogue of his kind. A werewolf with a nasty stalker streak...

Warning: This story contains hunky werewolves, librarian fetishes, Southern humor, smart-ass women and men who think that's sexy, magic, medieval legends, disco music and flatulent Boxers. (The dogs, not the underwear.)

ParaMatch.com
By MK Mancos

She can match anyone. Except the man she can't resist.

Dating in today's world is tough enough. Pair it with a paranormalady, and Lucille Wainwright is living the recipe for loneliness. Born a talentless witch in a family of legendary spellcasters, she's managed to carve a niche for herself with ParaMatch.com, a matchmaking service for paranormal beings.

What she lacks in the magic department, she more than makes up for with her uncanny ability to conjure committed relationships out of any combination of traits and backgrounds. Until now.

Enter Jager Cronus, deposed king of the Titans and successful paratrader. As a client, he's a nightmare. As a man, he's irresistible. When he demands a date with her to the annual Legion Halloween Dance, she's hard pressed to refuse. With her professional ethics warring with a deep need to prove herself, she gives him two more chances to find love.

That's all the opening Jager needs. After all, he didn't survive his downfall without learning a few things about prevailing in the face of the stiffest negotiations.

Now he's about to negotiate the deal of a lifetime—a future with Lucilla.

Warning: Contains inter-species romance, love potions, fallen Greek Gods, super-morphing wizards, and a male strip-tease.

The Ghost Shrink, the Accidental Gigolo & the Poltergeist Accountant

By Vivi Andrews

It's not smart to piss off a poltergeist...

It's bad enough to be sexually frustrated. But as a medium, it means until Lucy Cartwright gets some, she's doomed. Oh no, not to death. Worse. To nightly visitations by recently deceased, wanna-be Cassanovas without the bodies to back it up. Then a living, breathing fantasy arrives on her doorstep, and Lucy thinks her dry spell is at an end.

Much as he would like to be Lucy's personal gigolo, PI Jake Cox has a job to do. He's been sent to prevent her from getting laid until a particular horny phantom—and key witness in his mob investigation—pays her a visit. The real challenge? Keeping his own hands off Lucy long enough to get the job done.

Or the lonely, geeky ghost of a murdered mob accountant could rip a hole in the fabric of the universe...

Warning: This book contains cheesy pick-up lines, amateur stripteases, and voyeuristic intentions—all by dead men. And the living behave just as badly...

Witches Anonymous
By Misty Evans

Can a bad witch go good in thirteen steps? Not if Lucifer has his way with her!

Amy Atwood is a witch. Not the harm-none kind...the Satan-worshipping, devil-made-me-do-it kind. But after catching Lucifer in a particularly wicked hex act with her goodie-two-shoes Wiccan sister, Amy does what every self-respecting witch would do. She pops a Dove chocolate in her mouth, ends her affair with the devil, and swears an oath never to use magic again.

She wants to be normal. Human. Even if it means no more fun—and she's looking for a nice, normal guy to complement her new lifestyle. And ice-cream-loving firefighter Adam Foster looks like perfect hero material.

Lucifer, however, isn't about to be nice about letting her go. Stalked by Satan, manipulated by the angel Gabriel—and surprised by Adam's true identity—Amy finds herself up to her black hat in trouble of Biblical proportions...

Warning: Welcome to temptation. Sexy Lucifer is going to enchant you. The original Adam is going to charm you. And the angel Gabriel is going to scare your socks off!

Tickle My Fantasy

 A Samhain Publishing, Ltd. publication.

Samhain Publishing, Ltd.
577 Mulberry Street, Suite 1520
Macon, GA 31201
www.samhainpublishing.com

Tickle My Fantasy
Print ISBN: 978-1-60504-453-8
Carolina Wolf Copyright © 2009 by Sela Carsen
ParaMatch.com Copyright © 2009 by MK Mancos
The Ghost Shrink, the Accidental Gigolo &
The Poltergeist Accountant Copyright © 2009 by Vivi Andrews
Witches Anonymous Copyright © 2009 by Misty Evans

Editing by Laurie Rauch
Cover by Natalie Winters

Carolina Wolf, ISBN 978-1-60504-374-6
First Samhain Publishing, Ltd. electronic publication: February 2009
ParaMatch.com, ISBN 978-1-60504-384-5
First Samhain Publishing, Ltd. electronic publication: February 2009
The Ghost Shrink, the Accidental Gigolo &
The Poltergeist Accountant, ISBN 978-1-60504-391-3
First Samhain Publishing, Ltd. electronic publication: February 2009
Witches Anonymous, ISBN 978-1-60504-397-5
First Samhain Publishing, Ltd. electronic publication: February 2009
First Samhain Publishing, Ltd. print publication: December 2009

Contents

Carolina Wolf

Sela Carsen

Dedication

As always, to my wonderful, patient husband and children.

To Yukon, who is waiting at the Rainbow Bridge and who could clear a room without lifting her head. To Oliver, who gets plain yogurt in his dinner.

To my Romance Divas, without whose whip-cracking chats this story would never have been finished.

And if you're ever in Columbia, SC, be sure to visit the Congaree Swamp National Forest, then have dinner in North Columbia at the real Solstice restaurant.

Prologue

The soft Carolina night cushioned Debra Henry's footsteps as she wandered down the lane. Just in front of her lay the Congaree Swamp National Forest. To prove it, a mosquito the size of a kitten landed on her arm and prepared to drill. She swatted it, and then grimaced at the squishy bug mess on her hand.

"Yech."

A cypress tree provided a comfortable resting spot as the sun's last rays bled a red death over the canopy of dark leaves. The silence surrounding her was the loudest thing she had ever heard, even blunted by the haze of humidity. The buzz of mosquitoes, the cicadas' trill, the howling of a lone wolf.

Her head jerked up. The wail piercing the dusk was not a good sound. Not a comforting sound. The echo died sharply in the dense air. *There are no wolves in South Carolina. There are no wolves in South Carolina.* Debra made a smart about-face and, with a swinging speed-walk, headed back to the visitors' center. Though darkness closed in behind her, she refused to break into an actual trot. At least not yet.

Great. The center was closed. No park rangers. No people with big freakin' guns. Not that park rangers carried guns, she reasoned as she dug in her pocket for the keys to her dust-covered station wagon. Maybe they had tranquilizer darts, though.

The skin on the back of her neck crawled. Instinct from deep within crackled to life and she turned. There it was. A huge black wolf, its eyes glowing gold in the reflection of the single light outside the visitors' center. A waft of the swamp sifted into her brain, breathing and growing, clean, dark water and the essence of primitive life. The fragrance that lived deep in her soul. He brought it all back to her.

Debra held her breath, spellbound for an eternal moment. Then it ended. The wolf faded back into the underbrush and left her standing, oddly bereft without its presence.

This was going to be an interesting place to live.

He watched her get into her car and drive away. He raised his head and breathed deeply, sifting her unique scent from the noxious exhaust fumes, as well as the other, more familiar smells of the night forest.

He knew that scent. He had known it all his life, although he had never before encountered it. It was the scent that sealed his fate and wrote his destiny. His mate.

The wolf loped back into the swamp and down a path he knew would lead him home. She might not yet know it, but her future was certain.

Chapter One

"Don't you worry about a thing, Debra. They're gonna love your proposal and give you all the funding you've ever wanted. We'll have the best small-town library in the entire state by the time you're done with this council meeting."

Charlene King reached out a manicured hand and fluffed Debra's hair. "With this new haircut, any man would be a fool to say no to anything you asked." She spun the chair around so Debra could look in the mirror. "There you go. What do you think?"

Debra stared at her reflection. Hair that she had always considered plain old brown seemed to shine with copper and amber highlights. The frizzy ends were gone, cut off to tickle the back of her neck. Her head felt strange and light, as if a weight had literally been lifted off her shoulders.

"Charlene, I don't know what to say. It's beautiful."

The other woman smiled, and then snorted. "It's about time is what it is. I can't believe you've had that same boring old hairstyle since you were in high school."

"It was practical." Debra shrugged. "But this, this is wonderful." She got out of the chair and twirled around the empty salon. "I can't tell you how great this feels. They'd never recognize me now."

Charlene wasn't Culford's top stylist just because she knew how to wield a can of AquaNet. Information flowed within the walls of her beauty shop faster than she could say *high-speed Internet connection*. She never passed up an opportunity for good gossip.

"Who's they?"

"I'd say my family, but since mama's passed on... I guess it would be just my ex-fiancé, who shall henceforth be referred to as Weasel Bastard."

"Weasel Bastard. I like it," said Charlene. "Is he why you're here?"

"No," she said hastily, then curled in on herself a little. "Well, maybe. In a roundabout way." Debra bent down to retrieve her new, completely adorable purse. Big, square, shiny turquoise vinyl with big white polka dots and long white handles. It cut into her shoulder a bit when it was heavy, but it had been too cute to pass up the last time she'd been in Charleston.

"Let's just say that when I found out about Weasel Bastard's kink for college coeds, he plucked a few strings and I was out of a job. This position opened at exactly the right moment."

It hadn't bothered her as much as she thought it might. Well, she missed the job, but not the man. He was too...mundane. It would be easy enough to settle for him if she were normal, but her life was a lot more complicated than it looked from the outside. The few abilities she possessed, she guarded jealously. Her magic was small enough already without diluting it further with the wrong man. There had to be something left of her power to pass down to a daughter.

Not to mention, it made him mad that she could quote anything she'd ever read from memory. He was a small-minded man.

Charlene picked up a broom and started sweeping up the long strands of Debra's hair.

"You know what they say, sugar. When God closes a door..."

"He opens a window," they finished together.

"If I don't get to this council meeting, He might slam that shut before I've even started." Debra chewed on her lip and slid her glasses back up the bridge of her nose. Dumping a fairly significant budget proposal into the city council's lap always made her nervous.

"Don't you worry about a thing," said Charlene. "You'll do fine."

"I hope so. Myrtle said the mayor was back from his vacation."

Charlene gasped. "Gary's back? And Myrtle got the scoop?" She and the other acknowledged town gossip, Myrtle Painter, who had her own column in the local paper, had been tense rivals for years.

"I must be getting old. I didn't know." Charlene fixed a steady eye on Debra. "Just because that man has money, he doesn't need to be so obvious about it. I wonder how long it'll be before we all see photos of his trip in the newspaper."

Debra paid her bill and Charlene shooed her out the door. "You don't want to be late." Debra waved back distractedly.

The council room is too small, she thought as she squeezed into the last seat at the front table. The Presenters sign crowded her area, so she tried to keep her papers and handouts in a tiny pile. There was just enough space next to her for someone else to slide through. Unless it was the rotund Mrs. Abbott, who ran the Ladies Auxiliary with an iron fist in a pudgy glove. She wouldn't fit.

Nerves. She was rambling inside her own head. Debra shook herself and leaned down to rummage in her shiny new handbag for a pen when the last person arrived in the council meeting room. Shoes appeared in her line of sight and stopped. Big shoes. Chunky brown oxfords under plain khaki trousers, neatly pressed.

Debra took a breath and suddenly it seemed her body was in a vise. Unbearable pressure weighed down on her. Her ears stopped up so all she heard was the rushing of her own blood through her head. Her throat thickened and she struggled to exhale.

What she smelled stunned her. Turned her inside out. The fine hair on her arms stood up, the muscles of her thighs quivered and vibrated. Her nipples peaked in response and her breasts tingled. That scent shot straight to her womb, clenching and releasing in primal hunger. It was the scent of green, growing things, of fresh water, of moss and damp and earth. Over it all, like a fine mist of perfumed oil, was a spicy wild musk.

15

It was him. The man with the oxfords.

She shook her head, desperate to escape from the pressure. Was she having a heart attack or something? She'd never heard of angina triggered by fancy cologne.

Debra waited until her breathing settled before she sat back up, certain that her face was bright red. She pressed a hand to her chest, but everything seemed back to normal.

The man hadn't moved and now she was at eye level with his zipper. It twitched. Good heavens. She had to do something. Look somewhere else. They were in a public meeting, for pity's sake. Debra glanced around the room, but no one else seemed to be paying attention to her pheromone-induced meltdown. At least she wasn't staring at his...particulars...anymore.

She tossed her hair over her shoulder and stood to greet him. He didn't step back, so her nose ended up practically buried in his chest, inches away from that wild aroma.

And the god-awful ugliest tie she'd ever seen in her life. She didn't mind the random swirl pattern, but combined with the clashing colors, it looked like the designer had either been higher than a kite or needed serious psychological help. If she so much as took a deep lungful of air, her nipples would brush up against that hideous tie. She beat a strategic retreat, but only by a little. She was trapped between her chair and the table.

There was no way he could have missed her humiliating reaction to him. What a way to meet another council member. But none of the others had given her these problems. Even the mayor, the gorgeous, almost impossibly beautiful mayor, was easy enough to greet normally.

But this guy... She couldn't make herself look him in the eye, but staring at the tie was making her nauseous. Instead, she watched his soft white shirt rise and fall with each heartbeat. Watched as he took one long inhalation...of her.

"Maddox, honey. We haven't seen you in ages." Myrtle Painter's voice trilled up and down like a chain-smoking songbird. She turned her wrinkled eyes to him and struck a pose that might have looked provocative on her thirty years ago. Now, it kind of made her look like a wax figure left out in the sun too long.

"Maddox, honey," she repeated. "I want to introduce you to our new head librarian. Debra Henry, this is Maddox Moreau. He works with the park service at the Congaree Swamp and he's here to address some concerns about wild animal sightings."

Debra stared at his chest for another moment, then resolutely raised her eyes to his, looking over the tops of her glasses. She was cheating, but he'd never know. The glasses had slipped down her nose again and looking over the frames meant that she saw nothing but a flesh-colored blur and a flash of bright white teeth.

That teasing aroma was driving her nuts. And was starting to tick her off. She was mortified by her first visceral reaction to him, but he just stood there, smiling and smelling like sex in the moonlight. The unfairness of it irked her and goaded some snap back into her spine.

She faked a smile and nodded. "Mr. Moreau." Damned if she'd hold out her hand for a greeting, either.

"Miss Henry." A deep velvet voice rolled out of that chest and she fought to hold down a shiver.

Debra dragged her gaze from the blur of his face to Myrtle with her bleeding red lipstick and smiled again, trying harder to force more feeling into it. Myrtle might be old, but she was sharp.

"Ladies." His voice licked at her senses and Debra clasped her hands together to keep from clamping them over her ears, blocking out the sound that got into her brain and made itself far too comfortable. "Looks like the meeting's about to start. I'll see y'all afterwards."

And then it was over. As he walked away from her, the scent went with him and she was herself again. She exhaled. Wow. She never wanted to deal with that again. On the bright side, at least she hadn't lit up in sparks.

The public portion of the meeting came first, with citizen reports of unusual sightings at the edges of the woods. The people who spoke sounded frightened, and Mr. Moreau took their concerns seriously. He explained that though there may be large dogs or even coyotes in the area, there couldn't be wolves. Especially a wolf the shape and size they described. A huge, hulking creature that scared even the most vicious dogs. They made it sound like a monster. Not at all like the big black wolf she'd seen. It had to be a hallucination. A trick of the evening sun.

And he confirmed she was right. There were no wolves in South Carolina. At least not in the Midlands. Endangered red wolves were part of a Fish and Wildlife breeding program and had been released in northeastern North Carolina and in Tennessee, as well as in smaller numbers on coastal island habitats, but not around here.

After those issues were dealt with, the council took a quick break. Most of the public left, but the hunky park ranger stuck around. After they reconvened, she managed to set out her proposal and petition for a budget increase without ever actually *seeing* him sitting in the corner. It was easy. Every time she had to glance in his direction, she simply peered over the top of her lenses and everyone turned into a fuzzy, featureless blob. She'd never been grateful for her rotten vision before.

She finished her proposal and waited for questions. She couldn't blame the council for grilling her. The library needed new funds and a lot of them. The reference collection was woefully out of date—Ronald Reagan was in office the last time they got a new set of encyclopedias. And they were still using a card catalogue, for goodness sake. She also wanted a small portion for a PR campaign to get more people into the library.

It seemed the previous librarian hadn't troubled the council for new monies in nearly twenty years, which explained a lot about the state of the library, but Debra was determined to make it a vibrant part of the town. Knowledge was life.

After more than an hour's discussion, they tabled the issue until the next meeting and adjourned. Debra sat down, relieved that it had gone so well. Very few council members were outright opposed and she had a month to sway them. The mayor was on the fence and his vote would influence others, but she didn't want to approach him directly if she didn't have to.

She glanced over to the corner. The ranger was gone and the surge of disappointment surprised her. What nonsense. It wasn't as if she needed a man to be happy.

Her wants were simple. Do her job, read some books, walk the dog. She nodded decisively. That's exactly what she would do. Just because her body went haywire around a man didn't mean she had to do anything about it.

She stood up and began to walk around the room, sliding chairs under tables and picking up stray pens. Slightly compulsive, but it was habit. She'd been cleaning up after students in college libraries since she was a little girl, helping her mom at work. She didn't want to leave the council room untidy, even though she was exhausted after the pressure of the meeting.

Debra surveyed her handiwork with a small, satisfied smile, and then went to gather her own things. The door behind her opened and closed on heavy hinges and she sighed. No way her luck was good enough for that to be Mrs. Abbott, coming to discuss her membership in the Ladies Auxiliary. Debra turned. Nope. Not Mrs. Abbott.

"Miss Henry?" Gary Corvell, the mayor, stood beside the doors. "I wonder if I could ask you a question."

"Certainly, Mr. Mayor." Debra dredged up a polite smile. "How can I help you?"

"I was hoping to ask you out to dinner tomorrow evening. Perhaps the Mill, out in Boykin. Have you been there before?"

God had a twisted sense of humor. The Mill was a very nice restaurant, a special-occasion place in a picturesque location, but the idea of being stuck in a car with Gary Corvell from Culford all the way to Kershaw County inspired nothing other than faint boredom.

Elegant and charming, the silver in his hair added to his air of sophisticated *savoir-faire*. His beauty was almost disturbing, as if his uncanny perfection served to make everyone around him seem smaller and homelier than they actually were. He certainly played up the difference, flashing designer clothes and expensive accessories wherever he went.

Since she'd arrived in Culford, the mayor had been very welcoming, almost excessively so. He frequently *happened* to be walking through town in the morning when she arrived at the library. After the first couple of times he also *happened* to be eating lunch at Robin's Café and insinuated himself at her

19

table, she started brown-bagging it. He had never asked her out before tonight, though, and she wasn't sure what prompted him to finally act. Not that she would accept. Something about him seemed...off. That little prickle of energy she had picked up in the swamp pinched her.

Perfectly aware that she might be digging her career grave by rejecting the mayor, she squared her shoulders and looked him straight in the eye.

"I'm so, so sorry. I appreciate the offer, but I am otherwise engaged for the evening." Ok, so her so-called engagement involved a long bath and a good book. He didn't need to know the specifics. "But it's kind of you to ask."

The man's face tightened as if he'd been slapped and Debra's warning bells started tolling like a hunchback party at Notre Dame. The obvious rage was out of proportion to a simple refusal.

"Why would you do that?"

"Do what?" she asked, holding her ground. She wasn't about to let him intimidate her.

"Say no when I hold your library's fate in my hands? Is there someone else? Do you have some other man waiting for you somewhere?" His menacing whisper alarmed her.

Every muscle in her body pulled at her to cut and run. Fast. But he made her mad, so she stiffened her backbone and raised her chin.

"Mr. Mayor, my personal life is none of your business. Whether I choose to have dinner with you or anyone else has absolutely no bearing on our professional relationship. I hope that you'll give appropriate and unbiased consideration to my library budget proposal, but that is the extent of our dealings together."

Righteous anger flowed through her and her drawl deepened as she continued. "You ask why I won't go out with you? Because you have the sheer gall to presume that I would date you for the sake of a budget. That my favors are for sale. It is unworthy of you, sir. Good evening." She crossed her arms and raised her chin, skewering him with a dismissive scowl until he turned on his heel and marched out. The heavy door slid closed and she slumped. Crap. There went her beautiful library. She waited a few moments before she picked up her purse and hefted it over her shoulder. Even its utter cuteness couldn't lift her spirits. She had to lean against the door with all her weight to escape the empty room.

Maddox Moreau broke off his conversation with the last few council members who remained and followed as she stalked down the hall. Her warning bells sounded for him, too, but in an entirely different way.

"It was a pleasure to meet you, Miss Henry." His voice, sweet and deep as dark molasses, poured over her skin.

It was like she had some kind of radar where he was concerned. As he caught up, she realized he was hot. Not cutie-hot, but hot-hot. Waves of warmth billowed over her as if she walked next to a pulsing fire. She had to fight hard against the urge to stop and snuggle into the comfort he offered. This was a complication she did not need and the weight of it slowed her down.

Debra couldn't put it off anymore. Since her car was in front of Charlene's shop, she'd come in the back door. Everyone else was at the front of the building or already gone. She hadn't seen Mayor Corvell when she left.

Now she was alone with Maddox. The door was right in front of her. She could still run away if she tried, but it was best to confront this bizarre attraction head on and get it out of her system. At least this way there would be no witnesses if she did something stupid like try to crawl up his body like a needy kitten.

She inhaled, shockingly aware of how close he stood, of the way his breath moved over her hair. She straightened. Pushed up her glasses. And turned.

Sweet Baby Jesus.

It was entirely unfair that he should be so attractive. His eyes were the most amazing shade of smoky blue and smile lines bracketed his mouth. Straight brown hair fell adorably over his forehead.

Dang it. Even his nose was cute, broken and crooked, but still strong. Not fair. If her nose were crooked, she'd be *that girl with the crooked nose*. Not all goose-bumpy and sexy.

He'd said something, hadn't he?

21

Debra cleared her throat. "Likewise, sir."

"Have dinner with me."

Debra's raised eyebrows made wrinkles in her forehead, but she didn't care. "I beg your pardon?"

"Have dinner with me."

Too bad all those good looks were wasted on such a jerk. The nerve. After her fight with the mayor, this was too much. She gave him her most glacial glare.

"Allow me to introduce you to the mechanics of the interrogative statement, Mr. Moreau."

"Maddox, please," he interrupted.

She glared harder and continued. "The interrogative is used to ask a question of another person. Whenever possible, it should be qualified by a polite phrase, such as 'please'. For example, 'Miss Henry, will you *please* have dinner with me?'"

Smile lines deepened. "And will you?"

"Yes." She gasped and her eyes widened as she slapped her hand over her mouth. That was *so* not what she meant to say.

The lines blossomed into a full-on grin of triumph. "How does tomorrow night sound?"

The glare she gave him this time was far from glacial. What stupid impulse had taken over her mouth? Huge mistake. She didn't want to date anyone, remember? And if the mayor found out, she'd be back on the job market faster than she could say Dewey Decimal System. Maybe she could bargain with him.

"How about a cup of coffee instead?"

"At your house?"

"No!" She winced. Way to be subtle. "I mean, something a little less formal than dinner."

"I'm afraid not, Miss Henry. You agreed to dinner. I couldn't possibly accept anything less." He kept smiling that charming grin, though it had become a trifle fixed.

"I'm fine with a hamburger at the Sonic."

"Keep trying to talk me down and I'll take you clear to Columbia."

The state capitol was closer than The Mill in Boykin, but where the idea of riding through the Midlands with the mayor sounded both dull and creepy, being cooped up in a car with Maddox Moreau would probably drive her insane.

Debra gathered what little grace she could muster and smiled grimly. "That won't be necessary, I'm sure. Where would you like to go?"

"I have somewhere in mind. I'll call you tomorrow and let you know."

That was her cue to write down her phone number. Give him some personal connection to her. But she was ahead of him this time. Debra stuck her hand into a pocket of her bag.

"I'll be at the library. Here's my card."

A business card was supposed to be impersonal, but he took it gently between two long, strong fingers and lifted it to his nose, as though it was a precious love letter imbued with perfume. He smiled and Debra became short of breath.

She had to get out. She stumbled backwards into the heavy double doors. "Right. So. I'll, um, talk to you tomorrow then. 'Kay. Good night, Mr. Moreau."

"Maddox," he called after her, but the door clanged shut.

Chapter Two

Debra nearly drowned in the early autumn humidity. At ten o'clock at night, the temperature had dropped to eighty degrees. She put her hand over her chest to calm her erratic heartbeat. Big presentation, confrontations with two different men. Why didn't the universe space these events out so she could catch her breath a little?

Upset and confused, she dug in her purse for keys as she walked across the darkened town square. The nerve of that man. Those men. If she were honest with herself, the mayor had frightened her a bit. She didn't know that much more about the park ranger, but at least he hadn't scared her. She was just going to have to watch herself carefully.

When she heard the rustling, she wanted to put it down to a roaming cat or possum, but her newfound instinct for danger clanged wildly in her head. She stiffened, her fingers grasping the cold serrated edge of her keys.

A hulking black figure came out from the cover of the overgrown azaleas that surrounded the slightly shabby little gazebo in the center of the square.

He held out his hand and growled something, some liquid phrase that slithered into the air. The words slammed against her like a physical force, binding her in place.

Debra tried to open her mouth to scream, and realized her jaw was as locked down as the rest of her body. All she could do was wait for him to get to her. And scream in her mind.

Well over six feet tall, he didn't walk fully upright, but hunched, sharp-shouldered and long-armed. His face was inhuman, caught in an eternal hell between man and animal.

His jaw jutted, and unnatural fangs gleamed in the fitful moonlight.

"Not running away, bitch?" he rasped. He walked right up to her, not even bothering to sneak. "You can't do anything to me. You don't have any power over me." Foul breath washed over her face and she wanted to gag. "I know what you are," he crooned. One hand, hairy and claw-tipped, combed through a strand of her hair. "Witch. Bride of Satan. What's the matter? Can't get to your power?"

Debra's throat worked uselessly to refute him, but she remained unable to speak. Terror grew.

He leaned down and whispered in her ear, "Where's the Book, hellspawn? I need the Book. I have this power, but I need more."

A cry, low and pathetic, broke from her.

"Aw. So sad. So lovely. So evil. All witches are evil. They steal men's souls. They cloud men's brains. Good thing I'm not a man, then. I'm better. But to be the best, I need that Book."

His hand clutched her hair, yanking it back and causing a spear of agony to shoot down her neck. "Where's the Book?" he screamed, spittle flying from his misshapen snout.

Debra's heart beat so hard she thought it might shatter right in her chest. Panic, pain and helpless fury combined into a bitter lump of bile in her throat.

He knew. How did he know what she was? It wasn't like she hung a shingle on her front porch: *Witchcraft, Spells and Potions*. She didn't even know any spells or potions and her power was a pitiful, tiny thing. Barely a flicker and just enough to guard her secret. And pot, meet kettle. She might be a witch, but she didn't go around scaring people to death.

Her eyes darted to the darkness beyond them, sensing something else in the shadows. He saw the movement and laughed.

"What's the matter, trying to call for help?" He let go of her hair, but she still couldn't move. Couldn't run, couldn't escape, couldn't even lift her hands to shield herself from the blow. The back of his hand—rough fur that stank of unwashed beast—connected with her cheek and Debra's head whipped around. Stars exploded in front of her eyes and her mouth filled with

25

pain and blood. Tears tracked down her face and the monster laughed. Everything within her recoiled in disgust. He was enjoying this.

The laughter died abruptly at the sound of rustling leaves. He wheeled around and whatever power restrained her melted away.

She'd dropped her keys when he hit her and she fell to her knees, sweeping the ground with her hands until she touched them. The feral moan of an animal hungry for blood spurred her to clumsy speed. She stumbled the few feet to her car, one hand cradled to her cheek, and fumbled with the latch.

The sound changed. Slowly, she looked over her shoulder though her mind screamed at her to get in the car. Instead, she watched what emerged from the bushes.

Her attacker tried to escape, but a massive black wolf leapt, knocking him to the grass before circling his prey, growling and snarling. The monster stood up and feinted to the side, but the wolf was too fast, snapping those fearsome jaws around the rank creature's knee. Debra heard a wet crunch as the abomination screamed, but he didn't go down. Instead, he pulled something from a bulky pouch at his waist and thrust it at the wolf, who wrenched away.

The injury didn't slow the villain at all as he turned and hurtled towards Debra, screaming, "You're mine, devil's whore!"

Her thumb finally punched the door latch button and she slid into the car, slamming it before he reached her. Her eyes widened. The demonic thing was holding a knife, the blade glinting silver and deadly as it sliced toward her window. It never reached her.

The wolf's bulk slammed him sideways and they rolled together onto the sidewalk. The creature stabbed wildly at the wolf. Debra heard the animal cry out as one slash hit its body.

Her eyes were accustomed to the dark now. The wolf stumbled back and the creature limped away into the darkness. A glistening trail of blood sank into the thirsty earth.

Oh God. She had to get out of here. Her keys fell to the floorboard and she scrambled for them, uncaring that her head hit the steering wheel. She had them in hand when she heard the whimper.

The wolf stood staring at her, one front paw off the ground, dripping blood from its foot and its jaw.

It had saved her life. She could do no less in return. A flicker of something in her mind told her she was in no danger. Debra opened the door of the car and stretched out her hand slowly, slowly. The animal took one hopping step back from her and she stopped.

"I'm not going to hurt you."

The wolf swayed, then shook its head like a human trying to clear away a fog. Its form shimmered, shivered somehow, and Debra—practical, boring, only slightly out of the ordinary Debra—watched in fascinated horror as the wolf disappeared and the long, lean form of Maddox Moreau fell naked into her lap, out cold.

Chapter Three

Debra's fingers slipped off the key as she tried to start the car. She gripped the steering wheel until her skin pinched painfully against the hard plastic.

Maddox sat in the passenger seat, floating in and out of consciousness, his muscles twitching with each interval of semi-lucidity. She'd had a job hauling him into the other seat, but it finally worked and he was safely buckled in. Her demonic attacker was gone, leaving only a pool of dull black blood behind.

Debra shook her head. No, that hadn't been a demon—demons only existed in fiction. But she couldn't quite bring herself to examine the man next to her.

Man.

Wolf.

Something. But not what that creature had been.

Right now, she had her hands full with other problems. She tried the key again and the car started with a shudder. Where should she take him? An emergency room seemed wrong. If she wasn't completely insane, if what she had seen actually happened, she didn't think a local ER was prepared to deal with him. Anyway, how was she—or he—supposed to explain how he ended up buck naked with a knife wound in his shoulder, accompanied by the local librarian?

She could take him home with her. Debra didn't know where he lived, didn't know anything about him. Except that he was naked. And a wolf-shapeshifter thing. A werewolf. A naked werewolf. Sitting in her car.

Her gaze slid off the road to the man beside her. His eyes were closed again, but his mouth was tight, as if it held back the pain. Well, he wasn't completely naked anymore. Her cardigan was wrapped against the slash in his shoulder, but blood seeped through the cotton knit, staining the fabric an ugly purple.

Debra tore her gaze away from him and back to the road in front of her. It was wrong to ogle a bleeding, unconscious man, even if he was gorgeous. And naked.

Would you stop with the naked thing already? It's not like you haven't seen it before.

An image of Maddox, standing woozily in front of her the moment before he collapsed, flashed to the front of her brain.

Yeah, but none of the guys she'd slept with looked like that.

Maddox awoke to pain. He was moving. Apparently his body was functioning enough to help whoever he was using as a crutch up a couple of stairs and onto a front porch. A tiny hand on his waist and one on his chest. A sweet, southern voice saying words he barely understood.

"Now, you just stand right there for a second while I open the door."

It was her. His...he couldn't think straight. She sounded so pretty. Debra was the wrong name for her. She should be called Beauty. Or Lovely. Or Mine. He'd settle for Mine. There were other words, but he didn't think they were meant for him. She was talking to herself.

Aww. That's so cute.

The dog that met them at the door was not cute. He growled in wary aggression, ears flat against his rounded skull. Barely past the puppy stage, he nevertheless perceived the threat to his beloved mistress and did his best to warn Maddox away.

The trouble was, Maddox couldn't get away right now if he tried. Bastard had used a silver knife on him. He was lucky it was only a gash. Had the silver touched any vital organs, he'd be one dead werewolf.

"Hush now, Twister. He's hurt and we have to help him."

His savior, his unknowing mate, shushed the animal. The dog, which looked like a Boxer now that his vision was clearing, backed away, but continued to growl low in his throat. Maddox didn't blame him. He'd growl, too, if Debra had her hands all over some nude stranger.

She walked him to the couch and tried to help him down gently, but he was too heavy for her. Dizziness overwhelmed him and he fell forward, face down onto the cushions.

The next time he awoke, he stared over at a coffee table that wasn't his. He smelled blood and there was a hot weight on his legs. He looked down his body and found that his shoulder hurt like a sonofabitch. Debra had cleaned him up and put some tidy butterfly bandages over his wound to hold the edges of the skin together. She'd also draped a blanket over his naked ass.

"No dogs on the couch."

At the sound of her voice, he looked up and there she stood, carrying a mug of something in her hands. There was a smear on her cheek and her clothes were a wreck, but it hardly mattered.

Debra Henry was one of the prettiest women he'd ever seen. She'd cut her hair. When he saw her the other evening at sunset, it had been long—pulled away from her face and tied up in a ponytail. This swingy look that grazed her chin suited her better.

"What did you say?"

"I said, no dogs on the couch."

"Oh. Sorry." He tried to get up and she chuckled, a muffled sound.

"Not you. Twister."

The pressure on his legs shifted and he realized he'd been hot because the dog was lying on him.

"You're no dog. You're something else, but you are not a dog." He caught the merest hint of hysteria in her voice, but she seemed to be holding up. At least she hadn't shot him in his sleep.

He moved, trying to sit up, and she set down the mug to come and help him. Between them, he got propped up against a corner of the couch, but they were sweating by the time it was done. Part of the effort had been hiding the hard-on he got from staring at her breasts while she helped him. They were fuller than he'd thought at first, hidden under the loose, high-necked sweater she wore. Through the pain screaming in his shoulder, he smiled to himself. The girl was stacked.

But when she stood back, leaning a little on the arm of the couch to get her breath back, all thought of smiling left. The mark on her cheek that he'd thought was a smear of blood was actually a dark, swollen bruise.

"Your face."

She started, bringing a hand to her cheek.

"I remember now. The bastard hit you. That's when I lost it." Maddox felt the red tide of fury rise again and welcomed the sting of fur breaking through his skin. "I'll kill him."

In the receding space of his mind, he heard a dog bark furiously until Debra's voice intruded. Sharp, loud words.

"Cut it out! Stop it. Both of you."

Maddox came to himself, half off the couch, blood running down his arm and overwhelmed with nausea.

"I'm going to throw up."

She thrust a plastic bowl under him just in time before he disgraced himself. Debra knelt next to him, holding his forehead while he was sick. When he finished, he lolled back against the couch. She left with the bowl and returned with a cool cloth and a glass of water. Her face was pale and pinched.

"You don't look so good," he said.

"You don't look so good, either. You also don't smell so good." She swallowed and a tide of green rose and fell in her cheeks. "Sorry. I don't do throw-up well."

"I'd be worried if you did. Can you get me to a bathroom?"

She got under his uninjured arm and helped lever him to his feet. The blanket fell to the floor and there he stood, his dick still half hard from imagining her naked breasts as well as the adrenaline rush of the Change. He looked over at her and her eyes seemed to be glued to his partially erect state. Under her gaze, he stiffened further. Great. Maddox reached out and tucked a hand under Debra's chin.

"Hon, if you want that to go away, you're going to have to stop staring at it."

Chapter Four

Debra dropped his arm like he was on fire and he wavered without her support. Maddox caught himself against a wall, leaving a smear of blood behind.

"Sorry," he muttered. "I need a shower."

"You need a doctor," she answered. "And you're freezing. Why are you so cold?"

"No doctors," he said, ignoring the second part of her question. "I'll heal by morning."

Debra bent and gathered the blanket, pulling it up around his body. She stared at his chest the whole time over the tops of her glasses. He would have chuckled, but it hurt too much to be amused. That clever, subtle avoidance maneuver probably fooled most people.

Debra took up her position under his shoulder and led him through her bedroom into the master bath. The lights were off, but he saw clearly enough to make out the light cotton blanket, the rumpled pillows, the stacks of books on and around her nightstand.

The bathroom was clean, but cluttered with female paraphernalia—makeup, mirrors, creams and combs. The smells should have been overwhelming, but they were only a stronger, colder version of her. It wasn't until they combined with the essence of Debra that they became enchanting.

Debra, Debra. Pretty, bewitching Debra.

He didn't realize he'd said it out loud until he opened his eyes and she was staring at him.

"Do you need something?"

"What?"

"You said my name. Do you need me?"

Wrong question. The shower was running, heating the water and steaming the air around them, cushioning his senses until all he could breathe was her.

The silver was sapping his strength, stealing the warmth from his blood. The danger of silver was not only the damage of the wound itself, it also tainted the blood, draining the heat out of their bodies. Silver-killed werewolves froze from the inside out.

He lurched to his feet from his seat on the toilet lid. She had an enclosed shower big enough for two people with glass sliding doors—no tub to step over—and he stumbled inside, hissing as the water stung his skin with hot needles. The blanket fell again, this time with a wet plop. She reached in to get it out of his way, but he snagged her arm and pulled her all the way into the shower with him.

He needed her. To hold him, to help him, to be with him, to fill him.

She squealed when the water hit her full in the face, but he slid the shower door shut. Maddox pulled her closer and brushed the wet hair out of her eyes.

She spluttered, but her words weren't important. Nothing was important but his need. The moment her soaked clothes touched his skin, the cold went away. As long as she touched him, he knew he'd survive.

"Maddox, you're sick. You need a doctor."

"No. Need you. Just you." And he kissed her.

God. She tasted even better than she smelled—purer, simpler, richer, more complex. He could willingly spend decades sifting out the different flavors of Debra. She stood stiffly in his arms and he didn't know what to do about it, didn't know how to help her. Didn't know how to tell her what he needed from her now.

Maddox raised his mouth from hers and stared down into her face, water dripping from her eyelashes, running in streams down her cheeks, dangling at her chin before falling into oblivion.

"Please, Debra. Help me." He'd never begged before. Never needed to before, but he was sick and hurt and if she didn't help him now... He couldn't even finish the thought. She had to help him, even if she didn't know how.

He bent to her face again, but not to kiss her. Not right away. Drops of water slid over her skin as though they had the right. His tongue caught one beside her lips, and the taste of his mate exploded on his tongue, made him greedy for more. More drops enticed him and he lapped at her mouth, pulling her closer when she finally opened to him, letting him into her body. Accepting him. Trusting him.

There it was. As if a door opened and she invited him in, Maddox let his mind touch hers, its light sharp and pure and blinding.

He was stunned. Humans usually didn't have enough of a soul-light to heal themselves, much less anyone else. But there was brilliance enough here for magic like he'd never seen. And this part of her was untouched. She'd never let anyone into her heart before. It was all for him. He was too grateful to be greedy, so he simply basked in the glow, letting it flow into him, fill him until there was no room left for the poison.

In his weakness, her hands caressed and held him as tenderly as a healer, a mother, a lover. A woman. *His woman.* As the light overflowed him, he left her mind and came back to his.

His senses were clearing, the toxic metal leaving his body. Maddox looked over at his shoulder and watched the sluggish trail of tainted blood seep down his arm and drip to the floor, swirl into the drain. The last atom of silver left his body and he heaved a great draft of steamy air, finally warm all the way through.

"Thank you for healing me." Then the weakness took him.

This was so not normal. Not right, not...not anything. She was sitting, fully clothed, in a scalding shower. In her arms lay a naked werewolf who kissed her until she glowed, then bled silver into her drain and passed out.

And she wasn't screaming.

She should be screaming.

Twister butted open the bathroom door and stood there, wagging his stubby little tail, his head cocked to one side. She could barely see him through the steam on the shower door, but she laughed, a weak, sodden sound, when his broad pink tongue swiped a slobbery path up the other side of the glass.

She reached up and shut off the water, feeling the chill almost immediately. A towel hung on the other side of the shower door and she pulled it down to drape over Maddox's still form. His breathing was better, his color was up and the gash on his shoulder was...

No. This was not happening. Except it was. The cut was not only not seeping blood anymore, the edges of it were drawing together, leaving a faint pinkish line in their wake. She swiped water out of her eyes and looked again. His wound was healing right in front of her.

What had he said? "Thank you for healing me." How did he know? Debra's power was doing strange things lately. She'd never had the means or the motive to heal another until tonight, but he knew what had happened.

Maddox was out like a light and safe from harm sitting in the shower for now, but she was tired and shivering and soaked. Also, possibly psychotic. Her world had tilted. For some reason, the idea that there were other beings—not entirely human—shook her. She felt like an idiot. A blind idiot. After all, if there were witches, why couldn't there be werewolves? And monsters?

Her clothes left a growing pool on the floor. She grabbed a robe from the hook behind the door and held it in her teeth so it hung in front of her while she stripped out of her sweater and trousers. With another suspicious glance at Maddox, she pulled on the robe before she took off her underwear.

Twister stood, front paws in the shower, stretching his nose toward Maddox and giving him a thorough sniffing. When he came to the sliced shoulder, he licked it twice.

"Ew! Don't do that. That's disgusting. I've seen you lick yourself." She nudged the dog out of the way with her foot before she gathered everything up and shoved the whole mess in the washing machine.

She returned to study the man on the floor. How was she

supposed to get him out of there? And where was she supposed to put him when she *did* get him out? And what in heaven's name was she supposed to do with a werewolf in her house?

Debra reached out and touched his shoulder. His skin was again as hot as it had seemed a few hours ago—a few lifetimes ago—at the council meeting.

Werewolves must generate a lot of body heat.

But testing her theory didn't explain why she was tracing her fingers over his skin, up his shoulder and onto his collarbone. The strong set of his jaw drew her touch. The stubble of beard pricked her fingertips. The skin around his eyes was slightly lined. She recalled the way his face moved when he had smiled at her. You had to do a lot of smiling to get lines like that.

His eyebrows were thick, but not shaggy, and he needed a haircut. Well, not really. She liked the way the hair over his ears brushed against her fingers.

Debra snatched her arm back like she'd been burned. There was a *werewolf* sitting in her *shower*. Forget taking him to the hospital, she should have called Animal Control. And the *National Enquirer.*

She wiped her hands on her robe to mitigate the lusting effect of the hottie cooties before she prodded gently at his unwounded shoulder.

"Mr. Moreau, can you hear me?"

There was no response, so she tried again.

"Maddox." His brows drew together for a flicker of time before he opened his eyes halfway. His pupils were back to normal again and she could see the blue of his eyes.

"Huh?"

"You're sitting in my shower. Can you help me get you up?"

He groaned and nodded. Between them, they staggered to her bed, not even caring that he was nude. Honest. She didn't care a bit.

Uh-huh.

She covered him to his chin and straightened. The idea was to leave him to sleep it off while she had a nice cup of decaf tea and sat down with her notebook. She needed a list. A list of things to do, a list of questions to ask, a list of things that didn't seem possible.

It was going to be a really long list.

But his hand reached out from under the blanket and caught hers.

"Don't leave me."

Debra paused. The list could wait until he was fully asleep. She sat down on the edge of the bed and pulled his hand into her lap, stroking it gently.

"Rest. You'll be fine."

"C'mere," he slurred, pulling her down next to him. "Rest with me."

He pulled her off balance and her head hit the pillow next to his. He scooted backward and she rolled into the warm spot he'd left on the sheets.

"I shouldn't do this. I have things to do." The hot shower must have made her sleepier than she realized.

"You need to rest now. We'll both feel better in the morning."

Her eyes were so heavy. Debra nodded and slept.

In the middle of the night, her restless movements woke him.

"I'm hot," she moaned, kicking at the blankets. The knot on her robe had loosened, and she yanked at it, pulled off the heavy cotton and shoved it over the side of the bed.

Maddox lay perfectly still, praying she wouldn't wake up and scream, but she seemed to still be asleep. She flipped her pillow over to the cool side and settled back down, her breathing soft and even.

The body she revealed made his tongue go dry and his cock stand to immediate attention. She wasn't just stacked. She was built like a...disco music and the words "brick house" cranked up a mental soundtrack.

He tried to lift his hand. The desire to touch the silken skin of her side, to run his hands from her shoulder down to that round, smooth hip was overwhelming. Unfortunately, it wasn't overwhelming enough to beat back the healing sleep. The best he could manage was to drop an arm over her waist and pull her closer to him. Unconscious, she snuggled in and—thank you, Jesus—his almost painful erection nestled into the Holy Land, the valley between the cheeks of an ass he desperately wanted to grab. And lick. And bite.

After he slept some more.

Chapter Five

"Oooow!"

Maddox came awake snarling at the sound, but his disorientation melted at the sight of the lovely Debra, leaning up on her elbow with a hand to her cheek. Her face must have still been bruised from last night's attack.

The picture in front of him was unbeatable. Her back was a study in living sculpture, soft and strong. His hand still rested on her hip and there was no help for it. He stroked.

Oh yeah. Her skin was as smooth as he imagined. But for some reason, having her hip fondled by a naked werewolf seemed to freak her out.

Debra screamed, rolled over, and fell out of bed, landing on that luscious bare ass. Thankfully, it knocked the air out of her enough that she stopped screaming. The woman could shatter glass.

Maddox held out his hands in a peaceful gesture, but it didn't seem to help. She was scrabbling around, searching for her robe, when he realized she couldn't see to find it. Her glasses were on the bedside table and he picked them up.

"Here you go, hon."

She snatched her specs out of his hand and shoved them on. Too bad her next move was to dive for the robe, because he was enjoying the view. He'd never realized he had a fetish for librarians before, but she had the whole package. Beauty and brains, with guts and a great rack. What a combination.

"You...you..."

He wasn't going to take any points away for her confusion

this morning. After all, he had a lot of explaining to do.

Twister, who had come streaking off his doggie pillow when Debra hit the floor, decided that all was well, and stretched, gifting his humans with a gaseous emission guaranteed to blister paint.

"Jeeee-sus!" Maddox covered his nose and Debra fanned furiously, her eyes watering. He wrapped the sheet around his waist, the stench doing an effective job of withering his morning erection to a less embarrassing state, and went to open the windows while Debra flipped the ceiling fan to high.

"What are you feeding him?" he asked as he stood at the open window, taking deep gulps of fresh air. She joined him.

"Dog food," she choked out. "Good dog food, too, not that scary stuff from the Dollar Store. I asked the vet about it and he said Boxers are naturally...flatulent."

"Gawd Almighty. Put some plain yogurt in his food at dinner. See if that works."

"Why? Does it work for you?"

Her tone clued him in. She was angry. She'd gone from terrified to pissed in less than the time it took him to change species. Maddox rubbed the back of his head.

"Debra, I'll tell you everything—absolutely everything I know—if you'll go make a pot of coffee."

"I didn't realize werewolves drank coffee." She stood with her hip propped against the windowsill and her arms crossed under her breasts.

"There's a lot you don't realize. Do you have an extra toothbrush?" He wanted to distract her from hating him for a few minutes while he finished waking up.

"Toothbrush?" she repeated.

"Morning breath. Got anything I can wear, while you're at it?"

"I'm afraid I don't carry a large selection of men's clothing, Mr. Moreau." Now she was scaring him. He knew that voice. It was the one his mother used right before all hell broke loose. "What happened to your clothes?"

"You've seen me naked. You should call me Maddox." He put his hands on her shoulders to soothe her. "And I've seen you naked too."

For a small woman, she could put a lot of force into a downward stomp. Pain shot up his leg from his flattened big toe as she shook off his grip.

"There should be a new toothbrush in the drawer to the right of the sink. I'll be in the kitchen with coffee. You'd better come out with answers." She turned on her heel and stalked out the door. He'd have appreciated the view more if his foot didn't hurt so much.

Washed and brushed, he discovered a big T-shirt with a sizable hole in the armpit and a ratty pair of athletic shorts on the bed when he came out of the bathroom.

He was usually much better about shifting where there were some clothes to be had, but then he usually didn't get stabbed on his wild runs. Maddox followed his nose to the kitchen.

True to her word, Debra had made coffee and was busy setting out butter and jam for the toast. She took one look at him and burst out laughing.

"What?" He looked down. He'd pulled the shirt on as he was leaving the bedroom and hadn't paid attention to the front of it. Now, he wished he had.

"Nothing," she said, still snickering as she poured coffee into two sturdy mugs.

There was a mirror in the hall and he turned to check. He'd grown boobs. Not him, personally, but the sketch on the shirt was an outline of two pendulous nude breasts resting on top of an open book. The tagline said, *Read Naked*.

"You're getting me back, aren't you?"

"A little, yeah." She buried her face in the steam and she looked like an angel. God, he was a sap. Debra put the cup down.

"I'm sorry. It's not as if it's your fault you got stabbed. In fact, I ought to thank you. You saved my life."

Maddox sighed. He'd be lucky if he got out of this with just his toes crushed.

"Yeah. About that."

Her eyes narrowed. So did his.

"I guess I have a few things to tell you."

"Something weirder than a park ranger being a werewolf? Because frankly, you've about hit my limit of bizarreness for the day. Possibly the whole month." She took another sip. "And I haven't even finished my coffee yet."

There was nothing Maddox wanted more than to sit at the breakfast table with this woman every morning and drink coffee. The idea nearly gave him whiplash, since, before she'd showed up in his town, he'd been a lone wolf in every sense of the word. Happy and content, howling at the moon with a different woman every week.

Now, he was thinking white picket fences and a litter of cubs. May as well put a choke chain on him and snip his balls off—except he'd need those for the cubs. Of course, as soon as he told her everything she needed to know, she might be all too inclined to hold an impromptu neutering session. No puppies for him. Maddox couldn't think of a way to ease into this conversation, so he just started.

"First, I'm not a park ranger. I'm a wildlife management specialist. There's a difference, but it's not important right now. Second, that thing from last night. What did he want? Did he say?"

"Pardon me. Wildlife management specialist." She sighed and lost the sarcasm. "He didn't actually tell me what he wanted. He did something to me so I couldn't move. I couldn't even scream. I was so scared, I could hardly even hear him."

He rolled his shoulders, trying to rid himself of the feeling that she wasn't telling him everything.

"Try to think back. Was he looking for something specific?"

"No. He was just incredibly angry. At me."

"Why? Someone you know?"

He was pushing her and Debra hated being pushed. It wasn't enough he'd turned furry on her. Or rather, started out furry and turned human. He'd also slept with her and seen her nude. And now he was digging for answers about an incident she'd as soon forget ever happened.

Stubbornly, she bit into her toast to give herself time to

decide how she wanted to handle this. But a scratchy edge of bread scraped against the swollen inside of her cheek, reminding her of her injury. She hadn't even looked in the mirror this morning. She must be terrifying.

She swallowed. Terrifying. She'd been terrified. And that made her angrier than a few questions from Maddox Moreau did. He might be a beast, but he wasn't a bastard. But she couldn't tell him her story without breaking the oath to which she'd been born. She put one hand in her lap and crossed her fingers.

"Of course I don't know him. I don't know why he was so mad at me. He called me a witch, and something else. Not very complimentary, I think. Then he hit me because I didn't answer. I couldn't answer. Whatever he did, I couldn't speak." Her voice thinned in fury and honest fear. "He hit me because he could."

A low, deep throbbing filled her sunny kitchen and the hair on her arms stuck straight up. Debra looked over at Twister, who stood with his hackles raised and the fangs from his underbite dripping in anticipation. He was growling, but he wasn't the sole source of the sound.

Maddox. He looked human enough, no fur, no changing of shape, but his eyes... His eyes were molten gold and throwing off sparks. His lip curled in a snarl and she could have sworn she saw a fang. With his neck tensed to snap, Debra knew better than to touch him. But she had to get him back under control quickly.

She whistled, a sharp, piercing blast suited for hailing cabs in a noisy city. Twister whimpered and backed up. Maddox choked and blinked. His eyes turned blue again and his canine teeth turned back into the human sort of canine teeth.

"I'm sorry," he finally said, clearing his throat. "I've never been that quick on the trigger before."

"Well, I didn't think I could handle you turning furry on me at this hour."

"Turning furry. About that..."

Oh God. She really, really couldn't deal with this right now. Hysterical laughter bubbled right below the surface and she could feel her eyes stinging with tears.

"No. Please, no. I know I asked for answers, but I was

wrong. I don't want to know. I just want you to leave. I'm glad you're better. Please don't get stabbed again on my account." She stood, shoving her chair back. He stood with her, reaching out across the table, but she stumbled away.

"I...I have to go to work now." A tear fell.

"Please don't cry, sugar."

"I'm not crying. And don't call me sugar." She gulped in air to stave off the sobs. Funny how that sounded a lot like sobbing. She walked back to the bedroom with a man and a dog trailing behind her. "I want to pretend this never happened."

"That's not going to work, Debra. That guy threatened your life once. He'll do it again. He came after you for a specific reason."

She flipped through the clothes in her closet, scraping hangers over the metal rods to drown out his words.

"Are you sure you don't have what he wanted? Whatever he was after?"

Debra rested her cheek against the closet door, but winced away. His hands were light on her shoulders as he turned her to face him.

"He hurt you, Debra. I won't forget that." His thumb traced softly over the swollen heat of her skin. The gentleness nearly undid her. Her hands rested against his chest, over his quickening heartbeat, the muscles hard under her fingers.

The memory of his kiss in the shower rushed over her, but she couldn't let herself be swayed. She'd been taught from birth to hide her gift and her charge. She couldn't tell him. Not yet. It was too early. There were still too many things to consider. Too many questions left unanswered. She closed her eyes against the desire in his.

"You're right. I can't run from this. But I need a little time to think it through." She shook her hair back and straightened.

He eyed her cheek. "You can't go in to work like this. Will you let me heal it for you?"

She put her hand up to her face and felt the sore knot of bruised flesh.

"Please, trust me, Debra. I owe you at least this much."

She nodded shortly. "Go for it." A quick touch, a brief

opening of souls, and he would be done.

He lowered his head to hers and she drew back. "What are you doing?"

"I'm going to heal you."

"Strange, because it looked like you were going to kiss me."

His quick grin raised her temperature. "That's a bonus. This will work best if you kiss me back. Open up to me."

Her eyebrow went back up, higher this time. She knew what he was about, but it was worth almost anything to be this close to him again. His arms slipped around her shoulders and his heat enveloped her. Wild night scents of the countryside she loved flooded her mind and body. Her eyes closed, but images of Maddox in the shower flashed across her eyelids. When their lips finally met, she was more than ready, more than hungry, and as she tasted him, she moaned in relief.

He was gentle and tender, but it wasn't what she wanted. The brightness tried to distract her, but she wasn't having any of that. The bonds of proper behavior with which she had been raised shattered under her hunger and she pushed into his body, seeking more.

Maddox wrenched his mouth away, panting hard, his eyes beautiful and shimmering gold. "Heal first, then play. The light heals."

Primal instincts overshadowed her intellect. She barely heard his words, but sought his mouth again, eager for his touch.

"The light, Debra. When I kiss you, let the light come over you."

This time, the soft press of his lips took her where he led. The radiance grew again, surrounding her with peace and warmth. It was the place she had sought through the grief of her mother's death, through the upheaval of her life. The fact that it was connected to Maddox's kiss was, as he said, a bonus.

It washed over her until she calmed, then it faded, leaving quiet joy in its wake. She opened her eyes.

Maddox stood before her, his expression serious for all the tenderness of his embrace.

"I could fall in love with you."

Chapter Six

Debra dropped him off at the resource center at the park. He stepped out of the car, but before he shut the door, he turned to look at her grave, thoughtful profile.

"I'll pick you up at your place at seven. Have you been to Solstice? The food's excellent." Maddox waited.

He'd done everything wrong with Debra, but he'd had little choice. There hadn't been time to plan. From the second he'd seen her walking through the park, he'd known she was the one for him.

A sane woman would have run screaming, but she just watched him. Finally, she shook her head. "I haven't been there yet. Seven's fine."

"Debra, I'm sorry." Her eyes were killing him. So sad. But her lips tipped up a little.

"For what?"

"For dragging you into this mess."

"Maddox." She shook her head. "He attacked me, not you. I'm glad you were there. Are you sure your shoulder is better?"

He rolled it, testing for soreness. "All better. Thanks to you." Maddox hesitated. "So, see you tonight?"

Debra nodded. He closed the door and she drove off. It was good they had a few hours apart because Maddox had a lot of work to do.

At the council meeting, apart from wishing that being a werewolf gave him x-ray vision so he could see through Debra's clothes, he'd tried to assure the people that there were no wolves around. None but him, at least. Hearing about the sightings concerned him. He hadn't been anywhere near several of the places people had mentioned. And he sure as hell knew better than to flash his tail around humans. With all the rednecks around here, they'd shoot first and ask questions later.

After the attack last night, at least now he knew what he was dealing with. He walked into the deep shadows of the swamp and let the Change overtake him.

The Congaree Swamp National Park wasn't officially a swamp. It was a floodplain on the Congaree River, home to a large old-growth forest and a rich reserve of natural wetland wilderness. With over twenty-two thousand acres, the rogue had a lot of places to hide.

Maddox trotted out to one of the places near the edge of the woods where the beast had been seen and lifted his muzzle. The rogue stank. Far beyond a natural animal musk, the creature reeked of filth that obliterated the scent of the wilderness around him.

For miles, he traced the smell around the perimeter of the swamp, but every time he found a place especially heavy with the odor, it disappeared. Whoever this guy was, he was smart. He never tracked the scent out into the open with him where Maddox could follow his back trail. He must have only changed whenever he was under cover of the woods.

He followed one last trail that got heavier as it approached a small, older home outside the town limits. The beast spent a lot of time here, staring at the house. The area was rank with fetid rage and an unhealthy dose of lust. A movement in the fenced-off backyard caught his eye and he eased back into the underbrush.

Twister. The dog came out from his cool spot under the porch and approached him with a wary growl. His property. His territory. The wolf was an intruder.

Maddox stayed back, lest the dog begin to bark, drawing attention he couldn't afford. Whoever the rogue was, he'd been studying Debra's house. The hackles on his back rose with a tide of fury. No way was that son of a bitch getting to his mate.

He loped away through the bushes, back to his office at the center. He had to get back to Debra.

Debra jumped every time someone walked in the front door of the library.

The ostentatious building had originally been built as a home for the carpetbagging Yankee who swept into town after the Civil War, when there was little to be had in the South in terms of either cash or hope. He reigned as mayor with a hard hand until his Culford-born wife went gathering in the swamp one autumn day and served a lovely dish of sautéed mushrooms with his dinner that night.

Ludlow Corvell was laid to rest three days later with no mourners. His widow moved upstate to Greenville with a satchel full of cash. Her stepson, Ludlow Jr., took over as mayor, but deeded the house to the town. He said he was sick of his dead daddy always looking over his shoulder.

Through time, Corvell House served numerous functions for the city. It had, in fact, been the City Hall for years before the new one was built, leaving the home free to become a library. The original Ludlow confined his ectoplasmic activities to the small museum wing, so Debra never had any trouble with him. He wasn't a literary sort of ghost.

Today, however, the non-standard construction of the building meant that her desk faced an open portal for monsters and murderers.

She'd been distracted all day, thinking about Maddox (*Maddox naked, Maddox clothed, Maddox kissing, Maddox naked...*). Her mind stuttered and stuck there until she shook her head. She thumbed through a stack of books that traveled with her wherever she moved. Some of the books were modern hardbacks that looked like textbooks. Some, however, appeared so old they might turn to dust the moment anyone tried to turn a page. They wouldn't, of course. They couldn't. The knowledge contained in the books could never die or be destroyed. They were the physical representation of what she was—what her magic protected.

The Book.

Debra Henry, daughter many times removed to the great witch Morgaine, was a repository of magical knowledge. It was her task, as it had been her mother's and her mother's before her, to gather as much information about magic and witchcraft as possible, both new and old. Not that it did her much good. Generations back, her grandmothers had been strong in the Craft, but no more. She didn't have the power to wield it herself, only keep it for the One who would come after.

To do that, she had to keep it secret and keep it safe from those who would use the knowledge of the Book for their own purposes. Someone like that monster who had attacked her last night.

Somehow, he knew about the Book and knew that she carried it. And somehow, she was going to have to find the strength to protect it from harm.

Just her luck, Gary walked in the door. Debra sighed, keenly conscious of her budget, and gave him a reserved smile.

"How do you do, Mr. Mayor?"

"I'd like to speak to you in private, if you will, Miss Henry." His usually polished façade was a little the worse for wear. He was limping, but passed it off as a minor affectation by using an antique, brass-topped cane. The head was a snarling wolf.

Ever the gentleman, he placed his hand under her elbow as they walked, but his touch was hard and cold. She had the distinct impression of someone calling out, "Dead man walking," as they moved down the hall to the collection room.

She nodded to Gina McVay, one of the volunteers, and asked for privacy, knowing that within an hour everyone in town would hear about her closed-door meeting with the mayor.

She shook off Gary's hand and stepped back as far as she could in the cramped room.

"What's this about, Gary?"

"It's about you and me, Debra. It's about why you aren't seeing that last night didn't have to happen."

Immediately, she stiffened. "What about last night?"

"You have something that I want. I don't see why we can't come to an amicable agreement over it." He refused to meet her eyes, instead searching the contours of her face with a puzzled frown.

"What could I possibly have that you want?" Her blood

turned to ice. Could he be her attacker?

"Only you, Debra. I only want a little of your time and affection."

She almost slumped in relief. Whew. He was just your garden-variety obsessed stalker, not a big, furry murderous one. This she could handle.

"I'm sorry, Gary, but it's not going to happen." Better to cut it off cleanly, to leave him with no doubt at all that she was not interested.

He moved forward, crowding her. "I won't accept that. There is no one else in this town who is better for you than I am. I could take care of you. Make it so you don't have to work in this library. You could be with me all the time."

"Gosh. As fun as that sounds, I'm going to have to pass." An odd, prickly feeling spread over her skin, as if electricity gathered around her. Whatever it was, she welcomed the sting and bite of power.

Her whole life, her magic had been barely sufficient to guard her charge, but since the day she'd encountered that wolf in the woods, Debra had been changing. As busy as she was, she hadn't taken the time to sit down and sort it out, but something was different about her. Everything was sharper, clearer.

Last night's attack had taken her by surprise, but opening her soul to Maddox for healing had strengthened her further, unblocking paths in her spirit that had always been mere trickles. Now the trickles became rivers, rushing through her blood.

"I'm offering you every woman's dream, Debra."

"Your dream, maybe. Not mine. Don't you understand, Gary? Being a woman doesn't make me weak. I love working in my library and I don't want to be at your beck and call. And the fact that you don't get that is just sad."

Gary was the one stepping back now. He raised his arm to shield his eyes from the bright light that suffused the room. Where the heck was that coming from?

Oh. Debra checked herself. She was glowing like a nuclear plant in a third-world country. Uncertainty made the light falter, but she stood straighter, owning her gift for the first time in her life.

"Go away, Gary. Leave me alone. I don't need anyone to take care of me. I can do that on my own. What I need is someone to love me. I don't think you're capable of it."

The hand on his cane tightened and she could have sworn he growled, low and ugly. "You are going to regret this, Debra Henry. I want you and I'll have you. I don't like to lose." He pushed past her and through the door.

Curious heads poked around the stacks and he paused to adjust his gait and his tie. He glad-handed his way out of the library and Debra's stomach turned. A politician to the bone. It was like the man left a slime trail behind him.

The power she had gathered dissipated in tiny sparks, leaving her hollow and tired. She glanced at her watch, but the second hand wobbled. She shook her wrist, but it was no use. Oh well. A watch was a small price to pay for the rush of power she'd experienced.

All her life, she'd been the one in the background, learning and absorbing knowledge. It was her responsibility to Morgaine, but she took no joy in it. Instead she hid behind the task, using it as an excuse to never get close to anyone. Like her mother, she was the job, rarely indulging her desires, material or otherwise. She wore sensible, professional clothes in solid colors and classic styles. Getting her hair cut was just a whim, but she was glad she'd done it. Feminine and flattering, it made her feel better.

These surges made her think about herself in a new light. A light where being a whole person involved more than just her mind. What she'd said to Gary resonated with her. Being a woman was a genuine thrill and she'd been missing out. Grrl power ruled. She might have to start listening to Helen Reddy and burn her bra at this rate. Or maybe she'd just buy newer, prettier bras instead.

Still rattled by the encounter, she powdered her nose and smoothed down her hair before she went back out to her desk. Thankfully, it was almost time to go home. She had a pounding headache that even the thought of dinner with Maddox couldn't dim.

"Sugar, are you ok?"

Charlene King had a nose for conflict that would do a New York journalist proud. It was no surprise she showed up after the mayor left, just as it was no secret she didn't like him. That confluence of opinion made her a formidable ally within the confines of Culford society.

Since Debra needed all the support she could get to keep the library busy and well-funded, she was grateful to have Charlene on her side. Not to mention, her hair had never looked better.

"I'm fine, Charlene. Are you ready to check out now?"

"You bet. You know, I enjoyed hearing your plan to expand the library."

"Well, the council has to approve it first." And the mayor, she added silently. Her library was screwed.

"Is Gary Corvell giving you a hard time?" Charlene leaned in, giving off an air of confidentiality.

Debra tightened her lips. No way was she going to start gossiping about that jerk. That was trouble she didn't need.

"Honey, don't you worry about him. That little weasel has had it far too easy his whole life. Every Corvell son has been mayor at least once, since the original one built this house. And we've been watching the way he runs after you. It's not even decent." She fluffed her hair, and then patted Debra's hand. "Don't fuss now. We know you're not doing anything to encourage him, but if he tries to shoot down our new library, he's going to have some real trouble."

Since she was going blind from mortification, Debra could only focus on one thing at a time. "We?"

"Me and Mildred, of course."

Right. Charlene and Mildred—the two biggest gossips in town, as well as lifelong enemies—united on a course of action. Debra looked out the door to see if the Four Horsemen of the Apocalypse were trotting down the street.

"What is far more interesting is the way that young man from the Congaree Swamp was looking at you during the council meeting. He certainly seemed fascinated. And so handsome." Charlene winked broadly.

The memory of Maddox's kisses was worth an answering

grin. "I have no comment for the press at this time."

Charlene chuckled and gathered her books. "We'll see about that."

Debra packed her things, exhaustion making her steps heavy and slow. As she trudged out the door, a car pulled up in front of the library. It was Maddox.

"C'mon, Debra. I'll give you a ride home." He got out and came around to open her door. At least he'd changed out of her *Read Naked* T-shirt and crappy shorts. The jeans were old, worn and intriguingly butt-hugging. The green polo was not an improvement. The nasty color, somewhere between nuclear waste and radiator fluid, didn't help her headache.

She waved ineffectively toward her car. "What about—"

"Don't worry about it." He handed her into the seat, glancing up and down the street.

"What's wrong, Maddox?" she asked after he slid in behind the wheel. "Mmmmm, and what's that smell?" The whole car was redolent with the aroma of steak.

"That's dinner. I know I said I'd take you to Solstice, but that was before I figured out a few things. It's probably best that we stay in tonight. We have a lot to discuss."

The headache receded behind sharp concern. "What is going on?" His hands were tight on the wheel and a slight frown left a vertical slash between his brows.

The roar of the air conditioner grated on her nerves, so she reached over and snapped it off, rolling down her window instead. Immediately, the waning summer scents filled the car. Azalea blossoms and grilled steak, pine trees and hot asphalt.

"Are you feeling all right, Debra?"

"Just a headache. Strange, because it's not like I have any stress in my life right now." She closed her eyes and let the wind blow away the pain.

When they pulled up in front of her little house, she heaved a sigh. Home, at last. She got out and unlocked her door, with Maddox right behind her, carrying in dinner.

Greeting Twister after a long day at work took time and energy she could hardly spare, but his enthusiastic adoration made her feel a little better. She put his dinner—mixed with a little plain yogurt she had in her fridge—outside and closed the screen door, getting some cross-ventilation going.

"Come here," said Maddox, leading her to the tall stools lined up under her kitchen counter. "Have you eaten today?"

Debra shook her head. She'd been too nervous to eat lunch and the toast and jam from this morning hadn't lasted long.

"These are still warm, so let's eat. Almost like a real date."

"Do you think we'll ever have one of those?"

"I don't know." His easy smile was back. "Sitting in a public place, always interrupted by waiters. Dinner at home can be a lot more fun." He rummaged through her cabinets, found plates and silverware and unloaded the contents of the take-away boxes.

"I went down to Robin's instead. They're the only place in town that cooks their steaks rare enough for me." He uncorked a bottle of red wine and poured for both of them. She sipped then took a larger swallow.

"I ordered yours medium rare. I hope that's ok."

Debra cut off a bite and put it in her mouth. It melted away and she groaned in pure, visceral pleasure. "Perfect."

Maddox turned down the lights. The evening breeze took the edge off the day's humidity.

In between bites of steak, sweet potato fries and creamed spinach, she retrieved her notebook and pencil and sat down again.

"You said we had a lot to discuss. Why don't we start?"

"Going to take notes as we eat?"

"That's the plan." Depending on what he had discovered about the lunatic who had attacked her last night, she might be able to use her newly recharged power to protect both herself and Maddox. Her ability had to be good for something besides making her glow like a nightlight.

Maddox grunted and finished chewing. "Ever read any medieval French literature?"

"No, not really."

"A knight named Melion is the subject of a twelfth-century story out of Brittany, in the north of France. Back in the day, they actually had more ties to Wales and Britain than they did with France, so a lot of their mythology is mixed up with that. Even the Breton language is closer to Welsh than French."

"And this is relevant how?"

"Settle down." He sipped his wine and thought for a moment. "Ok, long story short, Melion is the original werewolf. He is where we began."

Debra leaned forward. Now they were getting to the good stuff.

"Have another bite and I'll tell you more. You need to eat."

"No, no. This is good. Keep talking."

"Eat first, then I'll talk." To prove his point, he took another bite and chewed slowly, making exaggerated yummy sounds. She rolled her eyes. *Fine, then.* Debra put down her notebook, cut off another bite of steak and practically swallowed it whole.

"Nuh-uh. This is truly prime beef, Debra. Enjoy it. Savor it. If you eat too fast, you'll regret it."

"You're trying to kill me, aren't you?"

"No, I'm trying to slow you down. A lot of things have been thrown at you and I want you to take a step back before you overload."

She hung her head and closed her eyes. He was right.

"I hate it when you're right."

"I know. I'll try to lob a few your way."

For the first time since she'd seen him in that old T-shirt, Debra laughed. It was weak, but it was a laugh. She tucked in and ate her dinner.

Chapter Seven

Maddox hid a shudder of lust as he watched her eat. The woman was sex on a stick and she had no idea how she affected him.

Too bad she didn't trust him.

An acrid tinge of deception colored the air sometimes when they spoke. Mostly when they spoke about magic. Debra had power, but he couldn't quite figure out what kind. Tonight, he needed answers almost as much as he needed her in his arms.

She finished her last bite, her last sip of wine, and delicately dabbed her mouth with a napkin. Close enough. He took her hand and helped her slide off the stool.

"Before we get to the part where you have to lie to me about what you are and what you're protecting, I need to kiss you."

Her eyes widened and she tried to pull away, but he wrapped his arms around her. "I've been dying to do this all day long, Debra. I can't wait anymore."

Every dominant instinct he possessed, both as a wolf and as a man, surged forward and he bent her over his arm, his hand cradling the back of her head as he kissed her. Devoured her. Consumed her.

Her lips melted under his, the tang of the dry red wine lingering in her mouth. Maddox dipped his tongue inside to savor more and tasted the overwhelming flavor of passion. Debra came alive in his arms. Not content to be swept under him, she fought his lead, vying for control, and he relished the battle.

She hooked one leg around him. Her skirt was long and

slim, preventing her from moving higher, so he slid his hand down and yanked up the fabric, bunching it around her hips so he could grab her thigh and pull her in tighter to his body.

Thigh-highs. She was wearing thigh-high stockings. With garters. His knees went weak. His erection turned into a painful throb and he groaned, pulling away from her mouth to nuzzle her neck.

"You're killing me, pretty little Debra Henry."

"Likewise, Mr. Moreau." Her soft, sweet drawl ripped his heart right out of his chest, but her scent changed from the spice of lust to sharp regret. She hugged him, tucking her face into his shoulder. "I'm so sorry." Her arms sagged and the weight of her remorse pulled at him like a millstone.

He slid her thigh back down his leg and adjusted her skirt. "Please tell me what it is. I can't help you if you don't tell me."

"I can't. I'm so sorry, but I just can't. Telling you may put us in even more danger than we're in now. It's...complicated."

"You're a witch. I know. I smell magic on you, Debra. Sweet and sparkling. It's like champagne. I know you're protecting something and I figure it's got to be pretty big if you're not telling me, am I right?"

The hitch in her breath and the way she caught her lower lip in her teeth gave him the answer he'd already guessed.

"There are rules that have to be followed. It's not my secret to tell."

"I understand that, but we'll have to deal with it sooner or later." He nuzzled her cheek. "Maybe later."

Despite the lie that stood between them, he knew her down in his bones. It was bad enough when he'd only wanted her, when his plan was to woo her gently, but in the face of the danger and the power that surrounded them, they were well past a slow courtship. Something bigger than both of them was moving them together and he didn't want to fight it.

"I have this fantasy," he said, letting his hand wander down over her hips.

"Do we have time for fantasies?" Her eyes glazed, her lips parted, and she reached up to kiss him again. He licked at her mouth.

"We'll make time. This one should be easy for you. You're perfect for it, in fact." Her glasses had slid down to their customary spot and she looked at him over the rims. While getting her naked and spread was high on his priority list, Maddox still wanted to give her something she needed—a loving that was fun and lighthearted.

He spun her out on the tips of his fingers. "You're the sexiest librarian I've ever seen. Sharp haircut, hot glasses. Pretty blouse." He trailed a finger down the modest V-neck. "Tight skirt." His other hand palmed her ass. "Your shoes are a little on the sensible side. Got any hooker heels?"

She chuckled, a husky sound that fired his blood. "You have a librarian fantasy?"

"Only if you're the librarian." He reached into her open tote bag and pulled out a paperback. A romance novel, its cover a subtle, sensual twining of male and female limbs. He tossed it onto the floor behind her. Her head cocked in confusion.

"Oh, Miss Librarian. I dropped a book. Would you please bend over and pick it up for me?"

Debra eyed the book, then her lips quirked up in a sexy smile. Her hips rolled as she turned her back on him. Oh yeah. She was getting into it now. Rather than just leaning down for it, however, she bent at the knees and, spine straight, elegantly lowered herself to reach the book. Not quite what he had in mind, but he'd work with it.

Then she nailed him. Smooth and slow, her legs straightened. Her arm still touching the floor, her ass rose in front of him like a mirage out of the desert. Teasing. Taunting. Right about the time she began to lift her body, he stepped behind her, hugging her hips into his, savoring the slide of heat on heat. His cock was cushioned against those luscious cheeks as she stood fully into his hold, reaching back with her arm to pull his head down to hers.

His hands shook when he took the book from her and tossed it onto the couch. His arms wrapped around her waist as he nuzzled her neck.

"Why, sir, didn't you want that book?"

"I don't need to read love scenes, babe. Let's go write one."

He led her to the hot, dark bedroom and left her standing dazed while he opened all the windows to the night breeze, the ceiling fan stirring to lazy life. Debra swayed in her sensible shoes and he came back to her.

"That's much better. Now we can smell the night."

She sorted out the scents of the forest as they flowed through her room. The most powerful of all was the male musk that filled her head.

"All I smell is you."

A wisp of night-blooming jasmine whispered through the air and the mood shifted to something sweeter, softer. He folded her in his arms and she welcomed the tenderness. Her head rested against his strong shoulder. The softest kiss landed in her hair as his hands stroked her.

"Sweetheart," he murmured. They stood in the starlit dark a moment longer before his arms tightened. "Tell me more about these stories, Miss Librarian."

Debra laughed. "I don't need the fantasy to make love to you, Maddox."

"I know, but we've had a rough day. Do you realize we've known each other for only twenty-four hours? We've eaten two meals together. We've healed each other's wounds. We've showered and slept together. Let's take a little time to play. Do you really read those naughty books?"

She blushed and wondered if he could see in the dark. "A few."

"Fantastic. Let's see what you can teach me."

Ripples of magic skidded through her. Maddox wasn't focused on what he could do to lead, though he was one of the strongest personalities she'd ever encountered, but what they could do together. Every second she spent with him, she became more and more the best version of herself. Sexy, feminine and powerful.

She raised her face to his and tasted his lips. As heady as good whiskey, he plastered her against him, but it wasn't enough. She wanted to feel his skin on hers.

Debra reached under his shirt and pulled up. Their lips clung until the last moment, when the noxious green fabric came between them. He undid her buttons and, within moments, her shirt followed his to the floor.

"I was right," he groaned.

"About what?" Debra went after the button on his jeans, cursing her nails as they got in the way.

"These." He cupped her breasts through her plain, rather sturdy bra. Not seduction material, by any means, but he didn't seem to care. "I thought I might have dreamed these, but they're real."

She would have laughed at the naked lust on his face, but that required breath she didn't have to spare. She got the button undone as he slid his arms around her back and unsnapped the bra.

The straps slid down her arms and he drew it off reverently, as if unveiling a masterpiece. She felt like one. He had already seen her naked and he seemed to like the way she was put together. In his arms, she felt sexy and earthy.

She stepped back, allowing him to look his fill while she watched his face. His lips parted and his chest heaved like a bellows. Faded jeans hung off lean hips, the unsnapped button a sweet temptation. A fine sheen of sweat silvered his throat and she wanted to lick it off.

So she did. Old inhibitions died as skin met skin. He wrapped his arms around her and pulled her close, sliding his hands over her back, pressing her body into his.

His palms traveled lower, pulling her hips into his, where she couldn't fail to notice the erection encased by his jeans.

"I've wanted to see you again, touch you again." His words fell into the void of her mind and she nodded, incapable of speech. Maddox deftly undid the fastening of her skirt, letting it slide to the floor.

She stood before him in nothing but her stockings, garter and hip-hugging underwear. The thigh-highs were more a concession to the Carolina heat than any attempt at sexiness. That was, as he said, a bonus. Her shoes, classic, simple, sensible pumps, brought her a little closer to his height.

He growled and she shivered at the primal sound. With animal grace, he stalked her, circled her, inhaling long drafts of her. Without ever touching, he surrounded her like she was the center of a bonfire.

He stopped behind her and wrapped his arm around her waist, pulling her back against him. It left his hands free to roam where they wished, caressing skin that burned like fire under his touch.

As enthralled as he seemed, she expected him to dive straight for her breasts, but he surprised her. The curve of her hip and the dip of her waist absorbed his attention until she rubbed mindlessly against him, her hands grabbing the sides of his jeans to pull him ever closer.

Only then did his fingers begin a torturous trail up her ribs to flutter against the sides of her fullness, over the top, up to her shoulders, while she yearned for his hands on her flesh. She whimpered in need and he took pity, letting his fingers feather down to draw the lightest of circles around her nipples, raising her nerve endings to a painful pitch. Her own hands turned to claws as she worked to hold back, to let him do what he wanted.

"Maddox," she breathed.

His hold on her changed, pulling her back against him as he swiveled his hips and started tapping out a rhythm with his toes. He hummed an old Commodore's song as his tongue trailed over her shoulders. The buzz from his lips started an electric current in her body and though they were both laughing by the time he got to the "boom chicka wow, she's a brick house" part of the disco riff, she was ready to come apart in his hands.

He unhooked her garter belt and the nylons slid down her legs. His lips followed them down the backs of her knees and she shuddered. She nearly fell over when his lips traveled back up.

His tongue slid along the edge of her panties, his hands pulling her thighs apart so he could follow the seam between them. His hair against the inside of her legs was hot, smooth silk, drawing forth a creamy response.

She moaned when he blew hot air against her most sensitive spot. She groaned when he bared his teeth, scoring the fabric. She sobbed when he finally used his fingers to move her panties out of his way.

And when his tongue slid through the folds that parted at his touch, her knees buckled completely.

Maddox caught her before she fell and helped her backward to the bed. Her underwear and his jeans flew in separate directions. Who cared where they landed, as long as they were off.

Debra crawled backwards until she lay in the middle of the mattress, her legs parted, cradling his solid, muscled body. But he didn't move to enter her. Not with his cock, at least.

Propped on his elbow, he leaned down to suck her nipple into his mouth as his hand delved into her sex.

"You don't taste like anything else in the world. You are uniquely, completely Debra." He licked the skin between her breasts, and then latched onto the other one.

She was awash in sensation. His mouth, his hands, his heat and weight overwhelmed her. The words he said were music on the wave of exquisite agony she rode.

The breeze touched her damp skin and jolted her back to a keener awareness. He was heading back down her body and she didn't want to be too dazed to enjoy this.

Slow licks and nibbling kisses spread her outer lips to his exploration. Two fingers held her open for more and soon he feasted, each touch of his mouth sending her farther and farther into the reservoir of energy that had been stored within her for generations. His tongue flickered inside her, licking and stabbing as his thumb stroked around her clit in a deliberate rhythm.

Maddox was relentless, driving her up a sheer cliff with no safety net until finally her body twisted in on itself and she burst, falling into space, crying for mercy.

He slid back up her body until he held her close, soothing her, drying her tears.

"Shhh, sweetheart. Don't cry."

"I'm...not...crying," she sniffled between gasps.

"Of course not." That masculine grin, that self-congratulating glint in his eye would have made her laugh if she had anything left in her. They lay together, quiet and close until her breathing steadied.

Until his heartbeat quickened.

Balance. Yin and yang, masculine and feminine. The universe thrived on balance. Her needs were satisfied, but his weren't.

She stretched, reaching up to kiss him. His hand wrapped around the back of her neck, pulling her in ever closer until they fused together from head to toe.

Everywhere their skin touched felt like he was cuddling up to a live fuse. His tongue in her mouth, hers fighting back, trading the flavor of her sex.

He'd never tasted anything better, or anything hotter. That Miss Librarian act was no joke. Underneath her cool, elegant exterior lay a deeply sensual woman.

Seeing her naked in front of him tonight, displayed solely for his pleasure, was a thousand times better than the illicit glimpse he'd spied this morning. She was a goddess. Every wet dream he'd ever had centered on the sexy, lush feast lying next to him right now.

The one who was kissing her way down his chest like she had somewhere important to be.

Maddox was a simple man. A direct man. So when she nuzzled his cock with her cheek, when she looked up at him and grinned like the wolf who caught the bunny, all he wanted to do was fuck her into oblivion. It took unbelievable strength of will to wait while she kissed from one hipbone to the other, groaning when the head of his penis painted a hot, wet trail under her chin.

Not soon enough, she licked her way around the base of his shaft. When she began to press sucking little wet kisses up and down his length, though, he started praying for patience, because he wanted this to last until the world fell apart.

Just as he had done to her, her hands moved up his thighs, parting them until hot fingers cupped his balls. He moaned and threw his head back on the pillow, blind with sensation. Her mouth traced a wicked pattern on his skin until it reached the top of his cock. She paused. Maddox opened his eyes and saw that she was looking at him like a fat man at an all-you-can-eat buffet.

He wanted to see how much farther she'd go and when she

finally licked out with her sweet, pink tongue, he couldn't help himself. He arched forward, sliding through her lips, over her tongue, feeling the faint scrape of her teeth along the sides of his cock. And when she swallowed, he choked.

Maddox pulled out of her mouth, out of her grip, and let his brain take a back seat to biology.

He rose up on his knees and pulled her up with him, kissing any inch of skin he could put his lips on. He cupped her face in his hands and tried to swallow her whole, laying his most carnal, voracious kiss on her. Delighting in her hot, wet response.

"I need to be inside you. Can't wait." His words were an urgent monotone as he reached for his jeans and fished in the back pocket. He ripped open the packet with teeth only a little sharper than human and sheathed himself in record time. When he refocused on her, he discovered her watching him, apparently fascinated by the way he touched himself.

She licked her lips and said, "Next time, I want to put it on."

His hips jerked forward and he growled, riding the thin edge of control and losing it fast.

Still facing each other on their knees, Debra looked into his eyes and smiled in wonder. She put her hand on his face.

"They're gold."

"What?"

"Your eyes. They're gold. They're beautiful."

Whatever. Sex. Now.

"I wouldn't know. I'm color blind." Maddox put his hands on her hips and pulled her in, cradling his erection in the soft flesh of her belly, until she pulled away. She turned. Slowly. Twisting her body until she rested on all fours, she looked over her shoulder at him.

If he hadn't been in love with her already, he fell for certain at that moment. Debra Henry knew what he was and she accepted him completely. Both human and animal. And wouldn't he love to get all romantic with her, give her the words he wanted her to hear, do all the sweet, tender things women liked. But he was only himself, with no poetry in him. Nothing but desire and love all mixed together until he couldn't think. Until her gorgeous ass was the only thing he saw in his tunnel vision. He'd give her everything, anything. As much as love could give.

He licked a path up her back, tasting sex and sweat on her skin. He pushed her knees further apart and moved close, close enough to feel her heat on his cock, to slide it through the cream gathered there, waiting for him. Welcoming him.

He slid home in one long thrust. Through the tight, clasping muscles, into the endless, mindless heat. When his balls touched her smooth skin, he stopped.

She was perfectly still underneath him and he hesitated.

"Debra? Sweetheart? Are you ok?" Christ. What had he done? He didn't know anything about her sexual history, other than he was sure she wasn't a virgin. Had he gone too fast? Had he hurt her?

Her arms were stiff, her head bowed and she whimpered a word so faint that even he couldn't hear it.

"Debra?"

She said it again.

"Move. I can't come until you move, so move, dammit!" She looked at him over her shoulder, her face suffused with the same need that rode him. So he moved.

Gently at first, still uncertain, until their hips caught the same rhythm and she began to piston backwards onto him. He grabbed her thighs and pulled her closer, levering her up so he could give her what she wanted. What they both wanted.

There was no way he could last much longer and the one desire that stood clearly above the rest was that she had to be there with him when he finished. Maddox slid his hands around her through the heat and the sweat and the slippery sex until he found her clit. His shoulders tightened against the rush moving down his spine and he circled her faster.

Her cries rose in pitch and his thighs began to shake. Deeper and deeper he drove into her body, answering the need to take, to dominate, to fulfill his mate and bond with her until she bucked underneath him, her voice gone, her body a living flame.

Maddox shattered, each fragment of his soul like the shards of a mirror, reflecting the whole. Broken and free, he drifted—under her, over her, around her. She became the focal point and he gathered the splinters of himself, using her as the center. And in the circle of light, he realized that she did the same. Like an unending series of self-portraits, he watched as she put herself back together around him. They protected each other. He was her heart now. And she was his. Forever.

Chapter Eight

She was awake. And talking. He tried to listen, but his brain was still a little blurry around the edges.

"You being color blind makes a lot of sense. It explains a lot too."

"What's that supposed to mean?"

"You remember that tie you were wearing at the council meeting?"

"Yeah."

"It's ugly. It's worse than ugly. It's hideous. Appalling. Nauseating."

"You criticize my favorite tie? I love that tie!"

"Why? How could you love that tie? Please tell me your mother didn't buy it for you."

He snorted. His parents had moved to northern British Columbia years ago to study the wild wolf population and freeze their asses off. "My mother doesn't do stuff like that. I bought it. I like the pattern."

"You need serious mental help. Your shirt today is ugly too."

"Ugly is in the eye of the beholder."

"Yes, it is. I beheld it. It is ugly." She snagged her pencil and notebook off the nightstand, then crossed her legs and waited expectantly.

"You're relentless, you know that?" Maddox watched her through sleepy eyes. They'd napped for a bit after the most explosive sex of his life, but rather than start on round two, she was ragging on his colorblindness and taking notes.

"I know but...it's what I do."

"Your magical gift is being judgmental about my fashion choices and obsessive?"

She tossed a pillow at him and he caught it and stuffed it under his head.

"That's cute. You're funny *and* fuzzy. I gather knowledge. Information. Being a librarian is kind of a family tradition."

He rearranged his pillows and made himself comfortable. "What do you want to know?"

"Why don't you start at the beginning? Tell me about werewolves."

"My line is descended from the knight I told you about, Melion. He was the lover of the sorceress Morgaine when Arthur was still king. Melion's children bred true werewolves, men and women who could change into a wolf to roam and hunt."

"So only descendants of Melion can be werewolves? What if a human gets bitten?"

"Total Hollywood. A bite can't turn a human. Being a werewolf is pure blood magic. You either are one, or you aren't." He stopped and scowled. "Unless you're a rogue. People like that are abominations. They take the magic and pervert it. For him to become what he is, he had to trap, kill and skin a true werewolf. Then the murdering bastard wraps the hide around himself, uses a specific incantation and a generous helping of burned wolfsbane, and he becomes half-wolf, half-human. All monster."

Maddox looked over at the top of Debra's head as she scribbled furiously. He'd been absolutely right about her. Brains and beauty. A perfect combination.

"Where would someone find this knowledge about how to become a werewolf? I mean, I know a lot about magic, but I've never heard of that."

"It's not as if we share the info with any random stranger who asks for it. In fact, no one has pulled this particular trick in the last hundred years or so. I don't know how he found out."

She tapped the pencil against her teeth for a moment. "What are his weaknesses? How do we get rid of him?"

"His weaknesses are the same as mine. Silver to a vital

organ, a snapped neck, or taking his heart. Because he's not born magic, though, we can also take him out by destroying the skin he wears."

"But how do we get to him in the first place? I've never seen him before. Last night was the first time." She frowned. "At least, I think it was. A couple of days ago, I went up to the park for a walk and I saw..." She broke off. "Well, you said there weren't any wolves in South Carolina. Not big black ones."

"Only me." He grinned.

"That was you?"

"Yeah, that was me. I was trying to figure out a way to meet you as a human. Providence was on my side when you showed up at that council meeting."

Maddox stood abruptly. Twister was outside, snarling and barking at something in the woods.

"Debra, go get your dog."

"What? Why?" She stood as well, looking around in confusion.

"Just do it. It's not safe for him out there."

She slipped on her robe and hurried to the back door.

Maddox called the Change to him. Bred into his blood and bone, the shifting felt more like diving into a maelstrom than anything else. Exciting and exhilarating, he became an extension of the natural world. As a human, he walked on the surface of the earth. As a wolf, he sprang directly from its heart.

She called Twister, who reluctantly returned to her, but before she could close the door, Maddox stood at her knee.

He heard her gasp, but ignored it as he stalked out to the back porch. There it was. That rotting stink. The beast was out there, watching Debra. Waiting for her.

A grating howl, an eerie scream, scraped through the air. Maddox raised his nose and howled his answering challenge to the black night.

Bring it, asshole. She's mine.

"Oh, that's it. I am so over this." Debra had no intention of repeating last night's weakness. After this afternoon, she had no patience left.

"Move over, Maddox." She walked out onto the back porch to stand beside him. He tried to block her path, but she had none of it.

"Do you want me? Do you want the Book?" she yelled out to the intruder. "Well, you can't have us!"

This was what she had been born to do. She protected the Book. Energy rushed through her like a flood. Fury accompanied it.

Down she charged, Maddox surging ahead, ready to meet the black sorcerer with power of her own. Together, they faced their enemy.

The wolf leapt at the beast's head, only to be knocked a glancing blow. Preternaturally quick, he turned and sliced into the creature's arm.

First blood. The battle was on.

They struck at each other over and over, the beast's long, claw-tipped arms giving him an advantage over Maddox. But Maddox had his own strengths. He knew how to move quickly, darting in, slashing with teeth and claws, inflicting damage where he could until they both bled freely from a dozen wounds.

Debra's home was on the edge of civilization. Only a few steps separated her from the swamp. The fight rolled into the wilderness and she followed.

There was a limit to what Debra could do, though, no matter how strong she was. She could only defend, never attack. Her entire being was hardwired to the most basic premise of witchcraft—"an' it harm none". Not even to protect those she loved could she destroy another being. But that didn't mean she was doomed to cowardice.

The beast wanted her, did he? He didn't even know what she was, and she could use that to her advantage.

Maddox rolled away from another strike, a little slow to rise. It gave the monster the moment he needed to draw his blade.

If she was going to save him, now was the time.

"Hey, you!" She whistled a piercing blast, jarring both of the fighters, who turned to look at her.

And her.

Identical twins, each on either side of their circle. One approached Maddox, the other sauntered toward the rogue. Each deliberately provocative. Feminine power bloomed through the night, giving off the heady scent of sex.

Here was the source of her power, here at the core of her being. She wasn't merely female, she was Woman with all the strength it entailed. The eternal paradox, the unsolvable enigma.

Her arm reached out to trail delicate fingers over each male.

"What do you want?" she asked in stereo. "What's your deepest desire?" Jasmine, heady, strong and dangerous, surrounded her, blooming where she stepped.

"I want you," each answered, then they snarled at each other.

The beast continued, "I want your magic."

"But you can only have one," said the Debra who danced before him. "You must choose."

She raised her hands to the moon, drinking in the light. Around her, black water shimmered. The monster growled, his long tongue snaking out to taste her scent in the air.

"Choose," she chanted, continuing her dance around him, never touching him, never letting him close enough to touch her. She, the untouchable. The unknowable. The ultimate mystery.

"I want both." His voice, inhuman, rose in a gravelly whine. "I can have whatever I want. You can't stop me. You can't hurt me. I am strong."

Immediately, the dance stopped and all the scents and sounds of the forest died away. The Female knew her power and knew that she could not be owned and used by any man, no matter how strong. Her arms dropped to her sides as she looked at him sadly. "Yes, you are. Too bad you're also stupid." She whirled. "Now, Maddox!"

Maddox circled his Debra, keeping her close. He licked her hand and she knelt, looping her arms around his heat. "I know you," she whispered in his ear. "I've known you for centuries, descendant of Melion. Ages ago, you were my hero, my lover. As you are now."

This wasn't Debra. The woman beside him was not his Debra. "Where did she go? What have you done with her?" he whispered, trying to keep his focus on the enemy before him, the one who was dazed by the dance of a ghostly, sensual witch.

"She is I. I am she. Fear not, brave knight. Courage and cunning will win fair lady, not brute strength. She can do no harm, and so she baits him, waiting for you. Trusting you. Will you fail her?"

Maddox shook off the weakness that gnawed at him. His Debra danced with a monster, but it was up to him to kill it.

Her call galvanized him. The beast was off-guard, the silver blade held in a lax grip. Maddox streaked forward and the monster raised his hand to protect his throat from the killing blow that never came. Instead, Maddox struck at his midriff, tearing off the pelt of the murdered werewolf.

The creature howled in agony, dropping to the ground as the evil magic drained from his body. He writhed, screaming, as his bones shattered, reforming themselves to a human mold. His skull twisted in a grotesque maneuver, shrinking back to a recognizable face as the coarse fur receded into his skin.

A naked human lay exposed to the elements, small and insignificant in his all-too-mortal body.

Gary Corvell.

The man's pale scent had been completely submerged to the beast. No wonder Maddox hadn't been able to identify him.

He returned with the pelt, which he softly laid at his Debra's feet. The other Debra knelt by Gary's motionless form and touched his head. He stiffened and moaned in pain then his eyes fluttered open. He jumped up snarling, but it just didn't have the same effect as when he was hairy and huge and disgusting.

Debra gasped and covered her eyes. Maddox snorted. The woman, the not-Debra, rose more sedately.

Gary crouched down, cupping himself while Debra's body shook with repressed laughter.

"It's not funny," screamed the formerly dapper little man.

"Actually," said the not-Debra, "it's quite funny." She raised her arms above her head and Gary cowered away. She raised an eyebrow at him—now he knew where Debra got that habit—and when her arms lowered, she wasn't Debra's twin anymore. Like enough to be sisters, but definitely different. The other woman was smaller, more compact, and her hair was darker.

"Why don't you tell us how you became the beast, Mr. Corvell?"

"I don't have to tell you anything." Gary tried a sneer, but it was like watching a pug snarl. Pointless. Maddox didn't even put any heat into his answering growl and the mayor paled.

"Where did you get the pelt, Gary?" asked Debra.

"Where do you think I got it? From Ludlow."

"Ludlow Corvell? But he's been dead since 1872."

"He's still around. You should know."

"How did he get the pelt?"

"I don't know. From someone in his family, I suppose. I was up in the museum area one day and he showed me where to find it in a box." Corvell shuddered at the memory. Maddox had seen the portrait of the old bastard. He'd shudder too.

"There was a book under the pelt with some old writing in it. I took it up to Duke to get it translated. It had the spell, so I tried it. I didn't think it would really work. But then it did. And it felt good to be big and powerful and scary."

"How did you find out about the Book? About me?" Debra inched closer to Maddox and buried her cold fingers in his fur.

"You have no idea, do you?" Corvell was starting to sound a little cocky, so Maddox growled again. "You reek of magic. It was weaker when you first came to town, but in the last few days, it's gotten stronger and stronger. There's no way *not* to know what you are. Controlling you would have meant controlling your power. I would have had all the knowledge in the Book for myself."

Debra looked at the other woman. "What do we do now? How can I protect the Book when he knows what I am?"

Maddox Changed and Debra's small, cold fingers reached out for his. The other one smiled at her.

"Do not worry, my child. It has been far too long since your mothers embraced what I am, what I could have given them. Haven't you figured out who I am yet?"

Yeah, he knew, and she scared the ever-living crap out of him. It was never safe for any male to stand too close to all that female power.

But his Debra stepped forward, fearless and brave. "I know you. You're Morgaine. My Mother. My Sister."

"The author of the Book that resides in your spirit. My magic, all my knowledge, lies with you. The magic we wield is older than any belief system. It comes from the earth, from the sky, from the water, from the fire. To take a memory is not a task undertaken lightly, but justice must be served."

She raised her hands to the moon again, but when her sleeves fell back, Maddox could see that her arms were covered in tattoos. Sigils. Wards.

Light grew between her hands and became a solid shape, a dark grid. When she lowered her arms, she held a cage inscribed with some of the same symbols she wore on her skin. Morgaine picked up the soiled and sad pelt, stroked it lovingly, and folded it into the cage.

She held her hand out to Debra and together they waded into the swamp, wet to their knees, and lowered the cage into the black water. The words Morgaine spoke rolled off her tongue, danced in his ears, flashed rainbows and lightning in his eyes. As the remains of the werewolf were swallowed, Debra joined in.

"Fire cleanses, fire purifies. Let the fire burn away the evil brought to use these many years ago. Let it burn away the memory of pain and power, of greed and death."

Green flickering light—what he had always called swamp fire—danced and flitted in the palm of her hand. Debra laid the fire down where the cursed fur had sunk.

"As the fire dies out, so does the remembrance of these evil deeds."

The ladies held hands again as they walked back to the shore and stood next to Maddox, watching the flames spark into nothingness.

Gary Corvell lay unconscious in the mud. At least he was

still breathing, which was awfully damn generous as far as Maddox was concerned.

"He has forgotten what he has done. I doubt others will be so forgiving now that he no longer possesses the glamour of the wolf's power. The wolf who was murdered so long ago can now rest easy," said Morgaine.

Debra ignored the pale body on the ground and looked at Maddox, tears shining in her eyes. "I'm so sorry, Maddox. I couldn't tell you. I'm charged not to tell any man. The women in my family have carried this knowledge for generations, but somewhere along the way, we forgot how to apply it in our own lives. The magic weakened. I knew about it, but I couldn't tap into it. Until I met you. Maybe it was your own magic that woke mine up. Or maybe it's because with you, I can be everything I'm supposed to be."

The great witch smiled. "As it should be. A woman's power is no small thing, but too many have made it so. We are meant to balance each other, not relinquish our will to that of another in the hope of gaining love. You would have found your power without him, daughter, but your magic will be all the greater for the love you share."

Morgaine turned to him and he stood his ground. "And you, Maddox. Son of my great love. Melion would be proud of you." She took his hand and Debra's. "You are not the ones who will wield the Book. Instead, you are the ones who will hold the circle around her. Your daughter."

Debra gasped, but Maddox just smiled. He'd known it the whole time. Debra was the one for him, the one he'd waited for.

Morgaine stepped back, leaving them holding each other. "Blessed be, Debra and Maddox. I'll see you again. In the meantime..." She glanced down at Maddox's naked body. The smile this time was all about feminine desire. "In the meantime, Debra, have some fun."

Two hours later, Twister started pawing at the back door, whining to be let in. Debra pulled a robe on over her well-satisfied body and let him bound into the house.

As she did, she saw a pale form scurrying along the edge of the treeline. She pushed her glasses further up on her nose and squinted. "Huh. There goes Mayor Corvell."

Maddox came up behind her, a towel wrapped around his waist. He slid an arm around her and planted a kiss on her neck.

"It's a good thing that man usually wears clothes, because he's pretty scrawny," she said, leaning back into his arms. "You think he'll be okay?"

Maddox shrugged and swallowed the bite of cold pizza he was eating. "Like I give a rat's ass. He'll be fine, but I bet he won't be mayor too much longer."

"Oh, good. I can get my library funding." She closed the door.

He dropped his towel, and then reached for the tie of her robe. "Yep. And you can fill it with books where wolves howl at the moon and everyone lives happily ever after."

She shrieked with laughter and ran to the bedroom. He howled and ran after her.

About the Author

To learn more about Sela Carsen, please visit www.selacarsen.com and check out her blog. You can also find her blogging regularly at Beyond the Veil—a group blog of paranormal romance authors at http://paranormalauthors.blogspot.com/. Send an email to Sela at selacarsen@gmail.com. She'll be thrilled to hear from you!

Look for these titles by
Sela Carsen

Now Available:

Not Quite Dead
Heart of the Sea

Print Anthology
Love and Lore

ParaMatch.com

MK Mancos

Dedication

To all those who believe love is the ultimate aphrodisiac.

Chapter One

"I have needs, you know?" Cornelius Thornton sat in the client's chair across the wide expanse of Lucilla Wainwright's massive desk. Even in a casual suit he looked like a predator.

He shifted his hunter's sharp gaze to look out the balcony doors. "It's difficult to maintain a relationship when every full moon I turn into a hairy beast who wants nothing more than to run into the woods and howl."

Lucilla planted a compassionate expression on her face and indicated the plasma screen television behind her. "After going over your questionnaire, I have compiled a short list of women I think you'll be pleased with."

He put his finger between his neck and collar. "I'm kind of nervous. This seems like a last-ditch effort for me."

"Nonsense. You're an attractive man. You hold down a good job. There's no reason for you to believe we won't find you a successful match."

He let out a long breath and nodded. "I'm just so damn lonely."

"I know, Mr. Thornton." She hit the play button on the DVD remote and the screen filled with the image of a woman who could stop rush-hour traffic. She wasn't just gorgeous, she was almost unreal in her beauty.

A low, seductive voice came from the speaker. "It's difficult for a man to commit to a relationship with me when he learns of my past." She tossed her long raven hair over her shoulder and looked directly into the camera as if making love to it. "They don't seem to understand that, for the right man, I'll be unbreakably faithful."

Lucilla glanced at Mr. Thornton and nearly laughed. If he thought howling at the full moon was bad, he looked ready to shift species in the middle of the afternoon.

"You approve?"

The poor man was beyond words. His mouth hung open as if he'd been rendered deaf and dumb.

"Would you like to meet her, Mr. Thornton?"

His lips flapped a few times before a low, growling "yes" came out.

"Excellent. Here is her contact information." She slid a postcard-sized printout to him. "I'll tell her to expect your call."

He stood and held out his hand. "Thank you, Ms. Wainwright."

"Save the thanks for after your date."

He gave her a most spectacular and devastating smile. When he was almost to the door, he stopped. "Um, what exactly is her paranormalady?"

"She's a succubus."

Mr. Thornton left the office with the air of a man who'd just won the sexual lottery. Oh, yeah, if he worried about having his needs fulfilled, he needn't worry any longer.

As her insides did a happy dance, Lucilla turned to her computer and consulted her schedule for the afternoon. She had some free time in which to review new client profiles and select possible matches.

Lucilla didn't believe in letting the computer perform that part of the service. Finding a true match for a client deserved the personal touch. When dealing with the precarious love lives of the city's paranormal element, one needed to have that special one-on-one connection. Many of the beings Lucilla dealt with on a daily basis were private in their interactions with the outside world. Having a committed relationship with someone who knew how it was to live with a paranormalady sometimes made all the difference in the world.

The intercom sounded.

"Yes?"

"There is a Mr. Cronus here to see you."

What is he doing here? "Tell him to come in."

Jeez. She really didn't want to have to deal with him today. Things were going so well. She'd made follow-up calls on three successful matches. The possibility for a fourth still hung sweet in the air. Now, Mr. Impossible-To-Match decided to come by and complain about the lack of compatible dates he'd been on.

Truthfully, Lucilla had doubts there was anything wrong with the women she'd matched with Mr. Cronus. The fault lay entirely with him. However, in the matchmaker business, it was impolitic to point that out to a client. Especially one who paid in cash. And Lucilla didn't come cheap.

She pulled up his file on the computer. There were several women he had yet to date. There was always hope that one of those would be his perfect match.

Jager Cronus ducked his head as he entered the office. He was the biggest man she'd ever met. As the deposed leader of the Titans, he claimed the mythologies maligned him. After the trouble she'd had matching him, Lucilla was almost positive the exaggerations were few.

"Lucilla." He crossed the room in a few long-legged strides.

He looked down at her from his great height of six-and-a-half feet. Granted, when one thought of Titans, one thought of giants, but in all honesty, their height had also been greatly exaggerated in the mythos. They were no taller than professional basketball players. But his height wasn't the thing Lucilla found so intimidating about him—it was his looks.

Drop-dead gorgeous didn't even begin to describe him. Tightness centered in her chest whenever she saw him. Though the fact he was so hard to please took points off.

Lucilla forced a pleasant smile and indicated for him to take a seat. "Can I get you anything?"

"Yes, you can get me an appropriate date."

The smile slipped slightly, but she ground her back teeth together and pushed on. "If you don't mind me asking, what was your objection to Ms. Hyde?"

"With a name like that, do you really have to ask?"

The word *jerk* did a serpentine inside her brain.

"My understanding is that she isn't in that particular form for long."

"No, but then I don't expect my dates to morph during the soup course." He raised a brow as if he were lecturing an errant child.

"I can see where that would be disconcerting for you." She clicked a few buttons on the keyboard and hit print. Two profiles sure to be doomed spit out of the printer.

"I haven't given up and I don't want you to either." She rose to collect the printouts. His gaze followed her across the room.

Mr. Cronus possessed the kind of stare that made a woman feel hot and naked. Even standing in the middle of a blizzard probably wouldn't cool the heat of his appraisal.

She looked at him over her shoulder. A connection too powerful to name passed between them. He started to rise, but Lucilla was quick to motion for him to sit.

"There are two new women who applied in the past few days. Maribon is a selkie with an impressive pedigree. Esmeralda is a djinn who has just fulfilled her contractual obligation with her master."

The look he sent her was skeptical. "I'll try them, but first I want you to do something for me."

If it moved things along, she'd agree to take up clogging. "What is that, Mr. Cronus?"

"Two things, then. First, call me Jager. Second, fill out a profile on yourself."

If she had taken a drink, it would have landed in his face. Luckily, her coffee cup was empty. "I don't think that's a very good idea."

"Oh, I think it is."

"Why do you want me to take the time to fill out a profile when I could be combing the database for more possible matches for you?" She already knew the answer to that question, but needed to hear him say it.

He leaned his big, sexy body over the desk. "I think you're the best match for me, and I think you know it, too."

There was no doubt in her mind their profiles would have a very high probability for a long-term match. She'd secretly crunched the numbers when he first applied as a client. The memory of which caused heat to creep up her neck and ignite the tops of her ears.

"Is something the matter, Lucilla?"

"No. No." She smoothed her hair, pulling it forward to cover the vestiges of her acute embarrassment.

"You look like you've done something wrong."

Lucilla cleared her throat. "Back when I first started the agency, I wanted to test the questionnaire software, so I took the profile quiz."

Jager grinned at her as if he'd caught her in the middle of doing a striptease. "Do whatever it is you do to compare it to mine."

Lucilla raised a brow at him. "I do all my comparisons by hand. It takes time and consideration. You just can't slap people together in a haphazard fashion. Computers can't give that personal touch my clients pay for."

"The personal touch is exactly what I'm asking for." The twinkle came back into his eyes. "But since you're the professional here, I'll make a deal with you. I'll go out with the selkie and the other, but you have to agree to go to the Legion Halloween Dance with me."

Even though she knew she looked as attractive as a freshly caught carp, Lucilla couldn't help but flap her mouth open and closed. The Legion Halloween Dance was the biggest event in Sleepy Hollow Woods. It was the one night of the year those with any form of paranormalady could go out and be themselves without fear of persecution from the Norms. The catch being that most people who were true Paras attended the dance only if accompanied by another from their community. The fear of going stag and meeting a Norm, falling for them, then having to own up to their affliction was too much of a risk.

However, there was always the chance he'd hit it off with either Maribon or Esmeralda and he'd back out of going to the dance with her. As a matter of fact, it was a pretty good bet he would.

Lucilla leaned back in her chair, crossed her legs, and then folded her hands in her lap. "Very well, Jager. If you agree to go on a date with my other two clients, I'll accompany you to the Legion Halloween Dance."

"I'll hold you to it." He stood, leaning over the expanse of her desk. Sexual power radiated from him.

If he held her to it, she'd go up in flames along with the holiday bonfire. Or melt into a puddle before he ever picked her up at her door. The man was too much.

No matter how much experience she had with men, it was all on the outside looking in. She understood the male species only insofar as to match them and collect her fee.

But Jager wasn't finished. He lifted one of those big, beautifully masculine hands and ran his knuckles over her cheek.

"What are you doing?"

"I wanted to see if you are as soft as you look."

"Yes, well." Lucilla ran a nervous hand down the pearl buttons of her silk blouse. "Do you want me to email the contact information to you?"

"If you wish."

Oh, she wished. Anything to get him out of her office and on his way.

Jager straightened then headed for the door. "You are, you know."

Lucilla's heart thumped against her breastbone. Oh yeah, she better pray he hit it off with one of the other women.

Lucilla's receptionist, Janet, came in holding a bundle of the day's mail.

"Is that all?" Lucilla watched her place it on the desk. If she wasn't getting junk mail in the post office box, she got spammed in her email. She shook her head and started sorting through the contents. Half of them went directly into the circular file, the others were too bizarre not to open. Like the advertisement guaranteed to rejuvenate hair growth on bald werewolves. What kind of a scam were they running? Most of the werewolves she knew would give their first litter of cubs to lose some fur.

That brochure went into the trash. She started to pick up the latest issue of *ParaWorld Weekly* when an ivory envelope with a metallic wax seal fell from the pages.

Her heart sank as the envelope dropped to the desk, breaking the seal into a thousand glittery shards. There was only one envelope that ever came to her in such a formal manner. She turned it over to look at the address written in ancient calligraphy.

Great. Just bloody brilliant. This was definitely the last thing she needed in her life—the annual summons for her attendance at the Witches Council's Open Forum. It was an embarrassment for both her and her family to sit there pretending she hadn't made a mockery of the craft.

Her failures were legendary.

She'd even heard that mothers, when confronted with a particularly hard-to-train daughter, had begun to say, "Don't be a Lucilla."

It was a nightmare to be considered the worst possible case scenario.

Well, this year she just wouldn't go. That's all there was to it.

Now, how to tell her family not only was she going to skip the forum, but that her prospective date for the Halloween dance was one of their species' greatest enemies.

Chapter Two

Jager hadn't felt so good in years. It was only a matter of time before the exquisite Lucilla became his. He'd never wanted a woman with such a hunger before. It consumed him from the first time he'd spoken to her on the phone to set up an appointment to review his profile. Her voice had that sensual quality that made a man break out into a sweat.

He shrugged out of his jacket then hung it in the closet. After the long day in the uncomfortable human confines of his business suit, he'd be glad to don the loose toga preferred by his people. He really didn't understand how the Norms wore the things they did. A man needed freedom to move as the ancient gods intended, not hamper his motion with stitched seams and noose-like neckwear.

The cotton fabric draped loosely around his waist then over his shoulder. A brief image flashed in his mind of how Lucilla would look dressed as a Greek goddess. Heat pooled low in his groin. His hands closed involuntarily.

Her skin had been so soft. A smile spread across his face as he remembered the look in her eyes when he'd touched her. The bright green had gone all hot like the flame from a chemical reaction. It had taken all his power not to pull her from her chair and ravage her perfect Cupid's bow mouth.

Oh, she'd be sweet as the richest nectar.

Comfortable in his native clothing, Jager moved to his home office to catch up on work. He'd spent so much time lately daydreaming over his dilemma with Lucilla, he hadn't been paying much attention to his business. Fortunately, he had an excellent staff to take up the slack, but as a deposed god, he was used to a certain amount of hands-on in regards to his ventures. As a broker in his own ParaTrader firm, Jager called all the shots, but his problems of the past had taught him one very important lesson—micromanagement.

He sat down to his computer, listening to the pleasant sound of the electronics whirling to life. A lot could be said for the Technology Age. The plethora of microprocessor-driven gizmos on the market made every man or woman as efficient as any of godkind, which was a good thing, considering most of his powers were tempered after his downfall.

His computer chimed, indicating he had mail. Heat speared him. Not because of a few hundred emails he received everyday, but because Lucilla promised to send him one. He clicked the envelope icon. Would the message have a personal note? No, probably not. Even though Lucilla was the most quietly sensuous woman he'd ever met, she was also the most professional. Any letter she sent would contain directions as to how to contact the women she'd matched him with.

By the fires of Hades, how was he ever going to get through two more dates he had no want to be on when the woman he wanted might be on a date of her own?

Jager scanned the contents of his inbox. Lucilla's email was sandwiched between a budgetary analysis by his CFO and the airline ticket confirmation for his trip to Japan.

His heart gave a disappointed drop as he read the greeting. The email was addressed to Mr. Cronus not Jager. Hope for a personal message dimmed.

He scanned the note. It mentioned only the contact information for both women being contained in the attached files. How unromantic.

He needed to find some way to capture her attention. So what if she melted when he touched her? That might mean she hadn't been with a man in a while and longed for *any* male to caress her lovely skin.

The thought alone had Jager shifting in his seat. If she gave him a chance, he'd touch her all over, wherever she wanted and needed it the most.

He downloaded the files, promising himself he'd open them later and read them. Before he clicked on the next message, he hit reply and sent her off a quick note.

That's Jager to you.

He was one of the few gods who didn't mind being called by his name. It was, after all, a name he'd selected after he was overthrown by his ungrateful son, Zeus. The need to put all the unpleasantness behind him seemed easier accomplished with a name change. Yet, he insisted on keeping the name Cronus as a reminder of all he'd lost.

The phone rang, bringing him out of the swirling mass of memories from eons of a godly existence. A brief glance at the caller ID had him wincing—Rhea, his ex-wife and the mother of his egocentric son. What in all the heavens did she want? Probably half his thriving business. She was always looking for a damned handout.

He let the phone switch to voice mail. Whatever she wanted she could say to a recording. He had no use for her. After she used him for his godly seed, she'd accused him of killing their children. Not so. He'd never harm his offspring. As a matter of fact, he'd always dreamed of being a father.

The woman was a menace to the Titan race.

The vision of another woman flashed through his mind—Lucilla, with her clear green eyes and forthright manner. There was no way she'd ever play a man false. No guile appeared in her gaze. No lies fell from her lips like honeyed endearments.

He bet when she loved, she loved full throttle.

A familiar stirring under his toga made him lean back in his chair. He needed Lucilla badly. This deep aching for her wouldn't go away until he stood with her in the circle and proclaimed his heart. It was a fanciful notion that, if any of his business opponents knew, would cause him no small measure of embarrassment.

They knew him as ruthless. Cold. Unfeeling. Not the sort of man who set his sights on a woman and decided without even knowing her to confess his undying love for her.

It was true, though. Ever since the first time he'd seen her.

At the time, he hadn't known the owner of ParaMatch and she were one and the same. That realization hadn't come until the first time he'd visited her office. No, the first time he'd seen her had been three years before, at the Legion Halloween

Dance.

As one of the organizers, she had been standing near the banquet table, discussing something with the caterer. She'd worn a dark-colored sheath dress that hugged her perfect figure. Tiny silver stars and moons glittered on the surface of the material, painting her like a midnight sky. Jager had taken one look at her, backlit by the bonfire, her golden hair piled atop her head, the nape of her neck exposed and vulnerable, and he'd fallen.

He'd spent the rest of the night looking for her, only to come up short. No one he asked had seen where she'd gone. No one even knew of whom he spoke. She hadn't seemed to make an impact on anyone but himself.

Jager took in a deep breath. The faint scent of burning wood clung to his senses as the memory faded.

He'd gone to ParaMatch looking for a mate—but more importantly, looking for her, hoping by some miracle she'd sought out the services of a respectable matchmaker to find her a mate. It was a long shot, he knew. But something in his gut had badgered him to take the risk, only to hit pay dirt the first time he'd walked through her office door.

He should have leveled with her weeks ago.

The phone rang again. He glanced briefly at the number. Maribon Seacrest. The selkie.

Might as well get it over with.

Jager took a deep, steadying breath and picked up the phone. "Miss Seacrest, I was just getting ready to phone you."

Chapter Three

Scents of brewing herbs hung heavy in the air of the duplex. Lucilla pushed aside a beaded gauze curtain, taking in a deep breath as she entered the industrial-sized kitchen of her Aunt Rebekah's apartment.

There had always been something old world about Rebekah's place. Warmth radiated from every crevice. Earth tones, red bricks and natural wood accents gave the space the look of a kitchen in some ancient castle. Plus, her aunt had expanded the room by taking out the living room and den. Now the kitchen and its massive prep area took up most of the duplex's bottom floor, along with a closet that worked as a drying room for herbs.

"Who's there?" Her aunt backed out of the drying room with her arms full of crackling stalks.

"It's Lucilla. I need to talk to you about this invitation I have to the Witches Court."

Rebekah Wainwright set the dry herbs down on a large butcher block counter in the center of the prep room. She blew a strand of bright red hair out of her face. "What about it?"

"I want to know why every year they insist on sending me the invitation when they know I have no intention of accepting? It's a waste of parchment and ink."

Not to mention, it never ceased to point out Lucilla's shortcomings as a talentless member of one of the most legendary witching families in the history of the craft.

Rebekah hitched a shoulder as if it didn't matter. "You're still a member of this family. According to the bylaws, you are more than welcome at the open forum at the annual Court."

The shade of a headache began in the middle of Lucilla's forehead then spread down to pierce behind her eyes. "Will you make my excuses to the council?"

Rebekah raised a henna-colored brow, pursing her mouth as if considering a deal. It was an expression Lucilla knew well and she had to resist a shiver. Asking for her aunt's help was going to cost her big time.

Strong, efficient hands began to untwist the ties on the herbs, working by experience. "There's a wonderful wizard who recently joined our spell circle. He's new in town and doesn't know many people. He needs a date for the Legion Halloween Dance."

Relief came at once. "Send him to my office. I'd be more than happy to find him a date. He'll have to fill out a questionnaire first."

Rebekah stopped her busy hands and looked up, stabbing Lucilla with a meaningful stare. "I didn't mean for you to match him professionally. I want you to go out with him."

Lucilla groaned. "I already have a tentative date for the Legion Halloween Dance." Not one she wanted, but a date nonetheless.

A shocked expression drew Rebekah's mouth into an "O". "You have a date for the Legion Dance?"

"Don't sound so surprised. I've been known to go out with the opposite sex on occasion."

Her aunt waved the comment away like a stink of burnt herbs. "I didn't mean it like that. You just keep your head buried in work all the time. You never allow yourself time for romance."

Lucilla smiled. Her aunt might be a tough customer when it came to her craft as a master level brewer, but she was also a hopeless romantic. It probably came from a lifetime spent making love potions and tonics and other magical potions for the Para world.

However, her aunt didn't understand that being a non-talent had Lucilla straddling the fence of two worlds. If she chose to, she could marry a Norm and have children. However, the possibility did exist that a stray recessive gene would reproduce the magic in her offspring. The idea of explaining that to a Norm husband didn't seem worth the risk. Dating and marrying a Para meant they would know of her deficiency. As they would know of her triumph with her matchmaking business. It was a respectable job, but there was nothing magical about what she did. Even Norms had a certain level of intuition they could call upon when needed. Besides, countless Para couples had her to thank for their successful marriages.

And yet Lucilla had no one.

"So who is your date?"

"Tentative date," Lucilla corrected. "You'll see at the Legion Halloween Dance. Or not. I'm hoping he'll strike an interest in one of my clients and back out. I really only agreed in order to get him out of my office."

Rebekah put her hands on her hips in consternation. "Hopeless." She shook her head, sending her springy curls flying in all directions. "I really wonder if the fairies didn't switch you at birth with some other child. Somewhere out there in the Norm community is a witch who doesn't know how to control her powers."

"Or who uses them to keep her interfering family in check."

"We only interfere because we love and worry about you."

"I love you, too. But I don't need you to matchmake for me. I'm a professional."

"Who doesn't use her services to find herself a man."

That damn telltale blush rose in her cheeks. "That wouldn't be ethical."

Her aunt noted Lucilla's high color with a low, "Ah, ha," then turned to the cauldron hanging over the fire in the hearth.

Lucilla picked up a lone sprig of lavender that had fallen to the floor. She put the potent beads to her nose, taking in a deep breath. The fragrance sent immediate calm through her body. "Will you call off the Court? I can't sit through another audience where everyone stares at me, wondering why I'm there."

"I have an elixir to cure paranoia, you know?" Rebekah spoke over her shoulder as she added some of the crumbled leaves to the boiling water in the cauldron.

"It's not paranoia when you *know* they're staring." Lucilla let out a long breath. Hopelessness washed over her. She crossed the room to the hearth, placing her hands on Rebekah's shoulders. "Never mind. I'll send my regrets along with the offer of free services for the annual benefit auction." She gave her aunt a quick kiss on the cheek then started for the door.

"Lucilla Morgana Wainwright, do not walk out of this house until we settle up."

Settle up!

That wasn't aunt to niece speaking, but witch elder to subordinate. It was Rebekah's way of pulling rank, using the coven bylaws' wording to stop Lucilla in her tracks. To *settle up* meant a bargain had been made and the time had come to make good on the particulars.

Rebekah stalked across the room, stopping only a foot in front of her, way beyond the borders of Lucilla's personal space. "Let Aramis take you out on a date. He's a good man. He's hardworking, respectable and handsome."

"Aramis?" Lucilla mouthed. How could anyone saddle a beloved child with such an awful name?

It was Rebekah's turn to blush. "I gave him your phone number. You should expect a call from him soon."

"Fine. I'll go to dinner with him, but I promise I won't enjoy myself." Lucilla started to leave, but then turned, pointing an imperial finger at her aunt. "Settle up. You have to tell the Court I won't be there this year."

Her aunt gave what might be construed as a nod.

Lucilla only hoped it meant the deal was sealed.

Chapter Four

Jager pulled up at the sprawling seaside mansion precisely at seven. Their dinner reservations were for seven-thirty. He only hoped she was a prompt woman. If there was one thing he hated it was waiting on the primping ritual to end while he cooled his heels looking at useless knickknacks in an over-decorated living room.

He'd often wondered why women found it alluring or even fashionable to keep a man waiting. The only thing Jager had ever found it was irritating as all hell.

The house stood on the edge of a cliff. One good mudslide and the entire structure would become one with the sea. But as a selkie, Maribon would no doubt enjoy returning to her watery home for good. Why she maintained a life on land, he didn't know. What he knew of the selkie race was that they were very protective of their seal pelts and went to great lengths to keep them from their lovers. Well, at least human lovers. Perhaps a Para lover was a different story for her kind. Even so, it wasn't a risk he'd take. His heart had already been given completely to the little matchmaker.

But a deal was a deal. He'd get through tonight, go out with the djinn, then sit back and wait for Halloween.

The door buzzer was an odd piece of hardware, shaped like a sea serpent. The chime was more of the sound of waves crashing on the shore than an actual buzz. Any relationship this woman had with a man would have to be done in the water behind her house. It was obvious the sea still held sway on her emotions.

She answered the door with a sly seductive smile, wearing

a black dress that fit like a second skin. Her eyes and hair were darker than the depths of the ocean. "Jager?"

"The one and only."

She gave him what amounted to a dazzling smile, but it failed to do anything for him. Not like Lucilla's smiles. "Let me grab a wrap and we can go."

At least she wasn't going to keep him waiting.

They arrived at Avalon on the Bay and were seated immediately. The maître d' treated Jager with deference, showing them to the best table in the exclusive restaurant. Fine chandeliers, candles in golden glass bowls, and deep, rich wood accents bathed the interior in a romantic glow.

Men seated at nearby tables stared at Maribon as she took her seat. She looked up at Jager with an appreciative glance over her shoulder as he held her chair for her. It looked more of an artful pose to him, used to expose the gentle curve of her throat. She really was a beautiful woman.

Now came the part of these first dates he hated the most— the get-to-know-you segment of the program. Considering he had no intention of repeating this experience with her, he failed to see why he needed to sit and listen while she extolled her many virtues like items on a grocery list. But he'd listen because it was the polite thing to do.

Silence stretched between them. Honestly, for a man who spent his life enduring the constant flow of acquaintances through his existence, he should have acquired the necessary small-talk skills. But he hadn't. Probably came from centuries of being an all-knowing deity. Who needed small talk when you could pick their brains at thirty paces?

"I've never been out with a Titan before." Maribon folded her arms and leaned over the table. The low, plunging neckline of her dress barely contained her impeccably pert breasts.

"There aren't that many of us around." Jager watched the waiter try to avoid looking down Maribon's dress while filling their water glasses. The poor man almost met his goal.

She fished an ice cube from her glass, running it seductively along her bottom lip. "Is it true that the bigger the better?"

He pretended ignorance of her innuendo. "You can't tell

from my ex-wife."

The tinkle of practiced laughter floated over the table. Her deep brown eyes sparkled in the light of the candle. "Your ex was a Titan?"

"As far as I know she still is."

Her perfectly manicured brows wrinkled slightly at the distinction of tense. She didn't appreciate the correction. "I've never been married before. It just never felt right."

Probably because all her dates tried to steal her skin. She no doubt had the damn thing in a safe somewhere so no man had the opportunity to entrap her. Not that he blamed her for taking such precautions.

"I wouldn't worry about the length of time you've been single, Lucilla is very good at what she does." Jager tried to sound reassuring. "I understand her success rate is very high."

"It would have to be, right?" The words hung on the air as they gave the waiter their order. When they were alone again, Maribon picked up a roll from the breadbasket and tore it into little pieces on her plate. "I mean she's a non-talented witch from a prominent family. If you ask me, she doesn't have a choice but to make a go of her business. A failure would be another black mark against her."

Check, please.

If she only realized what bad form it was to diss—was that the word he'd heard lately to indicate negativity—your matchmaker. Especially when she'd set you up with someone you were trying desperately to impress. And Maribon was trying. Too hard.

This dinner needed to move at mach speed.

"Lucilla has nothing to apologize for," he said over his wine glass, giving Maribon a steady stare. Hearing someone make disparaging remarks against the woman he planned to marry one day put him in a bad mood.

The waiter served their salads. Jager put his glass down then stabbed the unsuspecting lettuce, telling himself to cool down.

Maribon flipped her long fall of raven hair over her shoulder. "I didn't mean to insult her. I think Lucilla's wonderful."

A little too late to guard her words.

Luckily the dinner courses were served quickly. Jager continued to answer Maribon's various questions. He didn't expound on any topics, or offer any more information than what the question required for him to answer. His tactic didn't seem to dull her enthusiasm for enticement.

The desserts were served. Maribon ordered fresh strawberries with whipped cream. The provocative way she licked the cream from the berries should have garnered an "X" rating in the exclusive restaurant. Waiters stopped to stare, men at other tables ogled. Jager just wanted to get the Hades out of there. The woman had no couth whatsoever. Not like Lucilla. Lucilla was a class act all the way.

Later, when he walked Maribon to her door, Jager thought to give her a quick, friendly peck on the cheek so as not to make the evening end awkwardly.

Maribon had other ideas.

When he tried to pull back into his own space, she grabbed hold of him, winding her hands into his lapels, anchoring him to her.

He tried frantically to free himself, but the damn woman had more hands than a Hindu god.

No sooner had he freed his jacket from the clutch of her hand, she put a chokehold on his privates.

"Ms. Seacrest!"

"Mr. Cronus." Her voice went all silky as she started rubbing him.

He'd never been so disgusted by a hot woman in his entire life—and that said a lot.

He grabbed her hand, finally managing to free his junk from her over-amorous clutches. Jager straightened his jacket, ran a hand through his hair and started for his car before she took it in her mind to tackle him on the lawn.

Oh no, this date would not be repeated.

Chapter Five

Bells tinkled softly as a wind teased the chimes hanging from a tree in Lucilla's side yard. The haunting melody they played never failed to touch her in that deeply recessed place where her witch's senses were buried. It also highlighted the emptiness at not being able to perform even the simplest of spells.

There were times while growing up Lucilla prayed to all the goddesses that even a tiny flare of power would show in her. As a child, she'd failed every test to assess her ability. When all tests proved the obvious, she was apprenticed to her Aunt Rebekah to learn the art of brewing.

What a disaster that had been.

Though brewing didn't necessarily require a strong talent, the practitioner needed a certain amount of confidence while exploiting the herbs and water. Having known no success at any other craft-related vocations, she didn't arrive at Rebekah's kitchen with illusions of triumph in creating potions.

There was one particularly embarrassing incident that ended in Lucilla almost burning her aunt's kitchen down, and singeing the cat in the fallout. The Witches Council had not been amused. After that, she'd been banned from working near an open flame for a sentence of five years.

Lucilla wrapped her arms around her waist, hugging herself in remembered defeat. She'd been more than the black sheep of the Wainwright clan. Never before, in the entire family history, had there ever been a more spectacular failure.

And now her aunt wanted her to go on a date with a man who had proven himself not only as the most talented wizard to be born in over five hundred years, but whose recent innovations had him moving up the Council ladder at warp speed.

How would Aramis Blacktalon feel about going on a date with the biggest disappointment in all witchdom? Lucilla would never sanction such a mismatch in her office. But for her aunt to run interference with the Council, Lucilla would play along. She just had to remember all her failures led to the success of her business. The need to prove herself as a vital, even needed, member of the Para community ran deep.

The feeling of being stared at had Lucilla opening her right eye. Bright sunshine filtered through the red, yellow and orange leaves of the turning trees, painting the ground in dappled light. A large dog sat at her feet, looking up at her with his pink tongue lolling out of his open mouth.

"Hello." Lucilla held her hand out for the animal to sniff.

Intelligent gray eyes blinked at her. The dog wagged his tail then stood.

Lucilla pet his head. "You're a good boy."

He turned his head to lick her hand.

"Where'd you come from? I don't think you belong to the neighbors. I'd remember you."

He was an absolutely gorgeous animal with thick black fur, a muscular body and large white teeth. Whoever owned him took excellent care of him.

"Do you have tags?" Lucilla ran her hands through the slightly thicker hair around the dog's neck. She felt no collar or tags.

"Are you thirsty? Let's go get you some water."

Lucilla rose from the Adirondack chair and crossed the yard with the dog on her heels. She slipped into the house to get a bowl.

The dog waited at the screen, looking in at her. He tilted his head to the side, as if trying to understand what she was doing.

She quickly filled the bowl then set it outside on the porch. The dog sniffed at it then drank with noisy laps.

"You were a thirsty boy."

Lucilla started petting him again, loving the feel of his fur.

It was as luxurious as a mink pelt.

And definitely not right for a dog.

Her hand stilled.

The dog lifted his head, turning to look at her over his shoulder. If she didn't know better, she'd swear he had a teasing glint in his eyes.

He gave a deep bark then ran off toward the setting sun, disappearing into the lengthening shadows of the orchard.

A sinking feeling centered in her sternum—just below her heart and right above her stomach. No. He wouldn't. Would he?

Lucilla hurried back into the house, practically diving for the phone. Thank the goddess she had Rebekah's number on speed dial.

"This better be good. My youth elixir is going to thicken." The words were huffed into the phone under stress.

"I only have one quick question and then I'll let you get back to your brew. Can Aramis Blacktalon morph?"

"Lucilla?"

"Who else would it be?" Lucilla gripped the phone, looking out the door at the water dish. "I had a visit from a large black dog who mocked me."

"Mocked you?"

"I swear on the Witches' Codex." She ran her hand through her hair. "I saw him laughing at me when I petted him. He had this incredibly soft black hair. I couldn't keep my hands out of it."

The distinct sound of a muffled snort filtered through the phone.

"Are you laughing at me?"

"Darling, don't be so dramatic. So what if he took on an animal shape to visit you? Maybe he just wanted to get a look at you."

"Why would he do that?" Bewilderment made her voice come out in a whine. She winced. "Civilized people call and make a date, or arrange to bump into someone at the local coffee shop. They do not show up in an alternate form to sniff out a potential date."

Rebekah choked. "I'll call him and find out."

"Don't you dare!" Why did dating have to be so hard when she was a professional matchmaker? She owned the keys to the entire dating kingdom, for crying out loud.

"Then what do you want me to do?" Pans banged around in the background.

"Just tell me if he can morph or not." Sounds came from outside. Weird ones. Lucilla crossed the room to close the door.

"I'm pretty sure he can." There were rustling noises suggesting Rebekah moved the phone to the other ear. "He's one sharp practitioner."

Lucilla rolled her eyes and looked at the ceiling. "I'm feeling exceptionally violated at the moment."

"Just where *did* he sniff you?"

"I can't believe you asked me that." A sharp click interrupted the conversation. "Aunt Rebekah, I have another call. I'll ring you back in a bit. And take care of that youth elixir, I can hear it thickening from here."

Lucilla bristled as the café door opened and in walked a man with dark silky hair and clear gray eyes. His gaze surveyed the other customers before landing on her. A warm smile turned his face from merely handsome to truly stunning.

Her breath caught in her throat even as her temper flared. She stood, snatching her purse off the table.

Did he think she wouldn't know?

Aramis Blacktalon held his hand out, entreating her to stay. "Please don't leave, Lucilla."

"Give me one good reason why." She crossed her arms under her breasts.

He indicated the table she'd vacated with a subtle movement of his hand—one that told of countless hours casting spells and weaving dreams. "Can we sit while I grovel?"

"If you'd called me like a..."

"Like a what? A *normal* person?"

Lucilla blushed at her near faux pas. The least she could do was defend herself against the charge of nearly calling him normal. There was no worse epithet in the Para world.

She took the chair across from him. "No. I was going to say like a civilized being."

That same teasing glint filled his gray eyes, making them sparkle with devilish light. "I am sorry. It's just your aunt talked you up so much, I wanted to see if you really are everything she claimed."

"Ah, so you went to my house to trick me?"

When he smiled, he had the most charming dimple in his left cheek. "It wasn't supposed to be a trick, but you kept digging your hands in my fur and it was starting to turn me on. I had to get out of there before I embarrassed myself."

"I don't think I want to know what you mean by that." Lucilla frowned. Truly, she didn't want to know. The thought alone conjured up all sorts of visions better left unmentioned.

"My intentions were honorable. They just didn't materialize the way I'd planned."

"I find that hard to believe for the Council's new favorite son." She leaned on her forearms. "Exactly how long has it been since a magic work backfired on you?"

His movie star brow wrinkled. "Never."

Of course he had a perfect track record. What was he going to say when he figured out she was the worst non-talent in the witching community? Her family, even with their influence, was never able to keep the glare of her defect from the rest of their kind.

Had her aunt even told him?

Maybe Rebekah misled him into thinking she used powers to match people. Would she do something so potentially disastrous to a new or tentative relationship?

Lucilla started out of her seat. "I don't think this is going to work."

Aramis placed his hand over hers. "You don't know until you give it a chance."

"Do you know what I am?"

His steady gaze studied her, as if trying to guess what she meant. Strong male fingers gripped her hand a bit tighter. "A matchmaker?"

"That sounded like a guess." Maybe Rebekah hadn't told

him anything about her but what a wonderful person she was. If so, that should have been his first clue that something was wrong with her. No one was ever as good as advertised.

"It wasn't. I know you're a matchmaker. I just don't have any idea what else you could mean."

Oh, boy.

Time to drop the other ruby slipper on the guy. "You're exactly right. I am a matchmaker, but that's all I am."

Aramis laughed. "I find that hard to believe."

"Whether you do or do not is immaterial." She let out a long sigh. "If it's a date with the prodigal daughter of the Wainwright clan, you're going to be bitterly disappointed."

"Anyone who sees a stray dog and worries if he's thirsty or has a family missing him is not a disappointment."

Lucilla melted. So, Aramis Blacktalon was a really great guy. Granted, he was no Jager Cronus, but a good catch nonetheless. Lucilla didn't doubt the wizard's sincerity for even a moment. It was apparent in the look of his eyes and the touch of his hand on hers.

She gave a little shrug then smiled. "So, you want to get some coffee?" If nothing else he'd be a potential match for one of her clients. And after his furry prank, he owed her.

Chapter Six

Darkness flooded the neighborhood, interrupted by ornamental streets lamps made to look like antique gaslights. The street meandered along lazy curves like a blacktop river—the fact the Styx River ran along the back of the west-facing properties notwithstanding.

Lucilla drove towards her house, her mind a whirlwind of the day's events. Coffee with Aramis was the most fun she'd had in a very long time. Fun was important. Fun was what she watched everyone else have while she worked her non-talented fingers to the bone to match other people so they could have fun.

The road wound around a hairpin turn, exposing the front view of her house. The porch light of the old Victorian burned brightly, illuminating the dark yard. Out front, an unfamiliar car sat idling at the curb.

At this point all she wanted was to take a long, hot bubble bath and fall into bed. It didn't look like that was on the horizon. Who would sit in front of her house in the first place? She never gave out personal information to her clients, so it most likely wasn't one of them.

She pulled slowly into her drive, looking in the rearview mirror at the car as the driver's door opened. A tall, well-proportioned man stood. The light from the street lamp rendered his face half in shadow, but even from where Lucilla sat, she knew the identity of her mystery visitor.

Jager gazed over the top of his car and gave a hesitant wave.

Flutters like leaves stuck in a whirlwind flew around inside her stomach. She smoothed her hand over her abdomen in an attempt to calm the flying furies. What was it about Jager that made her body misbehave?

She motioned for him to come up to the house. It took him no time to get to her with his long strides.

He looked good. The dark suit jacket hung perfectly on his wide shoulders. He moved with elegant grace for such a big man. When he reached her, she looked up into his face, afraid he could hear her heart pound.

A rich, spicy scent filled her head. *Oh, Goddess weeping, he even smells good!* How was she supposed to resist him when he showed up at her door looking like the best fantasy she'd ever had? He gazed at her as if he didn't know how he'd come to be standing on her doorstep. And for the life of her, Lucilla couldn't think of a word to say.

Then he was there, kissing her mouth like a starving man. Lucilla put her hands on his shoulders, intending to push away from his unprovoked admiration, but only managed to sink her hands into his thick hair, holding onto him, afraid he'd let her go.

Her entire body melted against the wall of his heat. His tongue brushed against hers. A faint tang of cloves clung to his mouth. Why did he have to taste good, too? Now she'd never want to stop kissing him. But she had to. He was a client. His fees helped keep a roof over her head and food on her table. Kissing him was definitely unethical.

Lucilla managed to pull her mouth away from his. The maneuver didn't have the desired effect of stopping the kiss. It only served to give him an opportunity to run his mouth into her hairline, to kiss her temple and breathe hot breath into her ear.

Her nipples were so hard they ached behind the confines of silk and lace. Without conscious thought, she arched her back, rubbing them against him for relief.

"Lucilla," Jager moaned. "Please, don't send me out on another bad date when I already know who I want."

For a second she tensed, until she realized what he meant. She wanted to hear it. Needed to hear it. "Who do you want?"

He laid his forehead against hers. "I'm holding her right

now."

"If that's true, why did you sign up for my services?"

"I didn't know it was you." He put his finger under her chin, tilting her face up to his. "I'm not used to begging. It's not in my nature. But if you make me go out with the djinn, I'll be reduced to it."

A fallen god begging? It made for an intriguing picture, but Lucilla had never been that cruel. She slid her hand in his then turned to the door. "Why don't you come inside and we can discuss what we're going to do with you."

She led him through the living room and into the den. The room was filled with earthy colors, rich and warm. It was her favorite room in the house. Large, overstuffed furniture was grouped in the middle of the space to make for an intimate setting.

Lucilla indicated the sectional with a turn of her hand. "Have a seat and I'll bring us some drinks."

He released the button on his jacket and sat on the sofa. "You have a beautiful home."

"Thank you. I like it." She poured them both some brandy and carried it over to him.

She took a seat across from him, balancing her drink on her crossed legs. "Did something happen tonight to make you come over here and wait at the curb for me?" The words, *and kiss me*, echoed in her head, but she refrained from saying them.

He swirled the brandy around in the snifter. "I had a date with Maribon Seacrest."

A hand clamped around Lucilla's heart to squeeze. Wasn't that what she was being paid for? She'd only done her job in setting them up.

"I see." Her throat tried to close around the words. Even though it was obvious he hadn't had a good time on the date, it was like a knife going through her gut.

"The night will not be repeated."

"Oh, Jager." She hid her smile behind her hand. "You really know how to charm the ladies, don't you?"

He frowned. "What makes you think the failure of the date

was my fault?"

"Your track record. You've found fault with them all."
Warming to the conversation, she shifted in her seat. "How do I
know, if I go with you to the Legion Halloween Dance, you won't
say the same thing about me?"

"You *are* going with me to the dance. You've already
agreed."

"I *agreed* to it on the stipulation you went out with *both* of
my clients. Now you're here wanting to go back on your word."
Lucilla shook her head in mock pity. "I don't know, sounds to
me as if I may need to apologize to my other clients for sending
them on dates with you."

She watched his jaw tighten. He turned his head to avoid
looking at her. "I've never gone back on my word." When his
gaze connected with hers again, his eyes were hot, intense. "I
want you. I don't want to wait."

His words sucked all the air from the room. That was about
as plain a declaration as she'd ever heard. It was also a
challenge. Stalling for time, she took a sip of her brandy.

When she didn't reply, he set his glass on the low coffee
table and stood, moving around to where she sat. "Don't tell me
you felt nothing when I kissed you."

She started at his feet, letting her gaze travel the long way
up his body until she looked directly into his eyes. "I have no
intention of denying anything. But I'm not going to let you go
back on your promise either."

He went down on one knee in front of her. "Why do you
want to torture me?"

Lucilla laughed. "Is that what I'm doing? I don't mean to.
But you paid for my services and I'd be remiss if I didn't give
you the entire benefit of my experience and knowledge."

A low rumble came from deep in Jager's chest. "I see." He
plucked the glass from her hand and set it on the table next to
his. He let his large palms slide up along the outside of her
thighs. "I don't want to appear ungrateful, but maybe we could
find another way for you to demonstrate your experience to
me."

"Such as?" Heaven help her, but she couldn't think when
he ran his thumbs over her hipbones like that.

"Letting me know what it's like to date a woman who is as respectable as she is sexy."

"Me? Sexy?" She let him see just how funny she thought the notion.

"Unbelievably so." He leaned forward just enough to press his lips to her forehead.

Heat speared her to the chair. This was what a woman should feel like—the center of a man's universe, doggedly pursued by him until she felt consumed.

He ran his lips over her face. "Are you going to make me go through another date? Or do I need to fire you as my matchmaker so I can have you all to myself?"

"No. I'm not letting you back out of our agreement. You never know, Jager, you might really enjoy a date with a djinn."

"Not when I'll be thinking of you." He picked up her hand from her lap, bringing it to his mouth. He pressed a kiss on her fingers then opened them to place one on her palm.

She didn't know whether to be flattered or offended. "How do you know I'm not already in a relationship?"

He gave her a cocky smile. "Because you don't seem the type to accept an escort to the biggest social event of the season when you already have a man waiting in the wings."

Damn, he had her there.

"You're right. I wouldn't." She pulled her hand back from the steady caress of his fingers over hers. That simple gesture alone was beginning to turn her on. If he didn't put a squelch on it, she'd end up in bed with him.

He'd already as good as admitted the fact.

I want you. I don't want to wait.

A thought occurred to her then. He still hadn't explained why he had such a miserable time with Maribon. Lucilla raised a brow, cocking her head to the side. "What happened tonight to make you swear off another date with Maribon?"

Jager blew out a long-suffering sigh and backed away from her. "Are you sure she's a selkie and not an octopus?"

A comical vision of Jager trying to fend off the selkie's eager hands filled Lucilla's mind. "A little too forward?"

"And then some." He ran a hand through his hair then

leaned against the coffee table. "I'm not embarrassed to admit I'm a very sexual man, but I want to at least get through the first date before I'm stuck to a tentacle. I'd pretty much decided never to see her again before the salad course arrived, but when she attacked me at her door, groping me like I'm a ten-dollar gigolo, it proved she wasn't the type of woman I'd waste my time to see again."

Lucilla laughed. "Most men would feel privileged to say they'd taken a woman as beautiful as Maribon to bed."

"I'm not most men. If all I wanted was a conquest, I wouldn't be here now."

Lucilla took a deep breath and let it out slowly. If he wanted something more from her than a few dates and a quick tumble, he'd picked the worst person in the world to pursue. She doubted she needed to remind him of the feud between their peoples, but there were aspects of it they did need to discuss.

"Have you thought at all about the ramifications of a relationship between us? I may not have talent, but my family won't be pleased." She looked at her hands. "I couldn't even tell my aunt who my tentative date for the Legion Halloween Dance is when she asked."

"I didn't think it bothered you." His voice had dropped to a near-whisper. "Does it?"

Her gaze met his. Emotions too potent to deny swirled between them. "Not for myself. Any woman would be proud to be with you. It's my family's reaction that worries me. I've been such a disappointment to them..."

"How?" Jager demanded. He rose again, pulling her from her chair and into his arms. "You're the most amazing woman I've ever met. No one who knows you could ever believe you're a disappointment."

She swallowed. Twice in the same night, handsome, incredible men sought to tell her of her worth. She offered a gentle smile. "I was to my family. They had such high hopes for me, and I've failed them on so many levels."

"But it wasn't your fault," he protested.

The way he defended her against the injustice of her lot made her heart swell. History showed he knew all too well about being blamed for something that wasn't his fault. To be branded and pigeonholed for something beyond his control.

She'd blown out of the box the witching circles put her in when she'd opened her agency. Jager had started anew when he moved from fallen god to businessman. They really did have so much in common.

Lucilla rose up on her tiptoes, pulling his head to hers. Their mouths met in a kiss as hot as it was comforting. After she pulled away, she looked up into his gorgeous eyes. "You still have one more date to get through. That's the bargain. But I'll make it easy on you. I have a date tomorrow evening. If you want, we can make it a double and you might feel a bit more at ease meeting Esmeralda."

"And if she isn't available tomorrow night? Are you still going on your date?"

"Of course," she teased. "I don't break my agreements."

He gave a low growl in the back of his throat. "I'm not going to enjoy watching you with another man."

Well, if he thought he'd have a hard time watching her with another man, she wasn't going to have a good time knowing he was with a djinn. But she'd made the offer to get him through the date, so she'd follow through. And as a chaperone, she could ensure they didn't have too good a time.

Her ethics had been taking a nosedive ever since Jager Cronus walked into her office, but damn if he didn't fit her own profile match at close to one hundred percent.

Chapter Seven

Why did I let her talk me into this?

Jager looped one side of his tie around the other. A double date? What was he thinking? He didn't want to sit across the table from Lucilla and another man, pretending he wasn't jealous as all Hades.

At least he wouldn't be sitting at home wondering what she was doing and who she was doing it with. He'd already been doing that for months. However, he'd never been able to put a face to that shadowy vision he had of the man he thought she was with.

He wished he knew her date, or at least what to expect. After being blindsided by the hostile takeover of his unearthly reign, he promised never to be caught unaware again. Where did her tastes in men lie? Did she date Norms, or non-talent Paras?

The memory of her hot, sweet mouth pressed to his sent spirals of heat straight to his groin. She'd clung to him, her small delicate hands buried in his hair.

The doorbell rang, pulling him back to reality.

He walked downstairs, putting the finishing touches on his tie. The staff had the night off, so he was reduced to answering his own front door. The mighty had fallen far and wide. There was a time when he'd lived among the clouds on Mt. Olympus, before his life turned upside down. Everything he'd ever conceived was his at a thought. Now, he had to open his own freaking door.

A brief smile touched his mouth. Lucilla didn't have servants at all, or any powers to make life easier. She did it all herself. Maybe she indulged in a cleaning service, but that was it.

He looked out the peephole at his visitor. Zeus! What was he doing here?

Jager opened the door, but stood to block his visitor's entrance. "Hello, Zeus."

"Father."

"To what do I owe this unprecedented visit?"

"You didn't return my call. We have something very important to discuss."

"I thought it was your mother. But whatever it is, it will have to wait. I'm on my way out."

"Another of your agency dates?"

Surprise stole Jager's voice. He had no idea his contract with a matchmaking agency was public knowledge. But then his perfidious son probably watched him with an eye to taking over Jager's company as he had the heavens. What would Jager do then? Turn him over to the SEC and see him in a Norm jail?

"What I do with my private life is no concern of yours. Or your mother's." He waited a beat to let the hostility of the words sink in. "Tell you what, call my office in the morning and make an appointment with my secretary. I'll be glad to discuss your problem during normal business hours."

"This can't wait," Zeus insisted and pushed past his father to stand in the foyer. "Please. I'll only take a few minutes."

The light blond hair and gray eyes were something only a godly being could possess, they appeared so frighteningly unreal. Those were the only vestiges left from his traditional appearance. The trademark long beard and hair were gone, replaced by a smooth chin and hair gel. There was a soul patch just under his wide bottom lip. A Grecian map was tattooed on his right upper arm.

He considered the man to whom he'd given life before him. Was it such a small thing for a father to expect respect from his son? Was it too much to ask of one's progeny?

Freaking mama's boy.

Jager indicated the well-stocked wet bar. "Help yourself while I get my jacket. I don't intend to let you make me late."

He hurried to retrieve his jacket from the wardrobe. When he returned to the living room, Zeus was seated on the sofa, staring at a mural of *The Odyssey* painted over the fireplace.

"I love that story. It really was Homer's best."

Jager raised his brow, skeptical of Zeus's motives. "If you remember the tale, Odysseus's son fought side by side with his father in the final battle with the suitors. He helped his father keep his house together. He didn't dishonor him by trying to take the throne. Sons do that when they care for their sires."

Zeus looked down at his hands, linked between his spread knees. "She led me astray, you know?"

"That's not exactly a newsflash." Jager shrugged into his suit jacket. "Tell me why you were so anxious to see me."

"I think mother's planning a coup."

Jager paused in pulling his shirtsleeves through his jacket. "Who does she want to overthrow now?"

Zeus shook his head in disbelief. "I can hardly get my mind around it."

"Who?"

Clear gray eyes held Jager's.

"The Witches Council."

Why did everything always have to be so damned complicated?

Jager sipped his wine, looking over the table at Lucilla. Soft candlelight made her glow like the heart of a flame. He wanted her all to himself. Unfortunately, her date had the same idea. The djinn had excused herself from the table for the fifth time since they'd ordered their meal, so he was left to sit and watch while Aramis Blacktalon oozed wit and charm and all the traits her family would love in a suitor.

That was only part of the reason his mood turned sour as an unripe lemon. He needed to tell her about Rhea's bid to overthrow the Witches Council. Granted, he still didn't like the idea of one Para body having more power than another, but the Witches Council had done well in keeping all the Paras from being discovered by the Norms. They'd been doing so since the rise of paganism so many centuries before. As far as he knew, none of the other Para-kind actually cared that the Witches Council governed. It wasn't like any of the other groups organized and set up any form of self-administration. It was actually the sensible thing to do. If Rhea wanted to govern something, she should have put all her energy into organizing the Titans into their own council, rather than rallying them to war.

"Is something the matter, Jager?" Lucilla finally tore herself away from her date to notice him sitting at their table.

"I think Esmeralda had something more important to do tonight." Not that he cared, but it was something to say so as not to draw attention to his skyrocketed jealousy and worry over the possible Titan takeover.

Lucilla frowned. She pulled her napkin from her lap and set it on the table. "I'll go check on her."

Damn, now he'd be stuck at the table alone with a rival. What was he supposed to say to Aramis that didn't include a dissertation about how the wizard needed to back off from Lucilla?

Jager watched as Lucilla wound her way through the maze of tables to the ladies room.

"She's gorgeous, huh?" Aramis caught Jager's gaze as they turned back from admiring the view.

"Very lovely."

Aramis smiled like he had a dirty secret he wanted to share. Jager wanted to plant his fist in the guy's smug kisser.

"You're one of her clients?"

"Apparently."

"How's it going? Is the service worth the price?"

"She's the best there is." It was hard to speak around the ball of anger in his throat. Aramis made Lucilla sound like an overpriced call girl, not a professional matchmaker.

"I've heard that about her."

"You should sign a contract. She has a wide variety of potential matches to suit any taste."

"Are you writing her ads? I thought you were into Paratrading?" Aramis smirked then wiped the look off his face when the women returned to the table.

Smarmy character. What did Lucilla see in the guy?

Esmeralda—no last name—sat down at the table and tucked her cell phone into her jewel-studded handbag. "I'm sorry. I promise I won't leave the table again. The phone is turned off."

Jager shot a look to the djinn and then to Lucilla. Her lovely face was pulled into a frown. The mighty matchmaker must have laid down the law. "No problem, I know the demands of a high-pressure job."

Esmeralda turned a little red then glanced nervously at Lucilla and Aramis. "Yes. The job is very stressful."

Tension clung to the air like a rancid smell. Esmeralda squirmed in her seat, avoiding everyone's curious glance.

Lucilla returned her napkin to her lap as their food arrived. "What are you doing now that your commitment to your last master is fulfilled?"

Esmeralda twitched in her seat again. "Oh, this and that. Consulting mostly."

The vague answer didn't sit well with Jager. There was a lot more going on with her evasive answers than she let on. "Who do you consult for?"

She looked up from her plate, her eyes wide. "I'm an independent."

Aramis raised his brow, his fork poised halfway to his mouth. "On what?"

At least Jager wasn't the only one feeling the sense there was something going afoul during the less than cozy dinner. He turned his head to watch Esmeralda's reaction.

She shrugged a bare shoulder, flipping dark hair over her shoulder. "A lot of different things. When you've lived as long as I have and served so many different masters, you pick up quite a lot of expertise on a variety of subjects."

The maître d' approached the table. He spoke in a low voice to Esmeralda.

She stood. "I'm so sorry. I have to go." The apology fell from her lips like a hasty act.

After she left, with the sharp tang of exotic spices in her

wake, Jager gave Lucilla a pointed look. "You're a witness. Did I do anything at all to send her running away?"

Lucilla shook her head as if trying to process what occurred. "I don't understand it. You two had such a high probability match rate. I'm so seldom wrong about these things."

"You've been wrong for months," he reminded her.

Lucilla winced. "Jager—"

He held up his hand and gave her a slow promising smile, one that her date couldn't possibly miss the inherent meaning of. "I hope you know that fulfilled my obligation."

She lifted her wine glass and swirled the Merlot around before taking a sip. She looked over the rim of the glass, capturing him in her gaze. "I know."

Aramis raised a brow and studied first one then the other. "Am I getting in the middle of something here, because I'm definitely picking up some strong sexual undercurrents."

"Lucilla has agreed to be my date for the Legion Halloween Dance." *Take that, Spellboy!*

Aramis gave Jager a smile that only annoyed him more. "Is that right?" He turned to Lucilla. "How does your family feel about that?"

Lucilla covered her mouth with her napkin and gave a discreet cough.

"What was that?" His eyes twinkled in mischief.

With much dignity, Lucilla raised her gaze to meet Aramis's. "They don't know yet."

"That's what I thought." His words came out with a punch of laughter. "Think they'll mind?"

"I don't know. It's a dance, not a handfasting."

Jager felt the stem of the wine glass shatter in his hand. A jagged piece cut his finger, sending a drop of blood splashing on the white tablecloth.

"Jager?" Lucilla started to rise, but he waved her back down.

Jager took his napkin from his lap and wrapped his finger in it.

Stupid. He should have never let either of them see how

120

much hearing her say that bothered him. The little matchmaker already had him tied up in knots and they hadn't even gone out yet.

Jager waited for the waiter to replace and fill the glass before he turned the tide of the night. Now that his date was no longer hopping back and forth between the table and the foyer, he was in desperate need of a diversionary tactic. He dropped the bomb he'd been holding onto all night.

"Zeus came to see me this evening."

Lucilla gave him a cautious smile. "Really? You don't look pleased."

"I'm not." He directed his attention to Aramis. "I understand you are moving up the ranks of the Witches Council."

"I'm up for the next vacancy, why?"

"Because Zeus claims Rhea is organizing the Titans into a coup to bring down the Council."

Their reactions varied. Lucilla gave him a blank stare and Aramis rose from the table with a hasty excuse, sticking Jager with the check. But it was worth it. He now had Lucilla all to himself, even if by default.

After a moment of strained silence, Lucilla leaned over the table. "Are you sure? Do you trust Zeus?"

"I'd rather listen to him on this and look a fool if it's a lie, then stand by and do nothing while the Titans rip the Council apart. Granted, I know there have always been hard feelings between the Titans and witches, but nothing to make me want to see them harmed." He signaled for the waiter to bring the check.

"It's more than hard feelings, but you're right. If the situations were reversed, I'd have done the same thing."

The words gave little comfort to Jager as they left the restaurant. But maybe his honesty would see the way clear for her family to accept him into the fold. It was a huge gamble, but he hadn't gotten so rich in the Paramarkets by playing it safe.

Chapter Eight

Lucilla stood on her porch, looking up into Jager's tense face. "You did the right thing."

"Then why do I feel like I've just let my entire race down?"

She put her hand to his face, cupping his cheek tenderly. "No, Jager. I think you saved it."

He didn't look convinced.

"Look, the only people you've undermined are Rhea and her underlings. Even Zeus came to you for help. That says something."

"I did it for you."

Though his motives might be selfish, his heart was in the right place. Hers, however, had taken flight.

"Aramis will speak to the Council and they'll take precautions." She moved closer to him. "You've given them time."

"I suppose there is that. But there's always the possibility the other Titans will side with her in this."

"You've been in that position before and come out on top."

He backed her up to the house, pressing her between his hard body and heavy oak door. "Let me come in." He nuzzled the sensitive place behind her ear. "You smell and feel so good."

Lucilla knew inviting him in would result in only one outcome—they'd end up in bed. But she'd only agreed to a date, not to an affair.

As Jager continued to kiss a line down her throat, her resistance fled. His large hands rubbed her back, moving low enough to skim over the curve of her bottom. He pulled her closer. The ridge of his erection ground into her, right under her breast. Goddess, but he was a tall cauldron of brew. He thrust his hips slowly forward, moving between her cleavage. He moaned.

This had gone too far for a goodnight kiss.

He pulled back, breath puffing the hair around her face. "Tell me it isn't serious between you and Blacktalon."

"I hardly know the man. He's friends with my Aunt Rebekah."

He sent a long finger to trace her brow, cheeks and mouth. "You two looked pretty friendly."

"He's a nice man. A good man. I think I can match him with someone from my agency."

Jager gave a throaty laugh. "So you see him as a potential client, not a lover?"

"I see everyone as a potential client. It's one of the keys to my success." Lucilla gazed into his eyes. His were full of smoldering desire.

How long had she waited to know the potent pull of a man's passion?

"Let me come inside." This time the request came out as a rough plea.

Oh, who was she kidding? She wanted nothing more than to ride him like a broomstick on a full moon.

She turned in the circle of his embrace to unlock the door. Jager's arms came around her waist. His mouth descended on her shoulder.

Why did it take so long to unlock a door? Her fingers didn't want to perform the mundane task. All they wanted to do was turn and begin ripping Jager's expensive suit from his hard Titan body.

"Having problems?"

"Yes, and you aren't helping."

Jager placed his hand on hers. "Allow me."

They made it into the house, but stalled on the stairs. With arms and legs tangled, it was hard to navigate. Lucilla landed on her bottom. Jager followed her down.

"Are you all right?" It seemed a compulsory question since

Jager never slowed in his removal of her clothing to pay attention to her answer.

Lucilla didn't mind. Her hands were full of his jacket where she'd jerked it down his arms.

He moved off her only long enough to yank it off the rest of the way then gathered her close. His mouth opened on hers. His tongue invaded and retreated, moving against hers in sinuous motion.

Was it possible to have an orgasm from kissing alone? If so, she lay on the very brink. What Jager could do with his lips should have been illegal in all fifty states and most territories.

With their mouths connected, he unzipped her dress, sliding it down until her breasts were exposed to the heat of his body. The soft fabric of his shirt brushed against her distended nipples.

"Beautiful," he murmured then took one of them into his mouth.

Desire pooled in her belly. Jager used teeth and lips to stoke her higher, until at last she trembled.

With a jerk, he was off her and standing. He picked her up as if she weighed nothing and carried her up the stairs.

"Where is your bedroom?"

"End of the hall."

If his legs weren't so long, he would have been in an all-out sprint getting her to the bed. Once there, he laid her down and then stepped back, as if to admire the view. A devilish smile played along the corner of his wide sensuous mouth. His gaze drank her in as if he were dying of thirst.

Self-consciously, Lucilla began to tug her dress back up to cover her exposed breasts.

Jager shook his head. "No. Don't cover yourself."

She twirled her hand helplessly in front of her. "Then you have to lose your shirt. I'm not lying here topless all by myself."

"No. We wouldn't want that." He unbuttoned his shirt then slowly shed it.

Goddess, how she wished she'd turned on the central stereo system before coming up here. Somehow she'd gotten a vision into her head of Jager stripping for her to Santana's

"Black Magic Woman". Not that she knew anyone who practiced the dark side of the craft. The song just stuck in her head.

Even without the music, Jager's naked chest was an event worthy of applause. Her palms tickled in anticipation of touching that bronze expanse of muscular flesh.

He let the cotton slide off his shoulders. The man was a huge tease. And judging from the way he was working it, he was enjoying putting on the show immensely. His eyes sparkled with mischief.

Who'd have thought Jager Cronus was playful in bed? He'd always seemed so damned serious to her.

His shirt dropped to the floor with a final flourish. "Now it's your turn. Shimmy out of that dress."

Oh, hell, she should have known it was going to be tit for tat.

The hard part was struggling the rest of the way out of a sheath dress that fit like a second skin. Sexy was the last word that came to mind. She'd probably look like a fish trying to scale itself.

She took in a deep breath, holding in her stomach, and leaned against the ornate headboard. Tilting her pelvis up, she slipped the dress over her hips. Jager leaned over and tugged the fabric down her legs. She lay there in nothing more than a scrap of black lace and seed pearls.

"Those are some kind of panties, Lucilla."

"I thought I'd dress for the occasion."

He started onto the bed with his knee. Lucilla raised a finger and waved it at him. "This is a no pants zone."

"Well, in that case."

The dropping of trou was done with less finesse than the shirt. The evidence as to why shone through the silky fabric of his boxers.

Lucilla heard herself gulp audibly.

What had she gotten herself into with this man? Sure he was a Titan, and by definition he had to be big. But saying Jager was well-endowed was like saying the Golden Gate was a footbridge or Niagara Falls had a little water problem.

"Is that fear I see in your eyes?" The concern in his voice

touched her. So did the hand he ran up her leg, right to the inside of her thigh.

"Apprehension. Fear is not in my vocabulary."

"Glad to hear it." He stretched out beside her, his hand making lazy swirls over the front of her decorative panties.

Her breath caught as his fingers moved lower and lower toward that achy place deep inside her.

It occurred to her that she lay on the bed with her arms at her sides, letting him feel her up, when she had all that gorgeous maleness within reach that she hadn't even begun to explore yet. By rights she should be taking advantage of the opportunity before her and drive Jager right out of his ever-loving mind. It wasn't as if she were an untried virgin. She'd had lovers.

Well, a few. Some. Not many. All right, she didn't have that much experience, but she had enough and she had a very fertile imagination.

She rolled onto her side, facing him. How would he react if she did the same thing to his boxers as he'd done to her panties? Probably come unglued at the seams.

Lucilla started at the top of his chest, feeling the ripple of muscles and bone across his front. He was smooth, but tough. It was an odd combination she had a hard time defining. But oh, so masculine.

He had no hair on his chest. She'd always loved a hairy chest, but for some reason, on Jager she didn't miss it. He was perfection. Like a statue she'd once seen in a museum. All smooth, defined and perfect. His skin felt hot to the touch. Burning.

She ran her hand down his pecs, grazing her nails over his nipples.

He sucked in a breath, releasing it on a pleasured sound.

She flattened her hand and moved it down his stomach, heading for the gold.

Just as her hand reached its goal, she looked up into his face. His eyes were dark pools of desire. His jaw clamped tightly as if he held back strong emotion.

When she wrapped her hand around his silk-clad erection,

he lost control.

Lucilla ended up underneath him, her panties hanging off the bedside lamp, his big body on and in her.

She'd been wrong to be apprehensive. It was amazing.

He touched her everywhere at once. There wasn't a part of her sensitized flesh neglected as he thrust into her. She lifted her legs to rest high on his hips. His big hand held her in place. Their mouths collided in a kiss so deep and tender, her back arched in response.

How was she ever going to get close enough to him? If she lived inside his skin, it wouldn't be close enough for her.

"Look at me, Lucilla," he murmured, tearing his mouth from hers.

Her lashes fluttered open to gaze into his eyes.

"Yes, like that, my love." He thrust deeper, harder, hitting that special place that shattered her on impact.

"Jager." The sound of her voice surprised her. It was raw, desperate. Hot. It was a cry for mercy and a plea for more.

"I'm here. Always." And he followed her down into the most carnal orgasm ever.

Chapter Nine

The first thing Jager noticed upon waking was that he felt like Gulliver sleeping in a Lilliputian bed. The second was the soft female body pressed close to his. Snoring.

He smiled. Lucilla would be so embarrassed if she knew she snored.

It wasn't bad when measured on the Snore-a-Tron scale. No, on the contrary, it was kind of girly. If a snore could be considered such a thing.

All that gorgeous hair of hers had come down when they'd made love. It curled around her shoulders and down her back. Godiva hair. How in the world did she ever get all that pinned up into those tight bun things she wore? And she claimed to not have any magic.

She gave one last snort and woke. Her brows came down into a sharp "V". "You snore."

It was useless to hold back his incredulous laugh. "I do? That was your snorking that woke you. I was already awake."

"If you're awake, why isn't the coffee made? Chop. Chop. I run a tight ship here, sailor."

Instead of hopping to, Jager gathered her into his arms. "I'd rather have morning-after sex with the woman I love."

Lucilla looked around. "Is she here? Tell her to go make the coffee then."

"You're a grump in the mornings. Cute. Deliciously disheveled. But grumpy."

Somewhere in the depths of the big house, a phone rang.

"No," Lucilla whined and slid under the covers, pulling

them up over her head.

"Do you want me to answer that?"

"No." She snuggled back into the curve of his groin. "Stay here."

She didn't need to ask him twice. He wrapped his arms around her, holding her to his chest.

"What is on the agenda today?" he whispered in her ear.

"Sleep."

"How about I get dressed and get us some breakfast. When you're more awake we'll decide."

"Coffee." The word ended on another snore. And she was out.

So his perfect woman had two little faults. He could work with them. After she woke up and got going, she was the most charming person he'd met in a very long time. Her bedroom skills were unparallel. Another point in her favor.

Jager gathered his clothes and helped himself to her shower. All her soaps smelled of some kind of flowers. He used them anyhow, but rinsed twice. How embarrassing was it to be the former God of your own religion and go around smelling like you just stepped off an episode of *Queer Eye*? The only way to wear a flowered scent like a man was to have it put there by a hot woman rubbing up against you. At least that's the way he saw it.

When he went outside, Zeus had his behind parked on the hood of Jager's car. "That was one long-ass date, Dad."

"You jealous?"

He raised his brows over the tops of his sunglasses. "She's definitely hot stuff, but is it ethical to sleep with your matchmaker?"

"Is it *ethical* to overthrow your father and steal his heavenly throne?" Yes, the rebuttal was a bit childish and Jager, by rights, should have been over it millennia ago, but he had a hard time dealing with the betrayal by his own son.

Zeus hopped down off the car. "I told you I'm sorry. What do you want from me?"

"I should be asking you that. Why have you brought yourself all the way out here?"

"There have been some developments since last night." Zeus walked around to the passenger side as Jager hit the remote locks. "I'll tell you while we roll."

"I'm going to get breakfast for Lucilla and myself and then I'm coming back here to enjoy it in her company. You may talk while I get the food, but after that you're on your own."

"Fair enough."

Jager got into the car and started the engine. He turned to his son seated next to him. "This isn't going to become a habit with you, is it?"

"What?"

"You showing up at mealtimes."

He shrugged wide shoulders. "A guy's gotta eat."

They drove across town to a bakery that made the best bagels in all of Sleepy Hollow Woods. He had them made into breakfast sandwiches and bought some extra-large coffees. Two for Lucilla.

"Here, make yourself useful." Jager handed the to-go bag and coffee holder to Zeus when they got into the car. "Did you really want to talk to me about the latest developments or were you just trying to get me to buy your morning meal?"

Zeus steadied the bag with one hand and ate with the other. "No. I have genuine news."

"Let's hear it then." It was hell being held hostage for a sausage and egg bagel.

"At least one of the other paraspecies is going to side with Mom. I heard her discussing it on the phone after I left your place last night."

The knowledge left a big hole in Jager's gut. He doubted he'd be able to eat now. "Change in plans." He hung a U-turn and started back to Lucilla's place. "You're going to sit and tell Lucilla and me everything you heard."

Lucilla heard the front door open and voices in the entranceway. One was definitely Jager, but the other she didn't recognize. She'd just finished her shower and dressed. Her wet hair was pulled back and piled up in a claw clip.

She shoved her feet into a pair of wedge shoes and headed

down the stairs. When she moved, reminders of the night before's bedroom gymnastics made themselves known in the form of muscle cramps. Damn, it had been way too long since she'd indulged. Much too long.

She found Jager in the kitchen, sitting at the table with a man who looked in his late-twenties to early-thirties. He had that just-off-the-beach look to him, other than the overdose of product in his hair that looked more like skateboard culture or *Dragon Ball Z*.

Jager stood when she entered the room. The young man let out a sigh and followed suit, acting like it was an imposition on his personal style to show good manners.

"Good morning," Lucilla said.

"You're much more awake than when I left." Jager reached over and grabbed her hand, pulling her to him. He leaned over and kissed her tenderly.

"The thought of breakfast and coffee will do that to a girl." She glanced at the bag. "What did you bring?"

"Coffee, sandwiches and Zeus."

Lucilla gave the man a closer look. So this was the man who'd dared wrestle heaven from his father and sided with his mother in the conflict? Punk.

But that still didn't explain his presence at her kitchen table.

"He has some information about the coup." Jager pulled out a chair for her. "You might need to sit down for this."

"That bad, huh?"

"Well, it ain't good." He took a place next to her then turned to Zeus. "Tell her what you told me."

"My mother is negotiating with another of the paraspecies to side with the Titans. I think she might be going for broke on this one." He lifted his coffee and took a sip.

Lucilla glanced back at Jager for confirmation.

He gave a slight shrug. "We have to narrow down which group is politically motivated enough to want to see the Witches Council fall."

Lucilla had no idea. The Council had always run the affairs of the Paras. Why did the others want to change the order of things? Not that the Witches Council had a corner on the market of government. There was enough room for all of them to have representatives.

"Do you think we should open negotiations and set up a multi-species consortium? Maybe Rhea just wants the Titan voices heard." From what she knew of Rhea, that was as unlikely as a Para being allowed to run for president.

Zeus gave her a look as if to say *"get a grip"*. "My mother wants all or nothing, though I do like your idea."

Jager turned to her. "You deal with the gamut of Parakind. Ever caught an undercurrent that would suggest one group might be inclined to go against the Council?"

"Well, if they were, they wouldn't be likely to tell me." She picked up one of the unopened coffees and lifted the lid. Black and hot. She needed to blond it up a bit or it would never be drinkable.

"Maybe they did and you just don't remember. A gesture. A refusal to date someone different—"

Lucilla cut him off. "You're the only one in the last six months who's refused a date. Most of my clients are looking for a long-term commitment and are willing to give their dates a chance."

A sensual gleam came into Jager's eyes. "If you would have matched us from the beginning, I wouldn't have refused you a thing."

The blush started all the way down on her chest and swept upward. She rose to get milk and sugar for the coffee. Anything so she didn't have to sit at the table bathed in memories of Jager making love to her while his son sat across from her with that stupid knowing grin on his face.

Jager let out a low sexually-charged laugh. "Don't run from your feelings, Lucilla. I know you enjoyed yourself last night."

He was shameless.

"I don't remember running anywhere." She grabbed the condiments and returned to the table. "Now, if we can get back to the discussion."

Jager nodded. "I'll look at it from a business perspective, Lucilla can take the social, and Zeus..." He stopped and made a motion with his hand. "Do whatever it is you do."

"Spy," Zeus provided. He rose from the table, Styrofoam cup in hand. "I'll leave you two lovebirds alone. If I hear anything else, I'll let you know."

He started to go out the back door, but stopped and looked at his father with a wicked gleam in his cool gray eyes. "Keep it safe."

Lucilla's face became endangered of combusting. When the door closed behind him, Lucilla slapped her palm on the table. "He's awful."

Jager shrugged. "I wasn't much different at his age. Though I don't think I was near as arrogant."

Lucilla thought perhaps Jager had been more arrogant, but was humbled at his downfall. She chose not to mention that particular point.

She took a few steps, coming close enough to him to cup his face in her hand. "You're a good man now and that's all that matters."

His eyes went molten. "We're alone again."

"I did notice that."

Jager backed her up against the cabinet. He had a habit of trapping her against immovable objects for some reason. Like he thought she'd try to run away or something. Someday she might tell him she had no intention of going anywhere. But, for now, it was fun to keep him guessing.

"Are we going back to bed?"

He shook his head and lifted her up onto the countertop. "What's wrong with here?"

Lucilla draped her arms around his neck. "Nothing, I suppose. But sex on a countertop does have that clichéd feel to it."

"So does a bed, but you didn't complain about that last night." He began to kiss his way down her neck, pulling on the collar of her shirt for better access.

"Last night was our first time—"

"First of many."

Lucilla gave a half laugh, half moan as he connected to a sensitive spot behind her ear. The man definitely knew how to turn her on at light speed. But then, he'd once been a god, surely he had intimate knowledge of what pleased a woman. At the moment she didn't care, as long as she received all the benefits of his experience.

Jager raised his head from the hollow of her throat. "Where *do* you want to continue this?"

Two minutes later they were lying in the fallen leaves of the apple orchard, going at it like a couple of satyrs.

Though a light autumn breeze rustled the trees, at ground level it was a scorcher. How did Jager manage to put out so much body heat? The man must have been made out of muscles and flames. Everywhere he touched, he left burning pleasure in its wake.

A hard ball dug into her back, right above her tailbone.

"Mmm." She arched her back, trying to get away from the pain.

Jager moved deeper, pinning her to the ground.

She twitched again. "Ow."

He pulled away, his face awash in concern. "Sorry. Sorry." He showered her face in kisses. The next thrust sent the object digging into her butt cheeks.

She put her hands on Jager's chest and pushed. "Wait. Time out."

He moved off her and sat back on his knees. "What's wrong?"

Lucilla leaned forward, reaching behind her. Her hand connected with the remains of an apple, flattened from their ardent lovemaking. She threw the thing out of their range and held her arms out for him. "I'm good now."

"You're always good." He met her halfway then reversed their positions. "I'll protect you from violent fruit."

Tenderness moved through her. There wasn't anything about him she didn't find attractive. He was gorgeous, smart, sexy and just plain fun. So much fun. Goddess, it was the most attractive attribute he possessed.

Everyone needed to experience the heady excitement of having fun with their lovers. If laughter was the best medicine, it also was the most potent aphrodisiac. At least for her.

Lucilla stretched out along his large body, loving the feel of him beneath her. Happiness sang in her veins.

Jager placed his hand on her neck, lifting her hair. "You should see yourself right now. You're taking my breath away, you look so beautiful."

"I was just thinking the same thing about you."

He smiled knowingly.

It was hours before either of them uttered another word.

Chapter Ten

The room was already crowded by the time Lucilla arrived. She hated walking in late. Hated being the center of all attention. Even now, the many eyes of those assembled spied her at the door and turned to watch her enter and take her place in the family row.

"I thought you weren't coming?" Aunt Rebekah grabbed her bag from Lucilla's seat, where she'd stashed it.

Lucilla leaned over to whisper into her aunt's ear. "I wasn't going to, but after the bombshell Zeus dropped on Jager Cronus, I thought I should at least make an appearance."

"That's something else we need to discuss—the fact you're seeing a Titan." Aunt Rebekah pursed her lips in disapproval.

"It's a bit more than seeing him."

Lucilla didn't know her aunt's eyes could get so big, or her skin turn such a color, but obviously she was wrong.

"Lucilla—"

The High Wizard took his place on the dais, calling the meeting to order. Not a moment too soon either. Aunt Rebekah would have worried the point like a dog with an old shoe. Who was Rebekah to judge? She didn't know Jager personally. She hadn't stood basking in the light of his admiration. No, the only thing Aunt Rebekah had were thousands of years of bitter history that had nothing to do with Jager in the first place. He hadn't even been leading the Titans when the trouble started between their people.

Lucilla sat in her seat, stewing in indignation. She shot a frown in her aunt's direction. "Jager is a good man."

"His kind is plotting to wipe us out."

"His *ex-wife* is plotting. Not *him*. Big difference there." The words were forced out between Lucilla's clenched teeth. She crossed her arms over her breasts. Anger boiled like one of her aunt's brews right under the surface of her skin. It heated her neck all the way to her ears.

"Doesn't mean he won't side with them when the shit hits the fan," Rebekah whispered.

"As if he owed them any allegiance after what they did to him. Believe me, he hasn't forgotten or forgiven the treachery. If I know nothing else in my life, it's that Jager Cronus will do everything in his power to help us. He already is. What are you doing but hurling accusations?" A sudden sharp memory of their intense lovemaking from the night before scudded through her mind, igniting sparklers in her soul. "He's the best man I've ever met."

Lucilla hoped Aunt Rebekah didn't detect the little hitch in her voice at the end of her diatribe.

No such luck.

"You're in love with him," Rebekah accused.

"For longer than I wanted to admit."

Aramis slid into the seat beside Lucilla, effectively cutting off what was becoming an uncomfortable conversation. The Blacktalons had seating on the other side of the chamber, where the out-of-towners sat. "You aren't going to believe what I just heard."

"Try me," Aunt Rebekah said dryly. She shifted her gaze to meet Lucilla's. Irritation remained vivid in her eyes.

"Rhea has gotten herself a djinn."

A sinking feeling, as if someone had just pulled the plug on a drain and let all the water out, centered under Lucilla's breasts. "I have to go make a phone call."

One look at Aramis's face confirmed he thought the same thing she did. Now all she had to do was verify the identity of the traitorous djinn. Granted, there were a lot of them out there running around, but Esmeralda's behavior the week before had been odd, to say the least.

The djinn had never made it a secret they longed to have

powers like the witches, who were not beholden to the whims of a master. If Jager wondered what group would be politically motivated enough to side with the Titans in the coming conflict, he need look no further.

She rose from her seat, keeping her head low, so as not to call attention to herself as she snuck out of the chamber.

The phone on the other end was already ringing by the time she made it to the vestibule.

"Hello, sweetheart. Is your meeting over?" Jager's voice came through the line like melted butter and honey.

"No, just starting. Listen, Aramis just told Aunt Rebekah and me that Rhea has a djinn in her pocket."

A colorful array of expletives rolled out. Lucilla held the phone away from her ear. She nodded a hello at two old witches walking by as they gave her scandalized expressions.

"Jager? Jager?" she tried to get his attention. "Whoa, honey. Slow down. What was that? Baby, I don't think that's possible, no matter how limber she is."

Finally he let out a long breath and ended his tirade. "Sorry. Rhea knows exactly how to push my buttons."

"Apparently." Lucilla leaned against the wall between a display case of trophies from various regional witching contests and a statue of Merlin. "I think there's a good chance the consulting Esmeralda is doing is for Rhea."

"My thoughts exactly." He lowered his voice. "I'm going to call in a favor from Zeus. The boy owes me big time."

"What are you going to have him do?" Though she didn't particularly care for Jager's eldest son, she didn't want to see him come to harm.

"A little recon with the rogue djinn. He's a good-looking kid, a former god, and Rhea's son. I think it's pretty safe to assume Esmeralda might be persuaded to talk to him, if she believes he's on Rhea's side in the conflict."

"And if we're wrong and it's some other djinn?" Lucilla frowned when she noticed someone had stuck a piece of used chewing gum in the folds of Merlin's bronzed robes. She dug a tissue from her purse and picked it out. Was there no respect for authority figures anymore?

A purely male sound purled through the phone. "Then I have the satisfaction of knowing Zeus has one of my castoffs."

Lucilla smiled in spite of the truth stretching. Let him rewrite history if he wanted. It didn't matter to her, as long as he knew where he belonged now.

They said their goodbyes and Lucilla crept back into the chamber as the High Wizard Rowan Erlich made a mandate for the entire witching community to ready their resources should the Titans launch a surprise attack.

"What about the Legion Halloween Dance? It's less than a week away. Will it be cancelled?" someone in the crowd shouted.

Conversations erupted throughout the room. High Wizard Rowan raised his hands for silence. Then a spotlight landed directly on Lucilla while she tried to make it to her seat undetected.

"Why don't we let Lucilla Wainwright answer that question?"

The ground needed to seriously open up and swallow her. Now.

She straightened the front of her dress and fiddled with her hair, trying to control the nerves snapping throughout her body like frayed power lines. As the Dance Committee Chair, all major decisions regarding the annual event landed on her shoulders.

She cleared her throat. "If the Titans' complaint were with the entire Para community, I would perhaps see a need to cancel the dance. However, we only know of them going after the Council—no offense to our esteemed leaders—" Several of the Council members shook their heads at her, whether to acknowledge they were not offended or as a reflection of her hopelessness, she had no idea. "I have to therefore assume they wouldn't risk taking on the other species at a festival designed to include all Parakind. The fallout would devastate their bid to rule."

Aramis rose, coming to her side in solidarity. "I agree with Lucilla. If the Titans push too hard, they alienate the others. If they wish to rule, they can't do it by force. Not without a full-scale war spilling out to the Norms. The question is—would they hazard discovery?"

Lucilla put her hand up in the air. "I just want to stress one point, if I may. Not all the Titans are for the takeover. History shows us Rhea has attempted this once before and managed a successful coup. We should exercise extreme caution, but not paint every Titan with the same brush."

Whispers fluttered through the crowd.

Aramis leaned into her, speaking between closed lips. "Good way not to call attention to your boyfriend."

"Then can we expect cooperation from your Mr. Cronus?" High Wizard Rowan placed his hand in the long folds of his sleeves, awaiting her answer.

Her face burned. Every gaze in the room was glued to her.

This time, however, it didn't intimidate her. She lifted her head and shoulders and looked Rowan straight in the eyes. "Yes. You have his full support."

"Very well." He waved her to sit back down.

She remained standing. "Not so fast."

With the entire Witches Council watching, she walked with military posture to the front of the hall. "If I may address the assembly." She made it a statement, not a question. Her steady gaze penetrated into the eyes of Wizard Rowan.

"Make it short and succinct, please. We've a full agenda."

She turned to face the audience. She'd say what she had to say and take as long as she damn well pleased. After being the butt of their jokes for so long, she figured it her due.

"I know I've been the butt of jokes and ridicule for most of my existence, but I will remind you that I do come from one of the oldest and most respected of witching families. I've worked my non-magical fingers to the bone to make a success of my business. And I've succeeded. So, I demand my voice be heard on this issue. It's that important.

"Jager Cronus, along with his son Zeus, has agreed to come to our aid and side with us in the coming conflict with the Titans. That is true. We owe them our gratitude for bringing this matter to our attention, rather than letting us be blindsided by a war we never saw coming.

"Odd how that's possible in a group with such eminent

prognosticators. Or is this the true reason we've been at odds with the Titans for centuries? Because you knew this day would come?" She held up her hand to halt any heckling that might spring from those listening. And they were listening—raptly.

"In my business, I come into contact with all the para species. I know their quirks and foibles and there are none of them without faults. Including us. We have an opportunity here to create something better. Let's ensure none of the other species gets it into their heads to attempt a coup on this scale again. Enter into dialogue with them about organizing some sort of cross-species consortium to iron out problems before they come to a head."

"You're just saying that because you're dating a Titan," someone yelled.

Lucilla put her hand over her heart. "Correction. I'm in love with a Titan." There was a collective gasp. She ignored it. "But that's only part of the reason. The other is because I know it can work. There aren't any species in the Parakind that I haven't matched. Successfully. If it can work one-on-one, I know it can work in a forum of mutual respect."

Quietness filled the room, until the sound of a single person clapping cut through the uncomfortable void.

Aramis stood, continuing his solo applause. Soon, he was joined by Aunt Rebekah. Before long, the entire witching community were on their feet applauding her impromptu speech and the wisdom behind it.

Slightly embarrassed, but no less proud for standing up for herself and her position in the community, she started back for her seat.

"Wait!" Wizard Rowan's voice filled the hall. The applause died.

He stood from his place, hands resting on the dais. "You do come from a unique perspective, Ms. Wainwright, that is true. Your idea has great merit and shows a great love for not only this community, but all Parakind.

"It occurs to the council that—as you so aptly pointed out—you not only have intimate knowledge of all the species, but as an extremely successful matchmaker, you have their confidence as well. We can think of no better person to chair such a consortium."

They could have knocked her over with a levitating feather. If she'd ever questioned their respect, she need do that no more. She had it.

Lucilla was allowed to reclaim her seat.

The rest of the meeting faded into the background as Lucilla quietly made plans as to how best to protect the Legion Halloween Dance attendees and decide how best to select those individuals for the consortium.

On the way home, Lucilla stopped off at the party store to pick up her costume for the dance. She'd thought about going elegant again this year, but since it was the first time she'd be there on the arm of a handsome man, she wanted it to be different. Fun.

And sexy.

She'd called two days before to reserve a hot Playboy Bunny costume, complete with black hose and high heels. Jager wouldn't be able to keep his hands off her. Not that he needed much encouragement to grope her. It seemed a mandate with him. If they were in a room together, he found an excuse to capture, hold and fondle every place on her body he had access to.

Not that she minded. But one thing often led to another, and before either of them could offer a protest or catch their breaths, they were tumbling to the floor and making mad monkey love.

A hand waved in front of her face as the delicious contemplations fled.

"Here you are, Ms. Wainwright. It's due back on Tuesday. There is a two-hundred-dollar deposit that is refundable provided you return the costume in the same condition it was rented."

Lucilla frowned at the clerk. "Two hundred dollars? For a few scraps of material and some wire ears? I'm not renting a car here."

The young man pushed his glasses up on his nose. "There's a bit more to it than wire ears." He unzipped the garment bag exposing a long white and pink furry something that most definitely did not resemble anything Hugh Hefner would have had serving drinks in one of his clubs.

"Have you lost your mind? I was supposed to be a *Playboy* Bunny, not the Easter Bunny." Lucilla winced as a huge orange carrot that could have been seen from space rolled out of the bag, across the counter and landed on the ground with a bounce.

Goddess, this was not happening to her. She shook her head in denial.

The clerk lifted the carbon copy of the order form from around the neck of the hanger. "It says here *one medium bunny costume*. It doesn't specify what kind."

"Oh, so you just assumed it was the furry one who likes to hide eggs that get lost for months." She leaned menacingly into his pimply face. "Do I look like the Easter Bunny kind, kid?"

He shook his head. "No, ma'am."

"No, indeed. Now go back there and get me a Bunny suit."

He turned and fled, leaving the big plastic carrot where it lay.

Lucilla put her arm on the counter, resting her face in her hand. Why did everything always have to be so difficult for her? She just wanted to be sexy and fun for her man.

Her man.

The words alone made her all warm and fuzzy. Kind of like a pink and white bunny suit.

Laughter bubbled up from deep inside her.

Should she?

Oh, it would be too cruel for words.

Mischief like she'd never known before had her ringing the service bell.

The kid returned, shaking like he'd developed a nervous tic in the last minute and a half.

"Look, I'm sorry. I've changed my mind. I'll take the bunny suit. The furry one."

He gave her a cautious look. "A...are you sure?"

"Positive."

Lucilla handed over the hefty deposit and laughed all the way home.

Chapter Eleven

The night was crisp and clear. The crowds electric.

Overhead, a full moon hung low in the sky. In the center of the park, a bonfire blazed high into the heavens. People danced around it in costumes or formal wear. Food was laid out on long banquet tables, allowing partiers to graze at their leisure.

Jager wore a light cotton shirt that draped on his wide shoulders. His pants were a dark fabric with a drawstring waist. He looked both elegant and comfortable. Lucilla leaned into his chest as she watched the crowds. Her big puffball of a tail added extra padding where she needed none.

He'd been expecting a sexy bunny, too. She'd teased him about her costume as they'd lain in bed the night before and he asked her what she'd wear.

Just let them get through this one night. That's all she asked. But something deep inside her felt off about the evening. Though the sky shone clear, it was as if rain threatened on the horizon. And not a light, refreshing drizzle, but the mother of all thunder clappers.

Jager's arms came around her to hold her tightly. "Don't worry, sweetheart. I won't let anything happen to you."

"I know." She leaned back to look up into his face. Damn he was handsome standing there with the reflection of the flames painting his face in red and gold. She rested her big furry paws on top of his hands where they met around her waist.

A lump formed in her throat. He'd known from the first time he'd seen her she was the one for him. He'd told her that the night before, as he'd made passionate love to her.

Her breath hitched. She had to say something before it all came crashing down on them.

She turned in the circle of his arms. Screwing up her courage, she looked up into his face. "I love you, Jager. I think I have since the day I first looked at your profile."

"Lucilla." Her name had never been uttered with such raw emotion before. He drew her to him, his mouth descending on hers.

Suddenly, the night was on fire.

The beautiful bonfire exploded, sending dancers running for cover. Magic rained down from above.

A spark landed on her suit, igniting a small patch of fur. It smoldered with the stench of burnt fibers. Jager beat out the ember with his hand.

"Get out of here. I don't want you hurt," he yelled above the angry cries of the crowd.

"Forget that. Your ex-wife and her minions just cost me two hundred bucks and ruined my party. I'm going for blood." She picked up her plastic carrot, wielding it like a club.

She might not have magic on her side, but she had something a hell of a lot worse—rabid bunny hormones.

She reached up and pulled Jager down to her level. She gave him a hard kiss on the mouth. "Be careful. I'll see you after I clean house."

"You be careful." She started away when he pulled on one huge padded paw. "I love you, too."

Lucilla danced into the fray, looking for anyone who was over six feet tall and attacking the festivalgoers.

Bright sparks danced overhead, firefights exchanged between witch and djinn.

Lucilla came around the south end of the banquet tables and hopped up on them, looking for the heaviest fighting.

Oh, goddess.

Her Aunt Rebekah was busy trying to fend off a couple of djinn all by herself. Lucilla flew into the chaotic mass like the Bionic Hare, swinging her mighty carrot of terror. She fought her way over to her aunt. She kicked one djinn in the jewels, the other she dispatched with a swipe of her paw. They were heavier than they appeared and stuffed with something akin to boxing gloves.

When both djinn were down, she put her foot on one's chest, pointing into his face. "Looks like rabbit's feet aren't so lucky for you, buster."

"Lucilla, quit screwing around and help me." Rebekah had a hold of a female Titan's hair, holding her in place while trying to uncork a potion bottle with her teeth.

The Titan struggled to get away from the much smaller, but very agile Rebekah. One would think, with as much power and brawn behind her, she'd easily struggle out of Rebekah's grasp. But Rebekah had wrapped the Titan's long hair around her fist and used an enchantment to force her to stay still. The Titan fought against the magical bonds.

"Here." She threw the vial at Lucilla. "Open this and pour it down her throat."

"What does it do?"

"It'll knock her out."

The Titan shook with rage as Lucilla pulled the stopper out with her teeth and tried to decide how best to get the liquid down the throat of someone twice her height.

"Does she have to swallow it?" Lucilla sniffed at the contents and pulled back as noxious fumes made the images before her swim. "My guess is no."

Instead of attempting the impossible, Lucilla splashed it in the Titan's face.

"It burns." The Titan rubbed at her eyes then staggered. She fell like the giant from Jack and the Beanstalk. No more fe-fi-fo-fumming for her for a while.

"Excellent." Aunt Rebekah grabbed Lucilla's paw and hurried to help others. Djinn winked in and out of existence, faster than they became targets. Witches screeched overhead, dive-bombing the enemy like pointy-shoed Kamikaze pilots.

Rebekah and Lucilla hurried across the park as fast as Lucilla's fluffy feet allowed. They spotted Aramis and started for him when another Titan materialized in front of them. Lucilla looked up the length of the giant blonde woman. Her legs were longer than Lucilla's entire body. She picked up Aunt Rebekah by the back of her cloak, choking the brew master.

"Rebekah!" Lucilla jumped up, swatting at the Titan with her paws. It had no effect on the mammoth woman.

"Put her down," came a deep male voice from behind Lucilla. She turned to see Zeus staring at the female Titan with rage. "Haven't you ever heard the expression 'pick on someone your own size'?"

The Titan let out a growl and charged Zeus. But he wasn't playing games. He lifted a hand, turning her to a block of ice. Aunt Rebekah fell from a frozen hand, landing in the dirt.

Zeus hurried to her. "Are you all right?"

"I could have handled her," she complained.

Zeus smiled warmly. "Yeah, I know. Who do you think I was talking to about picking on people their own size?"

Lucilla watched, amazed, as her aunt got a gooey look in her eyes and allowed Zeus to help her to her feet. Then her attention was diverted as something big and angry, dressed in an expensive white shirt, flashed in her periphery. Lucilla lost interest in watching the battle. All her attention focused on the man who bore down on his prey like an eagle with deadly talons at the ready.

Jager pointed to the ground. She looked to see if there was something at his feet. But there was nothing.

He stalked forward, his gaze fixed on his ex-wife.

Rhea shook her head in denial of whatever Jager meant to do.

He extended his hand again. Even from where Lucilla stood, she could see power radiating out of his fingertips. Hadn't he lost all his godly powers after his fall?

The ground shook.

Long cracks appeared like a gorge through the center of the park. Lucilla couldn't hear Jager's shouted words, but their intent put fear on the faces of those who had.

"It's over, Rhea." Jager continued to force the ground to quake under their feet. It must have been a small trick left over from his days of ruling heaven and earth, but as a bluff, it was effective. "This little coup of yours is finished."

"Cronus, how can you turn against your kind?" Fear

widened her eyes.

"I owe no allegiance to you or our kind. I will, however, help to mend the rift between the witches and Titans." At her surprised expression, he sent another tremor moving through the ground and forced a lightning bolt to hit the ground. "Always you wanted more than your share. And even more wasn't enough. Your greed stops tonight."

He no longer had the power to send her away, but that didn't mean some of his newly acquired friends and soon-to-be family lacked the skill. "Aramis!"

The wizard materialized beside him as if the outcome of the evening had been preplanned. "You bellowed, your godliness?"

"Dispatch my ex to Hades. Let him worry about his mother for a while."

"No. Not Hades. He hates me." Rhea tried to stand, but another jolt to the ground sent her tumbling back on her behind.

"Too bad. You should have thought of that before you spent an eternity scheming."

Aramis reached down and pulled the Titan to her feet. He looked way up into her face and gave a dark smile. "Some days I really enjoy my power. This is one of them."

They disappeared in a flash of light.

Without their leader, the remaining Titans fled the field. The djinn disappeared like mist on the wind.

A loud cheer went up through the Parakind.

Lucilla ran to Jager. He turned just as she took a flying leap up. He caught her in his arms, holding her to him.

"You. Were. Amazing." She punctuated each word with a kiss.

"So were you. I saw some of the damage you did with that carrot. Remind me never to sneak up on you when you're holding vegetables. You could be downright lethal with celery."

Lucilla threw her head back and laughed.

Jager pulled her closer. "So, what do you say? You think we're a good match now, Lucilla?"

She sobered, holding his beloved face between her paws. "Oh, yes. Close to one hundred percent, I'd say."

"And your family? Do you think I've managed to put their reservations to rest?" Though he smiled, there was tension around his eyes. Worry. Her answer meant that much to him.

She smiled largely. "Marry me and find out."

"Lucilla." Her name said in that husky, passionate way was all the answer she needed.

As for her family, they whooped and hollered, gathering around them in a circle to perform a bonding dance.

Oh, yeah. They were with them all right. Amazing what a little cross-species cooperation could do.

They continued to kiss as the Parakind gathered more wood and built the bonfire anew. This would be one Legion Halloween Dance for the history books.

About the Author

To learn more about MK Mancos, please visit www.MysticKat.com or send an email to MysticKat1965@yahoo.com.

Look for these titles by
MK Mancos

Now Available:

The Host: Shadows
By A Silken Thread
Scythe

Writing as Kathleen Scott
Dragon Tamer
Solarion Heat

The Ghost Shrink,
the Accidental Gigolo
&
the Poltergeist Accountant

Vivi Andrews

Dedication

For my family, the most supportive collection of individuals on the planet. I am lucky to have you.

Chapter One:
The Larrinator

"Oh, please. Kill me now."

The half-naked figure jiggling in front of her seemed to take this as a compliment. "Yeah, baby, you know you want it."

Lucy Cartwright closed her eyes and wondered—not for the first time—what she had ever done in her life to deserve this punishment. Karma was a vindictive bitch, but this was taking things too far.

The pudgy, middle-aged stockbroker performing a striptease in her bedroom finished whipping his shirt around his head and flung it across the room. Keeping time to the booty music in his head, he bumped and ground his way in a little circle until his pasty back was right in front of her. The flabby ass that had spent more time in an ergonomic chair than hitting it in nightclubs bounced back toward her in nauseating invitation.

If he had been more substantial, he might have knocked her back a few steps in his enthusiasm, but tonight's visitor wasn't what you could call corporeal.

Lucy was a medium, which—no offense to Patricia Arquette and Jennifer Love Hewitt—did *not* involve helping the ghosts of murdered people find justice. Thank God. Lucy couldn't stand blood. Or death. Or anything involving blood or death.

Except, you know, the ghosts. That part was okay. Usually.

Helping loved ones contact the dearly departed was also not in her job description. There were people who did that, but she was in a slightly different line.

Lucy helped the deceased work through their issues and move on to the next plane. The white light. Whatever.

She wasn't really big on the whole theology of the thing. She'd met ghosts who practiced just about every major religion and hadn't really noticed any huge differences in their immediate afterlife. What came after the white light was none of her business. Lucy pretty much avoided the whole Heaven thing, which was easier than one might expect, considering she worked with the dead. She was not a priest. Or a minister.

Nope, Lucy was more of a post-life therapist. Helping people release the issues that were keeping them from moving on.

It was only recently that all of her clients had started wanting a release of a different kind.

"Larry," Lucy said in her calmest, most reasonable tone. "As, uh, *studly* as you are, I can't, uh, get with you tonight, buddy."

Larry shook it one hundred and eighty degrees and then performed a deep knee bend that was truly impressive for a man his size, his knees popping out to either side as his crotch slid down her leg.

Oh great, he's the stripper and now I get to be the pole. Lucy couldn't feel a thing—Larry wasn't that with it—but it was still a disconcerting experience.

"Come on, baby," Larry cooed in what he clearly thought was a sexy voice, but sounded disturbingly like the voice adults use when talking to infants. "Show the Larrinator how bad you want it."

"Badly," Lucy corrected automatically. "Larry. No matter how much I might want *it*, it isn't going to happen tonight. I hate to be the one to tell you this, buddy, but you don't have a body."

Larry laughed—it was actually a very pleasant laugh and Lucy felt a brief stab of pity. *Poor Larry.* Then he popped up out of his knee bend and began running his large, soft hands all over his vast expanses of jiggling flesh, making exaggerated sexy-faces as he petted himself. Pity took a backseat.

"No body? What do you call this, baby? I got a body for you right here, baby."

Larry's hands went to the fly on his trousers. Instinct made

Lucy reach out to grab his wrist to stop him from dropping trou, but her hand passed right through his arm without even the usual sensation of cold tingling. Larry just wasn't there.

"Larry, man, I'm sorry, but you're dead, buddy."

Larry laughed again and the trousers dropped to the floor. *Oh Lord.*

"Does this look dead to you, baby?"

Why did they always call her baby? And why could she never get through to them before they were standing—as much as ghosts could stand, anyway—in the middle of her bedroom, stark naked?

The Larrinator was standing at attention. Larry stood with his hands planted on his hips, all swagger and confidence where she was sure there hadn't been any in life.

Lucy sighed. "How about a hand job, Larry?" She thrust her hand out and it passed smoothly through the Larrinator.

Larry's image wavered, becoming a little more transparent. "Whoa. Heavy."

"Yeah, Larry, death is pretty intense. Would you like to sit down and talk about it?"

Larry shoved his lower lip out as he thought that one over, looking more like a lost little boy than a middle-aged stockbroker who had just died of a heart attack. "Do I have to put my pants back on?"

Lucy sighed, resigned. "No. Not if you don't want to."

Larry smiled cheerily and plopped down naked at the foot of her bed. Lucy straightened the comforter that she had thrown aside when Larry appeared in her bedroom in full stripper mode, waking her out of a sound sleep. She settled herself on top of the covers, leaning back against the headboard and smiling gently at Larry.

"So, let me guess, you don't want to be dead because you always thought you would have more time to live the life you really wanted. Are you disappointed that you didn't have a more adventurous sex life when you had the chance, Larry?"

"Exactly! I can't be dead," he whined. "I haven't ever been the sex machine I was born to be."

Lucy smiled supportively and settled in for a very familiar

conversation.

"If I have to have one more conversation about repressed sexuality with a naked ghost, I'm going to turn in my resignation and you can find someone else to torture."

Karma—Lucy's vindictive bitch of a boss—gave a husky little laugh that rippled through the phone lines and down Lucy's spine. Karma was pure sex. Walking, talking sensuality. Lucy was the girl next door who just happened to talk to the dead. And yet Lucy was the one getting nightly visits from horny businessmen. It just didn't make sense. Something was definitely whacked out in the cosmic flow of things.

"I can't control who goes to you, Lucy. I just open the door. If you're seeing an abundance of naked ghosts with sexuality issues, you must be calling them to you."

"I'm not calling them!" Lucy protested. "When Larry the stripper-stockbroker showed up, I was asleep, for cripe's sake."

"Oh? And what were you dreaming about?"

Okay, so it had been a pretty steamy dream. And yes, Lucy had been enjoying it a little more than strictly necessary. Her love life hadn't exactly been burning up the sheets lately, but to suggest that she *wanted* a bunch of dead guys coming on to her every night?

"My dreams are not the problem, Karma. Stockbrokers and accountants singing 'It's Getting Hot in Here' and pole dancing in my bedroom are the problem."

"Are you sexually frustrated, Lucy?"

"Oh. My. God. I am not having this conversation with you. Can you say sexual harassment lawsuit?"

"I'm only trying to explain why your clients appear to have developed a pattern of behavior," Karma said unflappably. "New ghosts are drawn to the medium who is most likely to understand their personal issues with death. If you are projecting sexual dissatisfaction into the universe, horny businessmen who want time to live out their sexual fantasies are going to respond."

"So you're saying this is my fault."

"There is no blame in this situation, Lucy. There is nothing wrong with these men going to you with their troubles. You have done your job admirably and helped each of them move on. You're one of the best we have. We don't want to lose you over something like this."

"I want them to stop." Lucy hated the whining edge in her voice, but it seemed to creep out whenever she felt helpless. Right now, she felt downright pathetic.

"Then you need to send a different energy into the universe."

"You're telling me to get laid."

"As your boss, I don't think I'm technically allowed to tell you to get laid..."

"But?"

"But if you want to see fewer horny businessmen suffering from repressed sexuality issues, then yes, you need to get laid."

Lucy banged her head against the wall a few times. "Sometimes I hate my job."

"No, you don't," Karma countered. "And even if you did, the money's great. Stop bitching."

Karma was right on all accounts. Lucy loved her job—as weird as it got, there was something inexplicably rewarding about that moment when the ghosts let go of their worldly troubles and ascended to the next plane of existence. And the money was fantastic.

Which was weird, frankly. After all, where did the money come from? It wasn't like they could bill the deceased. Lucy had been preoccupied with the money angle for a while now. Admittedly, keeping the sex-crazed ghost population down was a valuable service, but who was paying for it? The company she worked for, Karmic Consultants, performed a variety of other tasks, many of which she knew little to nothing about. Was there a high market demand for exorcisms? Did they support the entire business with aura readings and I Ching consultations?

"Lucy?"

Lucy snapped out of her musings. "I'm here."

"Look, I can shut you off for a few days. You can take a vacation, work on redirecting your energy."

Lucy cringed. Her boss was sending her on shore leave to get laid. "No. Thanks. I'll just, you know, keep on as I am. I'm sure things will change soon."

"Are you sure you don't want me to do anything? I could—"

"No. It's okay," Lucy said quickly, before her boss started pimping her out. "I'm fine. I'm great. No worries."

"Right. Well, if you change your mind…"

"Yeah. Later, Karma."

Lucy hung up the phone before her mortification reached critical levels.

Chapter Two:
Cox Gigolo Services

The incessant banging on the front door woke her.

Judging by her exhaustion, it was ungodly early. Judging by the clock on her nightstand, it was one-oh-two in the afternoon. Since her ghosts mostly visited her in the middle of the night and Larry the Stripper hadn't left her until after five in the morning, one-oh-two counted as ungodly early.

Lucy was largely nocturnal. She would occasionally go to bed at a normal hour like a normal person, but as evidenced by Larry's timely arrival the night before, her attempts at normalcy never lasted long.

Lucy tumbled out of bed and padded blindly toward the front door to stop the drumming, keeping her eyes closed as long as possible to maintain the illusion of continued sleep. The front door vibrated under the rain of blows coming at it from the other side. She yanked it open and squinted blearily up at the raised fist that nearly landed on her face.

"What?"

"Lucy Cartwright?"

"If you're an evangelist, I feel I should warn you that I already know about death, and you're going straight to hell for banging down my frickin' door."

Her eyes were still mostly closed or she never would have made that statement. The man who brushed past her into her apartment and slammed the door behind him did not look in any way related to God.

"Karma sent me." His voice was direct—a take-no-prisoners kind of voice. Very macho. "Did I wake you?" Very annoyed.

Lucy forced her eyes open all the way. Her first, most general impression was of immense size. He was well over six feet and, although he was bulky, it was the bulk of solid muscle rather than stockbroker flab—the worn blue jeans that fit him to perfection left no question there. This guy did not spend all day in an ergonomic chair.

Lucy took a step back to get a better view and try to get her breath back. He seemed to take up too much of the room, her cozy, uncluttered entry suddenly claustrophobia-inducing. He had black hair, cut shaggily, framing features that weren't smooth enough to be classically handsome, but were all the more striking for their rough edges. The rich caramel tan and up-tilted black eyes gave evidence of some liberal mixing in his family tree, but it was the attitude that really made him stand out. He exuded a sense of purpose and intensity that easily qualified him as the single most masculine person Lucy had seen in a month.

Although, admittedly, sexually frustrated ghosts didn't set the bar very high.

Lucy blinked slowly as what he'd said registered. "Karma?"

Something clicked into place in her brain and Lucy was suddenly very awake.

Oh God. Oh God oh God oh God. Karma had sent her a gigolo. She was a female John. *A Jane?* Lucy felt her face heating up and knew she must be turning seven shades of red, even as a sly little voice in her head cheered the fact that Karma had such excellent taste in gigolos.

"Karma sent you?" she choked out. She sounded like she was gargling frogs. Oh yeah, he wasn't going to be able to keep his hands off her now.

"Are you Lucy Cartwright?" he snapped again, his eyes raking down her body. He was very abrupt, for a gigolo.

"Um..." Should she admit it? Was he going to throw her to the ground—or the sofa—and have his way with her until all of her sexual frustration disappeared into a pool of liquid satisfaction the second he had confirmed her identity? He didn't want to have his way with the wrong woman, after all. Should she lie? Prostitution was wrong. Of course it was wrong. But he was so damn hot. Was it really so bad to do it just once? For the sake of her sanity? She *had* to get away from the strip-teasing stockbroker set. "Yes?"

"Is that a question? Do you not know who you are?" He sounded more annoyed by the second. He definitely needed to go to charm school for gigolos.

Luckily, her hormones didn't seem to care. They were already heating up and charging south.

"I'm Lucy," she said, nodding decisively—then ruined her newly confident image by taking a step backward and tripping over her own pajamas. His hands shot out, closing firmly on her upper arms and setting her back on her feet. The imprint of his hands burned through the silk of her pajama top. He was suddenly so close, his heat burning away all the oxygen in the room. Lucy found herself seriously reconsidering her moral stance on prostitution as her insteps melted away.

Then he released her and stepped back. When she swayed toward him unconsciously, he frowned and put out a hand to steady her. "You okay?"

"Fine," Lucy squeaked. How did one talk to a gigolo? "Um, what's your name?" she asked breathlessly, channeling her inner slut.

"Cox."

Cox. Of course. Lucy felt her face turning purple. She could *not* call her gigolo Cox. She'd never been able to talk dirty without giggling like crazy, and if she tried to say his name, she was going to sound like she was snorting nitrous oxide.

"Cox, like Madonna? Or do you have a first name? Or a last name?"

His eyes narrowed and a little frown formed between his eyebrows. What if he was having second thoughts? What if all he needed to derail a long and prosperous career as a deeply hot gigolo was one encounter with her? Karma would never forgive her if Lucy broke her gigolo.

A lock of hair had fallen over her eye. His frown deepened as he reached out to tuck it back behind her ear, and Lucy had a jolt as she realized what she must look like. She'd just rolled out of bed. Her hair must be sticking out at all angles and the men's silk pjs that she slept in were far from sex kitten material—anything sexier was *much* too encouraging for her sex-starved ghosts.

Staring up at her gigolo—she could *not* call him Cox—Lucy wished she'd taken the time for a brush...and a curling iron...and makeup... before answering the door.

"Jake Cox."

Thank God. He had a first name. Jake was a nice, normal name. She could moan, "Oh, Jake, yes, Jake, more, Jake," in bed for hours without any inappropriate giggling.

Lucy smiled cheerfully. "Jake. Hi." His eyes narrowed menacingly. "Ooo-kay. Cox it is. So, Mr. Cox..." Lucy snorted back a giggle, "...uh, what can I, uh, do for you?" *Or to you. Or have you do to me.*

"You're the medium." There was just enough disbelief in his tone to be insulting, but Lucy had long since learned to let skepticism about her profession roll off her back. He didn't have to believe in ghosts to make her eyes roll back in her head from sheer pleasure.

"Yep. And you're..." What was the right term? Did she call him a gigolo? Was that PC?

Mr. Cox thought she was pausing to let him fill in the blank. He jumped right in. "I'm a PI. I sometimes consult with Karmic."

Lucy frowned, trying to figure out what PI stood for. Pleasure Issuer? It didn't really matter. He could call himself Mr. Happy Pants if he wanted, as long as the sweaty, naked part of the afternoon started soon.

Mr. Cox kept talking, evidently expecting no response. "I'm investigating a series of murders, and Karma seems to think that the latest victim will be visiting you. Tonight."

Lucy froze. Okay, *what?*

It was a sign of how far into the gutter her thoughts had sunk that it took her a solid minute to realize that Jake Cox was not a gigolo, or a pleasure issuer, or any such thing. He was a private investigator. He consulted with Karmic Consultants and he was investigating a *murder*.

Lucy's face flamed with mortification as she ran through

everything she had said to him in the last five minutes, trying to remember if she had made a complete idiot of herself, or just a partial one. As her brain scrambled in one direction, her mouth went another.

"I don't do murders."

Cox snorted. "I'm not accusing you, Ms. Cartwright. I'm here because you talk to dead people, not make more of them."

"No." Lucy shook her head, still playing mental catch-up as her hormones stubbornly refused to acknowledge that Mr. Cox was not there for their personal enjoyment. "What I mean is I don't talk to murdered ghosts. They go to someone else. Someone who knows how to deal with vengeance issues and wrongful death. I get, uh, different cases." *Please don't let him ask what kind.*

"Whatever you deal with, Karma seemed pretty sure he was coming to you."

Lucy could only think of one possible reason why a murder victim would be knocking on her door—or rather, appearing in her bedroom. She hoped she was wrong, but she wasn't about to ask. There was no good way of asking a ridiculously hot man—who already thought you were a few bricks short of a load—whether the murder victim he was looking for was a repressed nymphomaniac. At least not without sounding like a repressed nympho herself.

Lucy tried to remember how to do her job. It had something to do with ghosts, didn't it? "So he, uh, he died three days ago?"

Mr. Cox nodded sharply. "Eleven p.m. So anytime after that, right? If he's going to show as a ghost, that'll be when he does it?"

Lucy studied him. She was used to people thinking she was loopy for talking to dead people, but Cox seemed pretty pragmatic about it. He just wanted to get the rules down. Cox looked like the kind of guy who would be big into rules. As long as he got to make them. She was quite willing to let him make the rules. Especially if his rules involved whipped cream and fuzzy handcuffs...

"Lucy?"

"It's not a strict seventy-two hour thing," she blurted. "I tend to get mine at night, so he probably won't show before sundown, but you never know. Some people are more punctual than others. Some ghosts, I mean."

Mr. Cox nodded again—he had pretty violent nods. Emphatic. Sure. Sexy. "I'll stay here then. In case he shows early."

"Oh."

It was not, strictly speaking, a brilliant response, but brilliance could not be expected of a woman woken out of a deep sleep to find a gigolo who was not, in fact, a gigolo pounding on her front door. At least, not if that woman was Lucy. She never woke up well and, at the moment, she was still preoccupied with the depressing realization that she wasn't going to get to cure her sexual frustration with the hunk of manliness standing in her living room.

And it didn't help that he was looking at her as if he couldn't decide whether he wanted to give her a straitjacket or an orgasm.

She was saved from further conversation when his cell rang. He glanced down at the caller ID and barked, "Karma," before turning away to answer it.

While he was distracted, Lucy escaped back to the bedroom to pull herself together.

Chapter Three:
Stud Muffins

Jake turned away, grateful for the distraction, when his cell rang. He flipped open the phone. "Yo," he grunted by way of greeting.

"*Don't sleep with her.*" Karma's voice crackled with desperate intensity.

"Excuse me?" Jake glanced back to where Lucy stood, but she had disappeared.

"You can't sleep with her. If Lucy gets off, then Mellman won't go to her tonight. You can't touch her."

"Jesus, Karma, what do you think I am? I just met the girl five minutes ago. Do you think I don't think about anything but how I can get into your medium's pants?"

The devil of it was, he had thought about it. Since Lucy Cartwright had opened her front door looking like she had just rolled out of bed—all soft and warm and sweetly muddled—he'd thought of little else but finding a way to roll her back into bed. Preferably underneath him.

Nothing about Lucy Cartwright was what he had expected. Mediums were supposed to be seventy-year-old women draped in scarves, who spoke in round, dramatic tones and filled their homes with incense and crystal balls. A young, wholesome blonde in navy silk pajamas did not fit the bill. Neither did her floral, *Better Homes & Gardens* decorating taste or the slight, lingering scent of baked goods that wafted through her apartment.

Jake had been off balance—and horny as hell—since the

moment she opened her door to him, but there was no reason for Karma to know that. As far as he knew, there weren't any mind-readers working at Karmic Consultants.

"I don't care what you've been thinking about," Karma snapped. "I just did a reading that showed some serious sexual fireworks, and if that happens, Lucy won't be any good to you."

Jake didn't bother to point out the inherent contradiction in what she had just said.

"Is she some kind of virgin oracle or something?"

"No, no, nothing like that. She just..." Karma trailed off and Jake checked his phone to make sure it hadn't dropped the call—Karma was *never* at a loss for words.

"She's what?"

When Karma spoke, each word was pulled out of her like taffy, slow and sticky. "The circumstances of Mellman's death, his lack of resolution in his sexual affairs, are what led me to believe he would be going to Lucy. Men who die with unresolved sexual issues often pay her a visit."

Jake nodded to himself. That made sense. If he died horny, Lucy would be his first stop in the afterlife. "But if I'm with her, he won't show?"

"You can be with her, you just can't be *with* her. In the Biblical sense."

"So keep my hands to my fucking self. Thanks for that vote of confidence, Karma."

"I don't know why I called," Karma said grouchily. "I knew you wouldn't seduce her, so I didn't even mention it when we spoke earlier, but then this reading seemed so certain."

Jake gritted his teeth, inexplicably annoyed by the assumption that he wouldn't have seduced Lucy, but he kept his voice carefully devoid of a telling hint of irritation. "Was there anything else?"

"No," Karma said then proved it a lie by going on. "But, Jake? If anything happens to my medium, I'm taking it out of your ass. I may not have kicked your ass in years, but that doesn't mean I can't still make you wish you weren't born."

"Love you too, sis."

He flipped the cell closed and looked up to find Lucy

standing barefoot in front of him in a little sundress, looking freshly scrubbed and twice as edible as before.

"You're Karma's brother?" She blushed as she said it. Jake had known her about five minutes, but he had already noticed that she blushed a lot, so he didn't read anything into her pink face.

He flashed a smile. "Did you think she had sprung out of the ether fully formed with no family of any kind?"

"I don't think I've ever heard her last name. I thought her brother lived in Phoenix."

"I moved."

Lucy nodded. An awkward lull fell over the conversation. She fidgeted and blushed and squirmed and Jake enjoyed her rosy-cheeked discomfort too much to alleviate it. Her neat little figure, which had looked damn good in men's pjs, looked even better sheathed in the snug cotton sundress, especially with her pale, bare legs on full display. Jake was perfectly willing to sit back and enjoy the view of warm, soft femininity. Lucy, however, was quite literally tying herself into knots, one leg wrapping around the other, her hands twisting together and, through it all, her face flushing rosy and warm.

Finally, she blurted, "Can I get you an orange soda?"

Jake blinked. "Orange soda?" Did he look like the orange soda type?

Lucy blushed again and shuffled toward the kitchen. "I know I'm supposed to offer you coffee or something, but I don't drink coffee. Or tea. Or anything hot really. And I don't have beer, even though you probably shouldn't be drinking on the job. If this counts as on the job. Waiting for the ghost to show so you can go on the job. I don't even know what you're going to do to him. What are you going to do to him? I ran out of milk. So no milk. Just orange soda. Or water. Do you like water?"

Lucy turned away from him to open the fridge, muttering something that sounded distinctly like, "Shut *up*, Lucy."

Jake grinned in spite of himself. She was adorable. A little kooky, perhaps, but utterly charming. He wiped the smile off his face—he didn't want her to think he was laughing at her—before she turned back around holding a liter bottle filled with neon-orange liquid.

"I love water," he said. Anything to keep that fluorescent chemical concoction out of his body.

"Water it is." Lucy turned to pull a glass out of a cupboard and Jake watched her putter around the kitchen, completely in her element.

"So what are you going to do with him, supposing he shows?" she asked. "Are you going to ask him who did it? Because I have to warn you, most of the ghosts I've met aren't terribly concerned with the details of their death. Although it might be different for murder victims. The ones who die naturally tend to be pretty obsessed with the unfulfilled things in their life rather than the reason they died. That's the real injustice—all the things they didn't get to do."

She extended the glass of ice water toward him and he took it, letting their fingers brush just to see her reaction. A little crackle of energy passed between them—not quite static electricity, but definitely electric. Lucy scurried back a few steps until the width of the kitchen separated them. She quickly began rifling through cupboards, pulling out mixing bowls and ingredients with a subconscious grace that spoke of serious repetition.

"So, you really talk to ghosts, huh?" he asked casually, leaning back against the counter to watch her hands fly through the familiar motions. "I still can't quite wrap my head around it. I guess you know the meaning of life, then."

Lucy shrugged without pausing in her mixing and measuring. "Not in the cosmic sense, no. I'm just about helping people accept their lives for what they are, release the baggage they are afraid to leave behind and move on. Sort of post-life therapy."

"So, you're a ghost shrink."

Lucy grinned impishly. "Yeah. They talk to me and their presence in our slice of reality *shrinks*." She giggled a little at the pun and Jake bit back a smile. She was too cute—especially with the little dab of flour clinging to the tip of her nose.

He nodded toward the mixing bowl in her hands. "What are you making?"

Lucy looked down at her hands as if surprised to find them baking without her permission. "Rum Cake Muffins?"

"Are you asking me?"

Jake thought she made a face, but she was turned half away from him and it was hard to tell.

"You still haven't answered my question," she said as she preheated the oven.

"About what I'm going to do to Mellman?"

She glanced at him over her shoulder, her eyes even bluer in contrast to the flour on her nose. "Is that his name? Mellman?"

"Eliot Mellman. Thirty-seven-year-old accountant and murder victim."

Lucy sighed. "I get a lot of accountants."

Jake thought about what Karma had said about the love-hungry ones coming to Lucy for satisfaction. "Yeah, I imagine you would see quite a few repressed number crunchers," he said, unable to keep the suggestive undertones out of his voice.

Lucy froze. "Oh God, she told you."

"About the sex thing? Yeah. Is that a problem?"

Lucy just groaned.

Jake studied her, puzzled. Lucy's cheeks were getting redder by the second and she stood staring down at the mixture in her hands, refusing to meet his eyes. She was obviously embarrassed, but he couldn't figure why. It was a compliment of sorts that all of the horny ghosts wanted her. He certainly couldn't blame them. Although it probably got old, night after night, ghost after ghost. There was no end to the horny men out there. There must be even more horny dead guys.

A sudden thought had Jake straightening away from the counter. "You just talk to them, right? You don't actually, you know, *do* anything with them, do you?"

"Mr. Cox!" Lucy exclaimed, scandalized. "They don't have bodies! And they're *clients*! It wouldn't be ethical."

"So, that's a no."

"Of course it's a no." Lucy glared at him and slapped a silicon muffin tray onto the counter.

Jake began prowling around the kitchen. In part to hide his smile at her adorable indignation. And in part to hide his body's reaction to her sexy, flour-coated domesticity. "So he shows, you talk to him, then what?"

"He sort of...transcends." Lucy waved floury hands vaguely in front of her face.

"And what? Disappears?"

"Yep." Lucy paused in the act of filling the muffin tray, staring off into the distance. "The actual transcendence is kind of pretty. Sparkly."

"I need to talk to him before you transcend him."

"*I* don't transcend him," she corrected. "He allows himself to transcend by releasing worldly cares."

"Yeah, whatever. I need to talk to him first." Jake frowned. "Will I be able to talk to him? Will I even be able to see him?"

Lucy shrugged, apparently unconcerned by this potential hitch in his master plan. "Probably. A ghost's presence is magnified by linking to a medium. If you aren't naturally sensitive to supernatural energies, he may look like nothing more than a wisp of white smoke to you. Though if Karma is anything to go on, the paranormal runs in your family, so you may be able to see ghosts even more clearly than I do."

"So I'll be able to interrogate him directly."

"You can't upset him." Lucy shot him a stern look that was somewhat less effective due to the flour that had spread from her nose to both cheeks and her chin. "When they're upset, sometimes it takes *days* for them to transcend. I do not want to babysit a ghost for a week just because you can't be tactful."

"Hey. I'm the picture of tact." Jake grinned his most charming, bullshit-innocent grin.

Lucy sniffed to show him just what she thought of that. "There will be no upsetting my ghost."

"Oh, so he's your ghost now, is he?"

"He's more my ghost than yours. No matter what he's a victim of. He's my responsibility until he transcends and I will not have you bullying him."

"I won't bully him," Jake lied absently, barely even aware of what he was saying. How was it that Lucy looked even sexier with her face covered with flour? She was a quirky, muffin-cooking medium, and yet he was in real danger of breaking his promise to Karma and irreparably fucking up the job. Literally.

He comforted himself with the knowledge that Karma hadn't said anything about what he was and wasn't allowed to do to her medium *after* Eliot Mellman made his appearance.

"So he shows, I talk to him—*without* upsetting him—and then you get him to transcend." *And then I seduce you.* Jake grinned in anticipation. "Done deal."

Chapter Four:
If You Can't Stand the Heat

Lucy took one look at that devastating grin and knew she was in trouble. Not the James Bond dodging bullets, running for your life kind of trouble, but trouble of the Moneypenny variety—unrequited lust with a man who knew exactly how mouthwatering he was and was going to tease you with his gorgeous body and wicked, flashing eyes until you melted into a puddle of hormones. Moneypenny should have gotten hazard pay.

Lucy looked down at the loaded muffin tray—baking was supposed to *relax* her, dammit—and mentally tried to navigate a path to the oven that did not put her in the line of fire, so to speak. He seemed to be everywhere. Long legs, massive shoulders, fantastic ass—every time she turned around, she saw something else to be tempted by.

And, oh boy, was she tempted.

Even if he was her boss's brother. And so far out of her league, she had no business even fantasizing about him.

Lucy knew what she was, and more importantly, she knew what she wasn't.

Lucy Cartwright was no sex goddess. When men described her, they used words like *cute* and *sweet*. She was *adorable* and *domestic*. And she had long since learned that the bad boys she lusted after took one look at her good-girl dimples and ran for the hills.

When she tried to be sexy, she looked and felt ridiculous, so she giggled. Sexy women did not giggle. They had throaty, sexy voices and throaty, sexy laughs. They probably had sexily scarred vocal chords from all the post-coital cigarettes they were smoking. Lucy was not a smoker—which seemed to mean both no lung cancer and no sex.

Some women were Aphrodite and some women were Martha Stewart. Unfortunately, Martha Stewart never got laid. Please God, *why* wasn't Jake Cox a gigolo?

Lucy slipped past the eye-candy in her kitchen, set the timer and shoved the muffin tray into the oven. Then she heard him breathing. *He's allowed to breathe, dammit*, she told her hormones, but they weren't listening. They were already summoning up fantasies involving breathing. And panting. And gasping.

So Lucy gasped, and swore, as her hand brushed the hot oven rack. She snatched her hand out of the oven, mentally cursing her stupidity, and slammed the door closed.

"Did you burn yourself?" Jake demanded, stepping forward and immediately taking control.

He caught her wrist and held it up for inspection. Seeing the vivid red welt rising on the back her hand, he tugged her over to the sink and turned on the faucet with a single-minded economy of movement that was somehow indescribably hot.

Dear God, I'm doomed. Even his first aid is sexy.

He temperature-tested the tap with his own hand before thrusting her burn beneath the cool, running water. "Keep it there," he ordered, already on his way to the freezer. He was back a moment later, a clean dishtowel wrapped around a bundle of ice. "Here, let me see."

He gently took her wrist and drew her hand out of the water, cautiously inspecting the burn. His attention was so focused, so intent, as he brushed the soft skin around the burn with his fingertips, careful not to touch the wound itself. He bent and blew cool air on her hand before gently pressing the ice pack over it, his concentration complete. Lucy couldn't help but wonder if he would bring that focus and intensity to everything he did. A delicious shiver ran down her spine.

"I know it's cold," he said, and Lucy was relieved he didn't suspect the real reason for her shivering—she was embarrassed enough already. "You need to keep it on there for twenty minutes or so."

"Thank you," she said quietly.

Jake shook his head abruptly, rejecting her gratitude. "My fault. I shouldn't have been distracting you while you were cooking."

"You weren't distracting me," Lucy lied, knowing she was blushing. Again.

"No?" He arched his eyebrows skeptically then reached up to brush the back of one finger against her cheek. "You have flour all over your face."

Lucy winced internally. Great. Now, not only was she as red as a turnip, she had the distinction of being a blotchy, flour-coated turnip with a propensity for burning herself. Oh yeah, he wasn't going to be able to keep his hands off her now.

She waited for him to laugh at her. She waited for him to turn away, writing her off as ridiculous. She waited...until he tipped her chin up, forcing her to meet his eyes. Eyes that didn't look mocking or superior, but rather curiously intent.

Oh my.

He brushed at the clinging flour on her cheeks, his calloused hands tentatively caressing. Lucy gazed up at him, trying to remember how to breathe, or think, or do anything other than stare at him with her heart in her throat and her stomach down around her toes. They were standing near the oven, but Lucy had a feeling the burning sensation rippling along her skin had more to do with the mountain of solid muscle in front of her than the oven behind. He smiled gently, his hands still cradling her face. "Even without the flour, you look pretty damn edible," he murmured, his voice low and intimate.

The world slowed and tightened until they were the only two people in it, and time was frozen in that thick moment when she *knew* he was about to kiss her. She stood paralyzed, hopeful, but not allowing herself to hope.

He bent toward her slowly, his gorgeous black eyes shuttered by thick black lashes. Lucy's eyes fell closed and she held herself perfectly still, desperate, waiting. When his lips finally touched hers, it was like putting a spark to a fast-burning fuse. A fuse attached to a stick of dynamite.

Lucy dove recklessly into the kiss, arching against him shamelessly. The first tentative brush of his mouth instantly became an urgent, open-mouthed exchange. She wound her arms around his shoulders and he gripped her butt in both hands, lifting her to get a better angle on her mouth, a better angle of her body pressed against his.

As soon as her feet left the floor, Lucy looped her legs around his waist, locking her ankles at the small of his back. Jake took two steps across the kitchen and pinned her against the refrigerator, the cool, smooth surface teasing her exposed shoulder blades where the spaghetti straps of her sundress left them bare. Lucy gave a little groan of pure, unadulterated lust, her hormones throwing an orgiastic party when Jake immediately echoed it. *Now, this is how a gigolo behaves.*

Jake grabbed the knees squeezing his waist with both hands and shifted her slightly for better access. The combination of his fingers teasing the sensitive skin at the backs of her knees and the sudden, grinding friction of his jeans where she wanted it the most was nearly enough to send her off right there. Lucy let her head fall back against the refrigerator, her eyes closing in anticipation of bliss as she sent a little prayer of thanks to the gods of nookie.

Jake immediately took advantage of the exposed line of her throat, his hands sliding slowly up her thighs as his mouth slid deliciously down her neck. Lucy dug her fingers into his muscular shoulders as his hands found their way beneath the skirt of her sundress. Deft fingers teased her through the soaked fabric of her panties and Lucy heard bells. She'd always thought that hearing bells was a metaphor, but apparently she just hadn't met Jake Cox, because the ringing in her head was very real. And loud as hell.

He stilled, his mouth pressed against the pulse point at her throat and his hands teasing the gates of heaven. His muscles clenched and he groaned, sounding pained rather than pleased. "Lucy."

"Hmmm?" Lucy tried to shimmy her hips to get him back into action, but he wasn't moving, and since he was the only thing holding her up, neither was she.

"Shit, Lucy," he groaned, bracketing her hips with his

hands to keep her still as his forehead dropped to her shoulder. "We need to stop this."

"Mm-hmm," Lucy moaned agreeably, grabbing his head and pulling his mouth back to hers for another kiss. She sent her tongue exploring, every ounce of willpower she possessed focused on making Jake forget whatever had made him stop. When he broke away, they were both breathing hard, the sound of their panting pierced by the shrill ringing of Lucy's imaginary bells.

Then she smelled the smoke. She knew that Jake was hot, but surely even he couldn't set kitchens on fire with just his presence.

"My muffins!"

With a dismount worthy of an Olympic gymnast, Lucy launched herself across the room, pausing only to grab an oven mitt before throwing open the oven door. "Crapadelic. They're burnt."

Jake was still standing with his arms braced against the refrigerator door. Lucy turned off the timer, whose persistent ringing had derailed them, and dropped the slightly crisp muffins onto the cooling rack. She ducked under his arm and slid between the mountain of warm, coiled muscle and the cool refrigerator door.

Lucy placed her hands on his chest and slid them slowly downward. "Where were we?"

Jake caught her hands before she could get to anything good, pulling them off his abs and holding her in front of him so the only point of contact was his hands manacling her wrists. "No, Luce."

His words landed like a slap. Lucy flinched. "No?"

Jake groaned, closing his eyes. "I'm glad the buzzer went off," he ground out. "God knows I needed something to stop me. Karma... I shouldn't have... We shouldn't have..." He shook his head abruptly, as if trying to clear it. Then suddenly he released her, quickly moving to the opposite side of the kitchen. "I'm sorry," he bit out sharply. "It won't happen again."

"It won't?" Lucy knew the pathetic, desperate whining tone had crept back into her voice, but she couldn't help it. She wanted it to happen again. She *needed* it to happen again. He couldn't just get her all hot and bothered and then walk away without fulfilling even one little fantasy. Could he?

Apparently he could. He turned and headed toward the living room, pausing in the doorway, but not even turning to face her as he said, "I think it's best if we aren't in the same room. Just come find me when Mellman shows up."

"Jake, *come on,*" she called, but he was already gone. "Crap."

Lucy stood in the middle of her kitchen, glaring at a pan of overcooked muffins, the refrigerator she would never be able to open without having sexual frustration flashbacks, and the timer that had ruined her afternoon. A few minutes later, her agitation calmed enough that she was able to think again.

Her first coherent thought was that she had just tried to mount her boss's brother in the middle of her kitchen while he was sort of on the job. Her sexual frustration had officially reached pathetic levels. With her luck, he'd probably report back to Karma about the attack of the nympho medium.

Lucy moaned. "Just kill me now."

Chapter Five:
The Accountant Nightlight

At two-twenty in the morning, Lucy lay in her bed trying to think of the Buddha. Or other Zen thoughts that did not involve stripping out of her navy silk pajamas and running naked into the living room, where Jake had crashed out on her couch. Attacking the poor, unsuspecting PI in a lustful frenzy probably wouldn't go over well. Even if it would be a great—*sweaty, orgasmic*—way to pass the time until he could interrogate her sex-crazed ghost.

The Buddha was not helping.

Lucy twisted around in her bed, silk rasping sensuously against her skin and *definitely not helping* with her persistent hormonal urges. She should have slept in jeans. Or cargo pants. Anything that was not slippery and oh-so-easy to slip out of.

Lucy rolled over and punched her pillow, burrowing down under the covers and wondering exactly how long she was going to have to suffer before Eliot Mellman arrived to put her out of her misery.

She didn't have to wait long.

A thump sounded in the darkness of her room. Lucy sat up and spun toward the sound, half expecting—hoping—to see Jake. Ghosts couldn't thump. At least, most ghosts couldn't. Moving physical objects was beyond most of them.

Eliot Mellman, it turned out, could thump things.

He hadn't been very big in life; his image was rail thin and not quite five and a half feet tall. His posture was apologetic, as if he couldn't be more aware of the unwelcome intrusion his presence would always be. In death, he still wore thick glasses and his hair was parted down the middle and flattened down with gel in what was possibly the least-flattering style ever invented.

Eliot stood at the foot of her bed, looking sheepishly at the ottoman he had tripped over.

And glowing.

Lucy blinked in surprise.

Only the strongest of ghosts gave off any sort of illumination. Eliot was better than a nightlight. He was glowing brightly enough to cast eerie greenish shadows on the wall.

As a man, Eliot Mellman had been stepped on so many times Lucy was amazed she couldn't see footprints. As a ghost, he was Godzilla.

Lucy wondered idly if all murder victims had firefly tendencies, which reminded her of Jake Cox sleeping on her couch. Time to get to work.

Lucy smiled soothingly at the newly dead man at her feet. "Eliot?"

Even if Cox hadn't told her in advance, she would have known Eliot's name. The name and circumstances of death just sort of came with the ghost, like a tag on a Christmas gift. In Eliot's case, the image she got of the death was a little off—like a photo of frantic movement that only showed blurry lines of activity, red-tinted and vague. Lucy usually got a nice crisp snapshot of those last moments, but for all she knew, all murders were red and unfocused.

Eliot twitched and looked up at his name, clearly surprised to be noticed at all, let alone known. "Yes?"

When he didn't immediately segue into a pick-up line, Lucy realized there was something different about Eliot Mellman. For one thing, he wasn't trying to mount her.

"Do you know what has happened to you, Eliot?" she asked cautiously. Some ghosts knew they were dead. Some didn't. She was betting Eliot was one of the latter, judging by his unchanged hangdog posture.

"I died?"

Okay, so he was in category number one. "You remember what happened to you?" Jake hadn't told her what he needed to ask Eliot, but she figured that question had to be on the list and she wanted Eliot to be comfortable with his new phase of existence before Jake started interrogating him.

"I was murdered." Eliot slumped a little more, pathetic and dejected. "I knew something was up," he mumbled. "She'd never been interested in me before, but I wanted to believe she was on the level. I just wanted to believe that someone could want me, you know?"

Lucy suddenly realized why Eliot's death had been a blur of frenzied activity. She felt her face heating in a blush, but managed to keep any trace of her shock and embarrassment out of her voice. "So, she, uh, she..." Lucy coughed and cleared her throat. "She...that is...ah..."

"Fucked me to death like a praying mantis. Murder mid-coitus. Bitch didn't even let me come first."

Lucy choked. This was a whole new level of sexual frustration. "So, you, uh, you know who did it?"

"Who murdered me? Big Joe Morrissey, probably."

He said it so matter-of-factly that Lucy was momentarily taken aback. Like he was talking about the results of a ballgame that was of no personal interest to him. It was only his murder, after all. Then she realized what he had said.

"Joe?" Something wasn't adding up here.

"Yep," Eliot said mournfully. "Candy never opens her legs without Big Joe's say so. I thought he was rewarding me, but I guess that was just wishful thinking. Poisoned pussy."

Lucy felt her eyes bulging out. "Poisoned?"

"Figure of speech," Eliot assured her. "She stabbed me with this needle thing she pulled out of her hair." He continued before she could formulate a coherent sentence. "It sucks, I guess. Being dead."

Lucy pulled herself together, blocking out the *Fatal Attraction* film reel running in her mind. "Right. You're right. It sucks. And I'd like to talk to you about that. Um, in a minute. Right now, there's someone else who needs to talk to you. About Big Joe Morrissey."

Eliot heaved a dramatic sigh. "I figured you were only talking to me because of Big Joe. Just like her."

Lucy hadn't ever been compared to a murdering fuck-puppet before, but she tried not to take it personally. Death could be very trying, so she gave Eliot the benefit of the doubt. She smiled sincerely and swore, "Eliot, it isn't like that at all. *You* are my primary concern. It's just there is someone else who needs your help. With Big Joe."

"Uh-huh." Eliot muttered, clearly not believing a word of it. He eyed her forlornly. "I should have known a super-hot girl like you would never be interested in me for me."

Lucy knew that she should not have been flattered by that comment. She should have been immune to ghostly flattery, laughed it off and called Jake in.

That's what she should have done.

Instead, she blushed and smiled and toyed with the sheet that had fallen across her lap. There was something inexplicably appealing about Eliot's compliment—rooted as it was in his own depression and insecurity. She wasn't usually moved by her ghosts' attempts to woo her, but then she didn't usually spend her days lusting after ridiculously masculine men who were not, in fact, gigolos sent to pleasure her senseless. She was horny. She was frustrated. And her self-esteem needed the boost.

So instead of calling in Jake and getting down to business, Lucy preened and said, "What a silly thing to say, Eliot. You seem like a wonderful man, er, ghost. I'm sure if we had time to get to know one another then I would find you *far* more interesting than Big Joe Morrissey."

Eliot wandered over to stand at the side of her bed, running ghostly fingers along the lampshade in an endearingly timid way. "Really?"

"Really." It wasn't even a lie. The murderer-pimp didn't really sound like her type.

The change in Eliot was immediate. The melancholy accountant pulled back his shoulders and shot her an oily smile. "So, what's your name, baby?" he asked in the same too-slick tone she had heard coating a dozen pick-up lines from countless dead businessmen.

But instead of rolling her eyes, Lucy smiled at the clueless accountant. "I'm Lucy. I'm a medium. I'm here for you, Eliot."

"You don't care about Big Joe?"

She knew she was using this sweet, pathetic ghost to feel better about herself, but she couldn't make herself stop. What would a little harmless flirtation hurt, anyway? She was making Eliot feel better. That was her job. Sort of. And it wasn't as if she were *lying*.

"I don't care about Big Joe, at all," she vowed. "If it were up to me, we'd just forget all about that nasty murder business and get straight to talking about you. Unfortunately, there are some other people who are real sticklers about murder and they'd like to have a few words with you."

"I just want you," he whispered wetly into her ear.

Lucy had been fidgeting with the sheet, feeling a little guilty about using poor Eliot, and hadn't noticed him leaning in to close the deal. At the sound of his voice directly beside her, she looked up and found him looming over her in full Casanova mode—his neck stretched out like a turtle peeking out from his shell and his lips puckered out in a fish face.

She gave a startled little yelp to find him so close to impact. Eliot yelped at her yelp, his confidence evaporating. His eyes flew open and his body flew backward—right into her lamp.

Lucy watched, stunned and not a little impressed, as Eliot *accidentally* knocked over a physical object, sending it flying to the ground with a resounding crash.

For a moment, the only sound was of Lucy's breathing as they both gaped at the shattered lamp.

"Wow. You knocked over my lamp."

"Oh, gosh, I'm sorry," Eliot dithered, kneeling on the floor and sweeping the shards into a little pile with his hands. "I didn't mean to."

"I know," Lucy said—but she wasn't trying to comfort him, she was too busy being in awe of what he had done. "You weren't even paying attention to it and you sent it *flying*. Most ghosts have to concentrate to make people feel a cool breeze, but *you* can move physical objects without even meaning to." She blinked at him, openly amazed. "Eliot, you're incredible."

He looked up at her, a slow, shy smile starting to spread across his face. As the smile grew, his glowing presence dimmed and flickered. Lucy would never know what would have happened next—that single moment of validation might have been enough for him to transcend—but before he could move on, her bedroom door flew open and Jake came charging through, gun drawn.

"Lucy! Are you all right? I heard a—What the hell?"

Lucy had told Jake a little bit about ghosts that afternoon. Based on her description of wispy white wraiths, he had no reason to expect a green-glowing nightlight of an accountant. And Eliot *was* his first ghost. That, at least in part, explained his reaction.

Jake stumbled back a couple steps until his back slammed up against the wall, his gun trained on the glowing specter kneeling beside her bed.

"What the fuck is that?" he shouted, never taking his eyes off of Eliot Mellman's ghost.

Eliot's head snapped up when Jake burst into the room. Confusion dimmed his expression. Lucy scrambled for words to explain Eliot to Jake and vice versa, but she never got the chance.

She knew the exact moment Eliot saw the gun. Fear flashed across his face, followed quickly by an eerie resolve.

"*I'll protect you, Lucy!*" he roared, surging up from his knees.

Eliot swelled in size until he towered over Cox, his glowing, greased-down hair brushing the ceiling fan. Light shot from his fingertips, and his glow grew brighter and brighter until Lucy had to shield her eyes to look at him.

The windows were all closed, but a howling wind suddenly tore through the room, whipping the drapes around like flags flapping in a hurricane. The doors to the closet, bathroom, and hall all began slamming, only to fly open and slam again.

Jake Cox braced himself against the wind, sighted on the blinding nimbus of light that was the Eliot poltergeist, and began firing, the sound almost entirely drowned out by the wail of the wind and the thunder of the slamming doors.

Lucy leapt to her feet on her bed and shouted to be heard

over the keening howl. "Eliot! *Eliot!* Bad ghost! Bad! Jake, stop shooting him! Eliot, stop it this instant! *Put down my nightstand!* If I wanted it on the ceiling, I would have put it there myself. Put it back right now! *Eliot!*"

Neither of the beings in her bedroom listened to her.

Jake systematically emptied his clip—the bullets passing right through Eliot and lodging in her floral wallpaper—then smoothly reloaded and raised his arms in preparation for putting a dozen more holes in her wall.

The mountain of pillows piled on her bed took flight, whipping around the room and bursting in a series of feathery explosions until her perfectly neat bedroom looked like the site of a bloodless chicken massacre.

"No, no, *no!*" Lucy yelled. She jumped off of her bed and directly into the line of fire between the two combatants.

Jake immediately pointed the muzzle of his gun toward the ceiling. "Lucy! What the hell are you doing? Get out of the way!"

"No!" Lucy shouted back. "No more shooting!" She spun around to squint up into the strobe-light brilliance where she suspected Eliot's eyes must be. "No more slamming doors and howling winds and *absolutely no more floating furniture!* I have had *enough.* Do you understand me?"

The storm inside her bedroom died down suddenly. Eliot shrank down to his normal size, his blinding radiance dimming back to his usual friendly green nightlight levels—though he continued to glare militantly at Jake, who returned the favor.

"He was shooting at you, Lucy," Eliot whined peevishly. "I had to protect you."

"He was shooting at *you,*" she corrected, then turned to glare at Jake. "But he shouldn't have been shooting at anyone. He's *supposed* to be on our side."

Jake held up his hands in mock surrender. "Hey, don't look at me. I didn't start firing until the furniture started flying."

Lucy turned her glare back on the peevish ghost. "That was a childish and completely unnecessary display, Eliot."

Eliot shoved out his lower lip in a pout, somehow managing to sulk and glower at Jake at the same time. "He started it," he insisted petulantly. "Bursting in here, waving a gun and screaming."

"I heard a crash," Jake snapped. "I had to make sure Lucy was all right."

Eliot started to puff up again, just a little. "That's *my* job. Lucy is none of your concern."

Jake snorted. "I hate to break it to you, buddy, but you're dead. How can you protect her if you don't even have a body?"

"Don't answer that, Eliot. Mr. Cox is *not* trying to goad you into showing him how you would protect me. In fact, as difficult as it might be to believe, Mr. Cox is actually the person I was talking to you about—the one who wants to talk to you. About your murder. *Don't* you, Mr. Cox?" Lucy snarled the last directly at the vexing PI.

"Yeah," Mr. Cox said grudgingly. "I have a few questions."

Chapter Six:
You Just Can't Trust a
Horny Poltergeist

Sitting at her kitchen table with a petulant ghost and grouchy detective was not how Lucy had envisioned spending her night—especially after Jake Cox had walked through her door that afternoon like a walking, talking gift from Cupid.

Lucy sat as far away from the two idiots as possible. Out of the line of fire, according to Jake's orders, and beyond Jake's reach, according to Eliot's insistence. Her little accountant nightlight took protectiveness to new levels, puffing up and turning up the wattage whenever Jake touched her, even if it was just a casual brush on her arm. Other than that, Eliot had shown no further signs of going poltergeist on them, and Jake's gun was back in his holster, although one of his hands hovered over it constantly.

Now if only she could get the two pig-headed men to stop bickering and cooperate long enough to get them both out of her kitchen.

"I'm not a rat," Eliot insisted stubbornly, his lower lip puffed out in classic kindergarten style.

"No, you're a ghost," Jake snapped irritably. "Joe Morrissey had you killed."

"Exactly! What do you think he'd do to me if he found out I'd ratted him out?"

"He can't do anything to you! You're already dead."

"You don't know Big Joe."

"I'm pretty sure he's not God, Eliot," Jake growled.

"No, he's the devil."

"He's a small-time mafioso with psychopathic tendencies and delusions of grandeur, and as his former accountant—"

"Hey, who said I was former?"

"You're dead, Eliot. Big Joe killed you. Get it through your head. As I was saying, as his *former* accountant, you are in a unique position to put him away for the rest of his life. And you don't even have to confront him. You can be the chicken-shit coward you are and still do your part for justice. All you have to do is tell me where Joe Morrissey's financial records are."

"And you'll do what?"

"I'll turn them over to the Organized Crime Task Force. The cops can't very well say they got tipped off by a dead guy, but if I get Morrissey's books for them, they won't look a gift mobster in the mouth. So where are they, Eliot?"

"What about Candy?"

"I'll do what I can to make sure she's prosecuted for your murder."

Eliot was shaking his head before Jake finished speaking. "I don't want her to suffer."

Lucy couldn't stay quiet any longer. "Eliot, she murdered you!"

"Yeah, but she also, you know." Eliot made a crude gesture with his hands. "I appreciate that."

"She only slept with you so she could kill you!" Lucy protested.

"Yeah, but she still slept with me. She shouldn't be punished for that."

"She should be punished for *murder!*"

"It wasn't her idea," Eliot pouted. "I'm sure she didn't want to. It was Big Joe."

Lucy couldn't help but roll her eyes. There were some things about men she would never understand. "Then will you let Jake put Big Joe in jail? Please, Eliot, tell him where to find Big Joe's books."

Eliot blinked at her limpidly. "For you, Lucy. I'll do it for you."

Jake rolled his eyes so hard he nearly fell off his chair. "Well? Come on, Romeo, where are they?"

Eliot sniffed indignantly, but when Lucy smiled encouragingly, he said, "There's a warehouse. Big Joe keeps all of his records there. There will be more than enough evidence to convict him."

"Where is it?" Jake demanded.

Eliot rattled off an address and Jake was on his feet before he finished. "I'm going to check it out." He pointed a warning finger at the ghost. "No transcending until I get back. You got that, Romeo? I don't trust you not to send me off on some wild goose chase, only to skip off to the afterlife while I'm off chasing my own ass."

After the front door slammed behind Jake, Lucy sent Eliot a sympathetic smile. "I'm sorry we can't work on resolving your issues until he gets back. I know you must be eager to move on."

"Not really."

Lucy's attention snapped to lock on him. "Not really?"

Eliot shrugged. "I don't care if I ever transcend. Why would I want to? I love you, Lucy. I want to stay with you. Forever."

Forever. Lucy had a sudden vision of spending the rest of her life sexually frustrated because a neurotic, possessive poltergeist wouldn't let a real man near her. It was not a happy vision.

Knowing precisely how powerful Eliot was, she didn't want to piss him off, but neither was she going to promise him a lifetime. Or deathtime. Whatever. They needed to get back on professional footing.

"Eliot," she began slowly, but he cut her off.

"We're meant to be together, Lucy. Can't you feel it?" He was glowing more brightly, giving off little pulses of energy that shivered across her skin, raising goosebumps on her arms. He shoved back his chair and walked toward her—no wispy floating for Eliot Mellman. He ran his fingers along her jaw and Lucy fought not to shudder. His touch was freezing, like an icy caterpillar crawling across her skin.

She swallowed her nausea. "Eliot, it's natural to want to

cling to life. Your attachment to me is just a symptom of that. Death is a big transition. No one expects you to move on before you're ready, but you can't stay in a plane where you don't belong just for me. I won't let you do that to yourself."

"You're worth it, Lucy," Eliot swore. "I would haunt the world a thousand lifetimes just to be with you for yours."

"Eliot, that's very—" *creepy, terrifying, appalling* "—sweet of you, but it wouldn't be right."

"If loving you is wrong, baby, I don't want to be right."

Lucy winced. She'd created a monster. A love-starved, green-glowing, pulsating nerd of a monster. "Look, Eliot, why don't we just wait until Mr. Cox gets back? I bet things will look differently after you know Big Joe will be punished for what he did to you."

Eliot snorted. "Sure. Let's do that. Let's just wait until Mr. Cox gets back, shall we?" He strutted across the kitchen.

Warning bells went off in Lucy's head.

"Eliot, what did you do?"

"Do?" he repeated innocently. "Why would you ask that?"

Lucy stood, shoving her chair back so quickly it toppled over. She didn't pause to right it. Instead, she marched over to where Eliot was admiring the way his light played across her crystal stemware. "Eliot, where did you send Jake?"

"To a warehouse," he replied with a catty smile.

"What's in the warehouse?"

"Records," Eliot said, then his face split into a grin as he went on. "And enough guards with Uzis to turn your mortal boyfriend into Swiss cheese."

"Eliot! Why didn't you tell Jake that?" Lucy was already running toward the bedroom, stripping out of her pajamas as she ran.

"He didn't ask," the ghost said, floating along behind her, pulled by the link between the two of them.

Lucy quickly yanked on jeans and a black T-shirt, ignoring Eliot's avid gaze and his little mumbles of protest as she clothed herself. "What were you thinking?" she asked him angrily. "He'll be killed."

"So? I don't see what the big deal is if he dies. I'm already dead. It isn't so bad."

"That is no excuse for sending him into a trap!" Lucy shoved her feet into her sneakers and grabbed her car keys, sprinting toward the front door.

"Where are we going?" Eliot whined, drawn along like a balloon on a string.

"To that damn warehouse to help Jake. I just hope we aren't already too late."

"Lucy," Eliot moaned plaintively. "I don't want to go. I just wanted him to get rid of him so we could be alone together."

"So you lied."

"I didn't lie," he protested. "The records are there. I just neglected to mention a few other details."

"Well, thanks to your neglect, Jake's life is in danger."

"That doesn't mean you have to go," Eliot complained. Then he paused, thinking. "Wait. If you die, does that mean we get to be ghosts together forever?"

"No," Lucy snapped. "If I die, I'm going on to whatever is next and leaving your sorry ass haunting my apartment for the rest of eternity. But I bet if Jake dies, he's going to hang around just long enough to kick your phantom ass."

Chapter Seven:
The Warehouse of Death and Taxes

Being inside the warehouse sounded like being inside the world's largest popcorn popper. Gunfire ricocheted and echoed in a nonstop patter of deadly explosions.

"This doesn't seem smart, Lucy."

"Shut up, Eliot." Lucy ran with her head down and ducked behind a crate. She could see Jake's legs sticking out from behind a crate in front of her. He was sprawled out on his stomach and she couldn't tell if he was bleeding—she couldn't see his torso at all, but she was sure it was him. There was no mistaking that ass.

Running into a firefight was stupid on more levels than she could count, but she needed to get to Jake—although by this point, he'd probably already figured out that the warehouse was used for more than just file storage. Still, if there was anything she could do to help, she was going to do it. She *liked* Jake and wasn't about to give up the opportunity to use him as her own personal gigolo once they were no longer being bombarded with bullets on all sides.

During a lull in the gunfire, Lucy launched herself from behind her crate, dashing toward Jake's legs. She skidded to a stop against the crate he was bent around, tucking herself out of the line of fire.

"Lucy! What the hell are you doing here?" Jake snapped, rolling behind the crate to sit beside her as he slid the clip out of his gun and jammed another one home.

"See? He's still alive. Can we go now?"

"Shut up, Eliot!"

"Go draw their fire or something," Jake growled.

The ghost hmphed and drifted away.

As soon as he was gone, Jake turned to Lucy. "Are you hit anywhere?" His eyes raked over her. "How did you get in here? Are the cops outside? Why did they send you in? Jesus, Lucy, what were you thinking?"

Lucy blinked at him, her brain suddenly rebooting after the half an hour of thoughtless panic that had brought her rushing to his aid. "The cops. That would have been smart. Damn."

Jake closed his eyes. "You didn't bring reinforcements." He groaned. "I'm down to my last clip, and you show up with no help other than the damned ghost who got us into this in the first place. How could you put yourself in danger like that?"

"I wasn't thinking," Lucy admitted. "I was worried about you."

"I'm touched. Next time you're worried, maybe you can bring me an AK-47 or two."

"I'll try to keep that in mind."

Another volley of gunfire exploded around them, deafening them for a few minutes as they cowered together in the dubious shelter of the crate. When she could hear him again, Jake was swearing fluently.

"If that ghost wasn't dead already, I'd kill him myself."

"In Eliot's defense, he doesn't really see death quite the same way we do."

"He sent me walking blind into fucking Fort Knox, Luce. I can't believe I was so stupid. I thought ghosts couldn't lie."

"I think that's demons. Ghosts are the imprint a person has left on the world after they depart it and people lie constantly, so it's only logical that ghosts would be deceptive. Besides, Eliot didn't *technically* lie. There is a lot of evidence in the warehouse. There just happens to be a lot of guards and a lot of guns also."

"Not to mention Joe Morrissey himself."

Lucy gaped at him. "Big Joe is here? Oh, no."

"I don't see that it matters. We're equally dead whether he's here or not."

Lucy grabbed his arm to get his attention. "Eliot can't see

him, Jake!"

"Big Joe is invisible?"

"This isn't a joke! Murder victims *cannot* confront their murderers. It's bad."

"Define bad."

"If we're lucky, he'll just maim Big Joe a little."

"I can think of worse things. And if we aren't lucky?"

"You know that part at the end of *Ghostbusters* where Rick Moranis turns into a mutant dog, and Gozer the Gozerian blows the top off a skyscraper and opens up a portal for all of the supernatural nasties to come through?"

"Eliot could do that?"

"If he went poltergeist on us and decided to call up some demonic force to take vengeance on Big Joe, that's the least of what he could do."

"Okay, yeah, that's bad. So we keep Eliot away from Joe." Jake looked around as much as possible without coming out from behind their cover. "Where is Eliot, anyway?"

Lucy glanced around, surprised. "He should be right here. He can't go far."

The gunfire stopped suddenly and for a moment silence reigned in the warehouse. Then a low rumble sounded, like a freight train coming, and the warehouse's foundation began to shiver and roll.

"Shit! It's an earthquake!"

"No," Lucy said direly. "It's Eliot."

Eliot drifted out to the end of his leash, pausing to examine the ethereal tether linking him to Lucy. He liked the link; it was like a psychic manifestation of their love.

It was unfortunate that she had been drawn to the warehouse by her sense of duty. Eliot would have preferred that she let the PI die—death was really not nearly as terrifying as he had expected it to be. If he'd known this was what death was like, he wouldn't have been so afraid of it while he was still alive.

Eliot drifted up above the crates, wondering how his life would have been different if he hadn't been afraid. Afraid of women. Afraid of risk. Afraid of Big Joe. Afraid of *life*.

He wasn't afraid anymore. His death would be different. He had Lucy. It was amazing how different the world looked when there was a sweet blonde smiling at him at the end of the day.

Lucy hadn't been smiling on the way to the warehouse. Words had been coming out of her pretty mouth that would have made a sailor flinch, and most of them had been directed at Eliot. He hadn't expected her to react so strongly to the PI's life being threatened. Women were a mystery.

Eliot glanced down at the love of his death and saw her bent in close conversation with the vile PI.

The PI was exactly the sort of man Eliot detested—tall, confident, probably disgustingly good at sports and anything else that society defined as *manly*. Eliot had never fallen into the manly category, no matter how broadly it was defined, and he had never cared for the members of his sex who did.

The PI was bad news. Unfortunately, Lucy didn't seem to see that. She was inexplicably drawn in by the PI's brawny, obvious charm.

Her infatuation would pass. Eliot wasn't concerned about that. The shimmering tether between them was proof of their entwined destinies, mortal and ghost.

Eliot drifted a bit farther and poked his head out from behind a crate, drawing a barrage of fire before he ducked back. The bullets couldn't harm him, but he hadn't yet grown accustomed to his invincibility.

Eliot stuck his head out again and felt another, darker tug yanking him away from Lucy. Both links drew at him, the effervescent purity of Lucy and the strange, murky force of a thick, oily rope, coiling around him. For a moment he was suspended between the two. Then the link to Lucy snapped. Without her, he was jerked forward so suddenly he knocked over a crate, but his momentum didn't stop there. He flew forward unchecked, directly into the gunfire. Dozens of bullets passed through him, but as he continued to fly forward, unaffected by them, the sound of guns firing slowly tapered off, replaced by the uneasy muttering of superstitious men.

Eliot's movement halted suddenly.

He stood in a small, clear area directly below Big Joe's

office. Around him, Big Joe's men stared at him with a mixture of shock and horror. For the first time in the company of these big, gun-toting mafiosos, he wasn't afraid.

Then he looked up and saw Big Joe Morrissey.

Chapter Eight:
Vengeance is a Dish Best Served in a Blender

Lucy's brain had a tendency to short circuit in stressful situations. That was the only explanation for what she did when she realized Eliot was about to do his Godzilla poltergeist act on a bigger stage.

Lucy jumped up from behind the crate and sprinted toward the eye of the storm.

"Shit! Lucy!"

She ignored Jake's harried shout behind her and kept running. Crates shattered and the fragments—along with all of the stolen merchandise inside—began whipping around the warehouse like debris from an indoor tornado. As Lucy dodged Eliot-shrapnel, she had a sudden sympathy for the food inside a blender.

Hardened criminals ran screaming past her in the opposite direction, but Lucy didn't hesitate. She bent her head and plowed through the storm, stumbling once as the floor dropped out from under her feet unexpectedly, only to roll up again with the next wave of Eliot's anger.

Lucy pushed her way through the cyclone, bent double against the force of the wind and avoiding being skewered by sharpened points of crate fragments by luck alone. Her eyes were fixed on the heaving floor, so her only hint that she was close to Eliot was the increase in the howling roar and a lessening in crate shrapnel.

Lucy looked up, squinting into the eye of the storm. Eliot hovered at the epicenter of it all, five times his normal size, huffing and puffing like the Big Bad Wolf. He flashed like a neon-green strobe light. His face was grotesquely distorted, abnormally swollen and yellowy-green. His mouth opened in a Van Gogh scream, though the only sound coming out of it was a high-pitched keen that sounded more like an air-raid siren than any sound a human voice had ever made.

"Eliot!" Lucy screamed up at him, bracing her feet to keep from being tossed about.

Eliot gave no indication that he had even heard her. All of his attention was focused on a dark, cowering figure in the office on the second story that looked down over the warehouse floor.

Lucy reached for the link between them, hoping to yank him back like a recalcitrant pit bull and surprise him out of his rage, but the link had been severed.

"Eliot!" Lucy screamed again, and got the same lack of response.

Strong arms wrapped around her and jerked her off her feet. Lucy found herself kneeling on the ground, her body shielded from the worst of the storm by Jake's bulk as he crouched beside her. "I'm hoping you have a plan!" he screamed in her ear.

What a coincidence. She'd been hoping the same thing.

"I'm open to suggestions," she screamed back.

"I vote for running like hell," Jake shouted. "Big Joe is on his own."

Lucy shook her head. Eliot was too volatile and he was her responsibility. She wasn't about to flee to safety—at least in part because if Eliot did what he was capable of, there might not be anywhere safe to flee to. She may not know how to stop him, but she wasn't going to start running.

"Eliot!" she screamed again. Again there was no response from the verdant poltergeist, but there was an echo.

For a moment, she thought it was her own voice, reflecting back from the open office above. Then a rail-thin woman with gravitationally improbable breasts stepped out of the shadows. She had short, shaggy, bleached-blonde hair and bloodshot, puffy eyes. She tottered forward in her spandex mini-dress and stiletto heels, screaming the accountant's name above the wail.

Suddenly, the cyclone of sound was sucked out of the warehouse like a reverse sonic boom, leaving an eerie quiet in its wake. "Candy?" Eliot asked plaintively, his voice distorted by his misshapen throat.

Candy trembled on her stiletto heels for a moment and then threw herself against the railing, sobbing melodramatically. "I'm so s-s-*sorry*, Eliot," she heaved brokenly between sobs. "I didn't w-w-*want* to. You were always so n-n-*nice* to me."

"Oh, Candy, I never blamed you!" the poltergeist assured her.

"Of course not," Lucy muttered to herself. "She's only the one who stabbed you in the heart while riding you like a bucking bronco. Why should you blame *her*?"

"Big Joe m-m-*made* me do it, Eliot! He threatened my l-l-little girl."

Lucy frowned. Okay, so maybe it wasn't *entirely* Candy's fault. She didn't look much more than nineteen, but that didn't mean she didn't have a daughter. Especially considering the company she kept.

The other figure in the office leapt to his feet, rushing forward to shove the groveling, sniveling Candy aside. "She's lying!" Big Joe Morrissey yelped hysterically. "Why would I kill you, Eliot? You've always been loyal to me!"

"That's what I've been wondering, Joe," the Eliot poltergeist growled. "Why would you want to have me killed?"

"I didn't! I wouldn't! How could I?"

"He said you knew too much about the organization," Candy chimed in helpfully. "He said that any piece of pussy who shook her thing at you could get you to spill all of his secrets. He said you were a liability 'cuz you were so pathetic."

"Shut up, you whore!" Joe screamed. Big Joe backhanded Candy, who didn't make a sound or even flinch as the blow knocked her to the ground.

"*Don't touch her!*" Eliot roared, the rafters quivering in response to his rage. "I may have had to stand by while you smacked her around in life, but in death I am a different man. You will not lay a single finger on her *ever again.*" The last two words boomed through the warehouse, rattling the supports that kept the office aloft.

"Eliot, please!" Big Joe wailed. "I am begging you. Is that what you wanted? You have Big Joe at your mercy, my boy. Whatever you want of me, it's yours."

"You killed me, Joe," Eliot said. "You don't have anything to offer the dead."

"Eliot!" Joe squealed, a stuck pig in Armani. "Eliot, you don't want to kill me! You're not a murderer."

"You don't know what I am," Eliot growled ominously. "But you're right about one thing. I don't want to kill you."

Candy looked up from where she had been thrown to the floor. "You don't?"

"Death is too good for you. I like death. I'm a fucking *god* dead. You don't *deserve* death."

"Oh, thank you, Eliot! Thank you! You're right! You're so right. I'm not good enough for death!"

Eliot continued as if he hadn't heard the mob-boss's whimpering thanks. "What you *deserve* is a lifetime of suffering. Don't you agree, Candy?"

"Abso-fucking-lutely," Big Joe's sex toy replied with relish. "Would you like me to castrate him, Eliot?" she asked cheerfully.

Big Joe whimpered as his eyes rolled back in his head and he fell to the floor in a dead faint. Candy nudged him, none too gently, with one spiked heel. "Pussy," she scoffed.

"Tie him up, Candy," Eliot instructed, his puffed-up poltergeist form slowly diminishing, the green strobe-light effect waning as he became less green and less deformed, reverting back to accountant geekdom. "Make sure you tie him good and tight."

"What are you going to do to him?" Candy made a beeline toward a cabinet along the wall and pulled out a length of well-used rope.

"Big Joe likes power and respect. So we're going to take away his power and make him a laughingstock."

"How?" Candy asked without looking up from her hog-tying.

"I'm going to take away his empire, turn him in with enough evidence to send him to jail for the rest of his natural life and when people ask him what his downfall was, he'll tell them that a dead man took him down. People will think he's crazy or a fool."

Candy looked up, but Eliot was no longer looming huge and green and intimidating. He was back to his normal size and standing on the warehouse floor, his illumination just a pale white sheen. Candy gave Big Joe one last kick and walked to the rail. "What about me, Eliot?"

Eliot smiled shyly. "Big Joe keeps the key to his safe on a chain around his neck. The safe is hidden under his bed," he said. "I think you've earned a bonus, don't you, Candy? Maybe just enough to buy a tropical island and disappear with your daughter."

"Are you *kidding* me?" Lucy jumped up and stalked toward her ghost. "She kills you and you're going to *reward* her? All because she tricked you into having sex with her?"

"She didn't *want* to kill me," Eliot said defensively. "It was Big Joe."

"She's still the one who stabbed you! Murder mid-coitus, you called it."

Candy began sniveling. "I'm so sorry about that, Eliot."

The ghost smiled and floated up to the balcony to pat her on the back. "I'm not sorry, Candy. I would have gone through my entire life terrified of living, if you hadn't killed me. Now I'm not afraid anymore. I stood up to Big Joe. *Me*. Eliot Mellman. I took down the big man. You did me a favor, Candy. I was wasting my life, but now I'm ready to enjoy my death."

A blade of brilliant white light pierced Eliot's abdomen. He looked down at it, blinking in confusion. "What the hell?"

His ghostly form began to rotate slowly in the air as more swords of light burst out of him in a rainbow array, each beam intensifying to a pure white.

"Lucy?" Eliot called out, panicky. "Lucy, what's happening?"

"You're transcending, Eliot," Lucy called from directly beneath him. "Relax, just let it happen."

"I don't want it to happen," he whined. "I want to stay with you. I want to be a ghost forever."

"You're ready, Eliot," Lucy said. "You forgave your murderer, even if she didn't deserve it. You protected me, even when I didn't need it. And you stood up for yourself. You said it yourself. You, Eliot Mellman, stood up to Big Joe Morrissey."

"I wasn't afraid," Eliot said wonderingly, but his voice was already breaking up and fading away. His ghost form coalesced into a knot of light then shattered, tiny sparkling particles exploding out in every direction.

Big Joe Morrissey, who had just come to, screamed like a twelve-year-old girl and passed out again. Lucy looked around for Candy, but she was already gone.

Chapter Nine:
What Have You Learned, Dorothy?

Lucy and Jake managed to find one crate that hadn't been reduced to splinters and perched on it side by side, ignoring Big Joe's whimpering pleas from the balcony and waiting for the authorities to arrive to cart him away.

While Big Joe had still been unconscious, Lucy had entertained the idea of painting his face like a clown or writing a phony confession, but when he woke up and immediately began babbling incoherently about exploding dead men, she figured his credibility would be shot without any additional help from her. Although painting his face would have been fun either way.

"Nice of Eliot not to kill him," Jake commented idly as they waited in the hurricane-struck warehouse. "It's a lot easier to explain finding him here babbling like a lunatic than the presence of a corpse."

"He couldn't kill him."

Jake turned toward her, a frown already in place. "You said it would be like the end of *Ghostbusters*. You made it sound like the freaking Apocalypse and now he couldn't have done anything?"

"I didn't say he couldn't have done anything. I said he couldn't have killed Big Joe. A murder victim cannot kill the person who murdered them. That sort of post-life eye-for-an-eye stuff would upset the balance of life and death. If Eliot had tried, he would have ripped a hole in the fabric of the universe."

"Ripping a hole in the fabric of the universe is okay, but taking vengeance on people who are actually to blame isn't?"

Jake asked incredulously.

"Ripping a hole isn't *okay, per se.* It's more a nasty side effect of breaking the rules."

"Thank God Eliot was feeling merciful."

Lucy snorted. "That wasn't mercy. Eliot liked being dead. He didn't want to share that with Big Joe."

Jake picked up a piece of crate shaped like a spike and spun it between his hands. "Is that normal? For dead people to get off on being dead?"

"No. Eliot was different. In a lot of ways. Most ghosts couldn't do the kind of damage he did either."

"But the—" Jake made a Big Bang gesture with his hands, "—that was normal?"

"Yep. That's transcending. He resolved his issues, released his worldly cares and moved on to whatever's next."

"He didn't seem like he wanted to move on."

"He accomplished what he needed to. He stopped letting people take him for granted. He stood up for himself and wouldn't let Big Joe walk all over him. He wasn't going to put up with injustice anymore and once he stood up for his beliefs, for what he knew was right, once he realized that he was worthwhile, he transcended. It was past time people started treating him with a little respect and stopped jerking him around. Stopped treating him like a child and giving him the most ridiculously convoluted mixed signals so you don't know whether you're coming or going—although you certainly aren't *coming* because *someone* is such a cock-tease and never follows through with what his body promises you."

"We aren't talking about Eliot anymore, are we?"

"You think?" Lucy snarled. "How *dare* you?"

Jake shifted to the opposite edge of the crate, eyeing her warily. "How dare I?" he repeated cautiously.

"You think you can just waltz into my life, get me all fired up and then just *walk away*? Just because you're too hot for your own damn good doesn't mean you can treat women like that."

"Lucy."

"Oh, don't *Lucy* me. Let me give you a hint, Casanova.

When you have a girl pinned up against a refrigerator panting for you, the absolute worst thing you can say to her is *it won't happen again*. It's the dimples, isn't it? It's because I'm too *cute*. You don't *think of me that way*, right?"

Jake grabbed her and shut her up with a kiss. His touch was even more scorching than she had remembered. By the time he released her mouth, her bones had been thoroughly liquefied by the heat.

"I don't know where you get this idea that I don't want you," Jake growled. He picked her up and dropped her onto his lap. "I've been having a devil of a time keeping my hands off you since the second we met, and the only reason I bothered to try was because I knew Karma would have my balls for earrings if I messed up her shot at the finder's fee on Joe Morrissey."

"So you want me?"

Jake shifted her on his lap. "Do you really need to ask me that?"

"Right. Stupid question." Lucy wasn't going to waste any more time talking. She speared her fingers through Jake's hair and pulled him back in for another kiss.

He let her have control for about five seconds before he took over, slanting his mouth over hers as his strong hands molded her body against his. One hand slipped beneath her T-shirt and closed over her breast, stroking, teasing at her nipple through the silky fabric of her bra. Lucy squirmed on Jake's lap, twisting around to straddle him, to give him better access and to get pressure against the best parts. She pressed her hips forward, the apex of her thighs rubbing against the ridge in his jeans through two layers of denim. Lucy moaned into his mouth and he growled, thrusting his tongue against hers.

Lucy arched her neck back, breaking the kiss, nipping at his lips when they chased hers. She yanked his shirt off over his head and nearly whimpered at the sight of his chest. He was all smooth muscle pulled taut beneath caramel tan skin. The broad, slightly bulging muscles of his upper arms flowed up into the wide expanse of his shoulders and down into defined pecs and abs so tight she could bounce a quarter off them.

"Damn, you're gorgeous," she murmured huskily.

Jake grinned wolfishly and reached for the hem of her

shirt. "My turn."

He pulled her shirt up slowly, his gaze intensifying with every inch of skin he revealed. He teased her stomach with the backs of his fingers, drew his hands over her ribcage, brushing the sides of her breasts, and then slowly slid his palms up her arms until his fingers were wrapped around her wrists and the shirt fell to the ground behind her. He didn't immediately release her hands, but kept her shackled by his fingers, her arms extended above her head as he bent his head and gently scraped his teeth across the upper curve of her breast just above her bra.

Lucy shivered and bit her lower lip as she watched him nibble and lick his way across her body, catching the front clasp of her bra between his teeth and releasing it as he bent her back and stroked his tongue down toward her navel. He released her hands, but all she could think to do with them was lace her fingers through the dense softness of his hair as his mouth slowly drove every coherent thought out of her mind.

When he pulled her mouth to his for another kiss, her bra had somehow vanished and he pressed her against him, skin to skin. A shiver of pure pleasure rippled through Lucy at the contact, and she wrapped both arms around Jake, holding him to her as firmly as he held her. Her hips slowly rocked against his, as they lingeringly explored one another's mouths.

She felt his fingers lightly trace the line of her stomach above her jeans, then the stronger pressure against her abdomen as he fumbled with the button.

The sound of the warehouse door slamming echoed in the cavernous room, along with the sound of dozens of footsteps.

"Police! Freeze!"

Lucy froze. Jake swore.

Chapter Ten:
Impatience is a Virtue

Lucy restlessly paced in her living room, waiting with no patience whatsoever to see if Jake was going to show up to put her out of her misery. It seemed like every time she got close to an orgasm, they were interrupted. The Fates were definitely against her.

Admittedly, getting it on in a destroyed warehouse with the cops on the way and Big Joe watching from the balcony had not been one of her greater ideas. Apparently, she had an exhibitionist streak she'd never known about. Any thoughts of propriety or the right time and place had vanished as soon as he touched her.

Maybe she would just avoid going out into public with him. Lucy figured that was the only way to avoid jumping on him in public places.

The cops had been in high spirits. Apparently, finding Big Joe Morrissey trussed up on a stack of evidence and a topless blonde straddling the hardass PI who sometimes worked with them was better than Christmas. Even though they all knew him, they'd made Jake hold up his hands until his *identity had been verified*. Jake played along, but drew the line when they tried to get Lucy to put up her hands, glaring down the officers until they agreed that Lucy could keep her arms crossed over her chest, since she wasn't packing.

She had blushed beet red the entire time, but took her cues from Jake and silently accepted the police ribbing.

When the cops finished their game and holstered their

weapons, the first thing Jake did was grab her shirt and drop it back over her head. He'd then pointed her toward her car and told her to go home, that he would take care of everything.

Lucy had expected to be stopped, had expected someone to want her statement at the very least, but the cops just waved, leering at her like the lecherous bastards they were as she drove off.

And now she waited.

Lucy hated waiting. Over and over again, she paced her apartment and analyzed everything that had happened over the past twenty-four hours. When she got to the part where Jake all but patted her on the head as he sent her away, she groaned every time. He hadn't said he was going to come see her when he was done, but he would. Wouldn't he? It had been nearly three hours, dawn had already broken, but Lucy wasn't even thinking about sleep. How long could it take to give a statement? He'd be in a hurry to get to her, wouldn't he? He'd come as soon as they released him, wouldn't he?

But what if he didn't want her? What if she had just been a convenient piece of ass, and as soon as she was out of his sight, she was as forgettable as the next disposable lay?

When the phone rang, Lucy vaulted over the back of her couch to get to it. "Hello?" she asked breathlessly. Desperately. She was officially pathetic.

Karma's wry, honey-coated tones rasped across the phone lines. "Honey, you need to relax. You're so agitated, you're keeping *me* awake."

Lucy had spoken to Karma at every hour of the day and night over the years of her employment with Karmic Consultants and she had never heard her boss even refer to sleep before. She didn't believe for a moment that her tension was upsetting the cosmic flow enough to alert her boss. "Is your name really Karma Cox?"

There was a long silence on the other end of the line, and then Karma sighed heavily into the phone. "My mother was surprisingly naïve for a hippie. She had no idea she was giving me a bonafide stripper name. I wondered if Jake would mention our relationship."

"You didn't tell me your brother had moved back from

Phoenix."

"It didn't concern you," Karma said flatly. "What concerns *me* is the fact that you took your ghost to confront his murderer. How exactly is that in keeping with the company bylaws, Lucy?"

"Jake was in trouble," Lucy protested. "You wouldn't have wanted me to leave him alone in the warehouse to die, would you?"

"No. You shouldn't have done that. What you *should* have done is call me. Or the police. Or *anyone,* really. The one thing you *shouldn't* have done is bring a volatile poltergeist into the situation. You're just lucky things worked out as well as they did and that Big Joe isn't in a position to sue for damages."

"Eliot did do a number on the warehouse." Lucy frowned into the phone, asking the question that had bothered her since Eliot had knocked over her nightstand, "How is it that he was able to manifest such physical energy? Most of my ghosts are barely there."

"How strong the ghosts are depends on more than just you," Karma replied. "There isn't an exact formula, but the general consensus is that the strength of a ghost has to do with how much energy they carry over with them at the moment of their death. Murder victims have stronger presences as ghosts, because their deaths are often the result of a struggle. Old men who die peacefully in their sleep will often transcend without even passing through the ghost realm."

"Well, Eliot's death was certainly active."

"And he had the poltergeist tendencies to prove it. In the future though, Lucy, the company would prefer that you not allow your ghosts to get quite so close to bringing about Armageddon."

Lucy flushed. "Right, boss. Won't happen again."

"Excellent. That said. Good work. And thank you for saving my little brother's ass, since he will probably never thank you himself."

"He won't?" Did that mean he wasn't coming over? Was she never going to see him again? Had Karma done a reading? Did she see the Fates tearing them apart before Lucy achieved the sexual satisfaction at his hands she so richly deserved?

"He's an ungrateful bastard," Karma continued lightly. "Now, since you've done your part with the Mellman case, you have my permission to work on changing your client list. We'll find someone else to handle the horny phantom population in the future."

"We will?" Lucy felt like she was missing some crucial piece of the puzzle.

"You bet. Goodbye, Lucy."

"Bye."

"Oh, and Lucy? Look on your front step." Karma cut the connection.

Lucy walked to her front door, wondering what surprise Karma had left on her doorstep this time. If it was a gigolo, she was going to be very disappointed. She only had eyes for a certain non-gigolo gigolo. Jake, the ungrateful bastard, had ruined her for other men. When she opened the door, she nearly walked into Jake's fist, which he had just raised to knock. Lucy smiled. There were worse things than having a psychic for a boss.

Chapter Eleven:
Hello, Handsome.
Goodbye, Larrinator.

Jake barely had time register the door opening before a warm, soft bundle of feminine flesh launched at him. He caught her instinctively as Lucy wrapped her legs around his waist and her arms around his neck.

"Howdy, cowboy," she purred, rocking against him enthusiastically before planting her mouth on his.

Jake's brain instantly incinerated from the warm, wet heat of her. He'd had a hell of a time explaining to the cops exactly what had happened in the warehouse without sounding as crazy as Big Joe, but now all of the tension from the last three hours drained out of him as he fell willingly into her mouth.

She broke the kiss and wriggled against him, making his eyes roll back in his head a little. She snagged his earlobe gently between her teeth. "I missed you," she whispered huskily.

"If this is the homecoming I get, I'll have to go away more often."

Lucy leaned back in his arms. With her torso angled away from him, her crotch pressed tighter against his, grinding hard. Jake groaned and closed his eyes in bliss. This woman was going to kill him. Luckily, she'd also be his first stop in the afterlife.

"You aren't going anywhere until you have fulfilled your promise," she said sternly.

"My promise?" he asked dazedly. He was too horny for riddles.

Lucy rocked her pelvis against the hard ridge in his jeans. "*This* promise."

"Sweet Jesus," Jake gasped out, and waited for his vision to clear.

"Take me to bed, Mr. Cox," she purred, his name sounding dirtier on her lips than he had ever dreamed it could.

"Yes, ma'am."

There was something deliciously wanton about jumping a man on her front porch. It was even more delicious when that man was Jake. For once, Lucy didn't care that she didn't look like a sex object. Feeling like one was far better than looking like one.

Jake carried her easily, as if she weighed nothing, his hands palming her ass and his body bumping up against hers as he strode back to her bedroom. He sat on her bed and she pressed him back onto the mattress, letting her hands run wild across his chest, shoving his shirt out of the way until he impatiently grabbed it and yanked it off in one quick move.

He reached for her, but Lucy was enjoying having control too much to surrender it just yet. She batted his hands away and pushed his shoulders back down. She knelt above him, straddling his waist, and stretched her arms above her head, arching her back sinuously. She reached down and slowly raised the hem of her shirt an inch, giving him a teasing glimpse of her stomach. He reached for her again, and Lucy dropped the shirt back into place to catch his hands. He let her pin them to the mattress, though he was strong enough to easily overpower her.

"Stay," she commanded teasingly, languidly releasing his hands and reaching again for the hem of her shirt. This time, he made no attempt to interrupt her striptease, though his gaze scorched every inch of skin she revealed. The shirt rose slowly above her navel, her ribs. She paused, giving him a teasing glimpse of the underside of her breast—a little reminder that she was braless, since the one she had put on that morning was probably still on the warehouse floor, if it hadn't become a banner at the police station by now.

"Come on, baby," he murmured encouragingly, and Lucy grinned wickedly.

"What do you say?"

"Please."

Lucy chuckled throatily and dragged the shirt up farther, shivering a little as the fabric abraded her nipples. She slipped the shirt over her head and tossed it aside with a flick of her wrist. She brought her hands down slowly, sliding them down the sides of her neck, slowly over her collarbone, down her chest to cradle herself, offering herself up to him.

Jake flipped her onto her back, tangling his fingers through hers as he dragged her hands away from her breasts to make room for his mouth. Lips, tongue, teeth, he scraped, suckled and licked until she was writhing beneath him. She arched, trying to get more. It wasn't quite *enough*, but he held her down, held her back, right on the edge of the *more* she needed.

His lips pulled at her nipple and she moaned, "Jake."

He chuckled, his breath hot against her skin. "What do you say?"

"*Please*," she whimpered, twisting against the delicious weight of his chest pressed against her abdomen.

Jake rasped out a rough laugh that sounded more like a growl and made quick work of her jeans, unbuttoning them with quick, deft flicks of his long fingers and then dragging the clinging denim slowly down her hips, thighs, knees and ankles, his hands roaming every inch of the way, until she was spread before him in only her pale blue panties.

Girl-next-door panties. Lucy felt a twinge of nervousness, as if he would suddenly realize that she wasn't a sex goddess and walk away, but she needn't have worried. Jake fell on her, his mouth hot on hers, and Lucy wallowed in the heat of his skin.

He was so *warm*. She wrapped her legs around his, enjoying the rasp of his denim against her sensitized skin as she burrowed into his heat. She felt his pulse pounding hard against her, vibrating through his chest and into her. He was a living, breathing furnace—both the pulse and the heat vastly different from the men she usually spent the night with.

His long fingers slid beneath the fabric of her blue girl-next-door panties and Lucy emitted a thoroughly un-sex-goddess-like squeak and pressed herself up into his touch. Jake scraped his teeth against the side of her neck and worked his hand deeper.

"Whoa, baby! Free show!"

Lucy jolted and Jake froze over her. She peered past his shoulder to where the nasal voice had come from and saw the vague, mostly-transparent form of a ghost hovering over the bed.

"You want a hand there, stud?" the ghost asked, his shimmering form giving the slight impression of a lecherous leer. "I've always wanted to try a threesome. Of course, I thought it would be me and two chicks, but beggars can't be choosers, am I right, champ?" The ghost drifted closer. "I bet I can make your lady scream."

Lucy did in fact scream. In frustration.

"I thought they only showed up at night," Jake growled, shifting his body to more completely conceal her from the ghost's view.

"Usually at night," Lucy corrected, all but whimpering. "But they pretty much show up whenever the hell they want."

The ghost suddenly appeared on the pillow beside her. "Hey, baby, you wanna feel what a *real* man can do for you?"

Lucy was used to such lines. She just rolled her eyes and tried to think how she could get her clothes without giving the ghost a show and transcend the little punk as quickly as possible so she could get back to Jake. They had been *so close*. Dammit.

Jake, however, was not used to ghosts hitting on her. And he definitely wasn't used to ghosts crawling into bed with her. He reared back as much as he could without exposing Lucy and pinned the ghost with a look of pure violence.

"Listen, Casper, you may be dead, but that doesn't mean I can't make you suffer. If you even think about laying one ghostly finger on this woman, I will perform an exorcism on your ass so fast it will make your god-damn hornball head spin. You get me? Now, get the fuck out and don't come back unless you want to see what hell looks like."

"Jake, he can't—" Lucy began, but broke off when the ghost yipped in terror and made a beeline for the closet door, flying directly through it. Through the link, Lucy could feel him cowering on the floor among her shoes, but at the moment, she really didn't care.

Jake groaned and dropped his head down beside hers on the bed. "Lucy, we have got to do something about these ghosts who are attracted to you. There must be something we can do to keep the horny loser set from barging in on us."

"There is," Lucy said, tipping her hips up against his. "Make me come."

Jake looked her straight in the eye and growled, "Done."

He whipped off her panties, hooked her legs over his shoulders, and bent to lick into her. Lucy's toes curled, her back arched, and she jaggedly screamed his name as she came from the first unbearably perfect touch of his mouth, but he wasn't done yet. He bit and licked, stroked and teased, working her higher until she shattered a second time, digging her heels into his back and keening senselessly.

When she could speak again, she panted his name and he looked up. "Inside me," she managed to gasp. "Need you."

Jake beat the speed record for stripping out of a pair of jeans and was back against her in a heartbeat. He fit against her and pushed inside slowly, stretching her with the almost pain that was so intensely pleasurable. Lucy moaned and her eyes fell closed, but Jake growled, "Look at me," in a voice that sounded barely human, and her eyes flew open to lock with his.

The intensity in his eyes coupled with the intense pressure of his body invading hers was overwhelming. Lucy trembled, afraid she was going to burn up and disappear, but Jake wouldn't let her. His eyes held hers, his focus pulling her along with him, making her match him stroke for stroke, moan for moan. They locked together, closer, tighter, unbearably, impossibly linked, until they exploded together, transcending every experience that came before, breaking them apart and fusing them together. One heart, one body, one spirit.

Lucy sighed, utterly replete.

Then sighed again, resigned. "I'd better go talk the ghost

out of the closet."

Jake grunted. Lucy figured that was the extent of his verbal ability at the moment. She patted his shoulder affectionately. He had a right to be exhausted; he'd moved mountains, erected pyramids, and rebuilt the world as far as she was concerned.

Jake rolled off her and flopped bonelessly onto his back. Lucy slipped off the bed and went in search of clothes that weren't in the closet, enjoying the feel of his eyes on her back as she puttered around the room. She finally settled on his shirt, wallowing in the scent of him that enveloped her as she pulled it over her head.

"Is this going to be a common problem?" he asked from his lazy sprawl in the center of her bed, nodding toward the closet where the ghost could be heard whimpering to himself.

"Karma said my client list would change, but I'm always going to get visits from ghosts," Lucy answered hesitantly.

"And they're always going to pop in on us uninvited, whenever the hell they please?"

Lucy squirmed, terrified that he was going to announce that she wasn't worth the trouble, grab his clothes and walk out of her life forever. "Probably," she admitted reluctantly.

Jake frowned and then dropped his head back to the pillow and sighed heavily. "I guess I can put up with a few ghosts." He shot her a devastating grin. "As long as I get you."

Lucy beamed at him and padded over to the bed. The ghost in the closet could wait. Her own private gigolo came first.

About the Author

To learn more about Vivi Andrews, please visit www.viviandrews.com. You can send an email to vivi@viviandrews.com or visit her blog at viviandrews.blogspot.com.

Look for these titles by
Vivi Andrews

Now Available:

A Shifting Dreams Story
Serengeti Heat

The Ghost Exterminator

Witches Anonymous

Misty Evans

Dedication

As always, this story is for Mark...my dear husband and best friend who never fails to tempt me with laughter and an occasional Dove chocolate.

Special hugs go to my sister of the heart, Chiron. Without her encouragement, this story would still be in the drawer.

And more hugs to my brainstorming partner, Nana, who brought Liddy and her crazy hair to life for this story.

Many thanks to my chocolate-loving editor, Laurie Rauch, for her expert eye for details.

Chapter One:
The Thirteen Steps

In a room full of witches, you'd think I wouldn't stand out. You'd be wrong.

My name is Amy Atwood and I'm a witch. Not one of those goodie-two-shoes Wiccans. No, I'm a Satan-worshipping, Devil-made-me-do-it witch.

However, after catching Lucifer performing a particularly wicked hex act with Emilia, my sister—a tried and true Wiccan—I turned my back on the Devil. I didn't exactly expect him to be faithful, but bewitching it with my sister? High ick factor. So, no more casting spells to entertain him. No more curses to carry out his desires. No more witchery of any kind.

That's why I was attending my first Witches Anonymous meeting. Glancing around at the faces staring back at me, with their raised eyebrows and thinned lips, I suddenly realized the last part of my introduction, about the Wiccans, I said out loud. In a room full of the goodie-two-shoes sisters.

Way to go, Amy. Stepping on broomsticks in less than thirty seconds. A new record, even for me.

Too bad I couldn't cast a spell and enchant them all, but I'd sworn an oath to stay clean. Because magic is a slippery slope. Even one small curse or spell could put me on the downhill slide back to Lucifer. So far, I was sticking to my oath. I was good now. Normal.

Human.

Yeesh. The thought made me shudder.

Anxiously caressing the square of Dove chocolate stowed in the pocket of my jacket, I gave the witches in the room my most charming smile, full of ear-to-ear goodness. I'd promised myself if I got through the meeting, I could have the chocolate.

And there wasn't much I wouldn't do for a Dove.

The door behind me opened, saving me from making a false apology. A tall, good-looking guy with a determined look on his face pulled up short as he took in the circle of women. His T-shirt was a bit too tight and his jeans a bit too loose, but his boots were high-quality leather with snappy silver toes peeking out from beneath the frayed hems of his pant legs.

That's what I call good*ness.*

His intense brown eyes looked intelligent when his gaze locked with mine. "Uh, hi," he stammered, his focus dropping to my mouth. It stayed there a second too long before returning to meet my eyes. Thank the devil I'd worn my plum lip gloss. "Is this room 12A? I was looking for the Harley Brothers meeting."

Men and Harleys? Now that was my kind of group. "I'm Amy." I stepped forward to extend my hand. "I was looking for that meeting, too. It must be down the hall."

The grin that passed over his face showed me one perfect dimple. He took my hand with confidence, his warm skin kissing mine like a lover as he pulled me toward him. I noticed an apple with an arrow piercing the core tattooed on his right arm.

"Let's get out of here, then," he said, "and let these fine women get back to their...whatever meeting."

Out in the hall, I put my hand over my mouth and giggled. "Your timing is perfect. You just saved me from being burned at the stake."

Up close, his brown eyes looked like the color of the Dove in my pocket. The dimple reappeared. "Rescuing damsels in distress is one of my specialties."

I'd never considered myself a damsel in distress. However, the dimple won me over, saving him from a sharp rebuke. I found myself wondering if his eyes got darker, like melted chocolate, when he got mad.

Or horny.

He took my hand again. Soft warmth enveloped it. "I'm Adam Foster."

Instantly, I thought of Bananas Foster. Yummy. My mind was already casting a circle of lust around us when I caught myself.

No spells. No charms.

No fun.

"Nice to meet you, Adam Foster." I took my hand back, wishing I could curse Lucifer and Emilia for forcing me to embrace goodness and normalcy. "I better let you get to your meeting."

"You're not coming?"

"No." I glanced at the door to Room 13C and shuffled my feet. "I swore an oath to be good. I have to go back to this one."

"Back to the stake, huh?"

"You could say that."

He gave me a nod. "Maybe after our meetings, we could grab an ice cream?"

A Harley-riding, tattooed man who wanted to go for ice cream? Normalcy wasn't all that bad.

And revenge on Lucifer, whether by stake or by mortal torment, was extremely satisfying. "I'd love to."

"Meet you outside later?"

"I'll be there."

As he walked away, I watched the back of his dark brown hair brush his neck and thought about touching that same spot with my fingers. When Lucifer discovered I'd taken a new boyfriend—a human one, no less—he'd be mad as hell.

Who says being a good witch isn't fun?

Inside the room, the good witches chatted in pairs. One lonely woman, with glasses covering most of her face, sat alone, staring at the others with a look of distracted interest. Weaving my way through the small groups to get to her, I felt the other witches' annoyance and fear pinging off me like little balls of hail. Instinct had me forming a protective bubble around my body until I pulled up short. Was protecting myself from negative energy too witchy? Deciding not to take chances, I ignored the energy hail balls and continued on toward the woman sitting by herself. As I stopped next to her, I plastered a smile on my face and pointed at the empty chair on her left. "This seat taken?"

Her eyes widened behind the thick lenses. Straightening, she glanced around at the witches nearest her who were watching the exchange. Was it my imagination, or did tiny bolts of lightning crackle in her hair? She pointed one short finger at the chair as if it were a boa constrictor and eyed me with suspicion. She seemed genuinely surprised. "You want to sit here?"

I nodded, doing my best to look harmless. "Yeah, if you don't, you know, have a partner."

"Oh." Again she stole a glance at the group around us and I saw her discomfort shift to something more determined. Something friendly. The frizzy curls in her hair seemed to relax a bit. "Actually, I was saving this seat for you. I'm Liddy."

She motioned me into the chair and I dropped like a rock, full of relief. "Nice to meet you, Liddy." Once the majority had returned to their conversations-in-progress, I leaned closer to her and said under my breath. "Thanks for the save."

"The save?"

"Yeah, you know, saving me from embarrassment in front of everyone. Me not knowing what the heck is going on and all."

She gave me a covert nod and cracked her knuckles one-by-one self-consciously. Again, I could have sworn I saw microscopic lightning bolts, this time emerging from the ends of her fingertips. "This is your first meeting, huh?"

"Yep." I settled back and crossed my legs, curious about the energy she was fighting to hold in. "So, what are we doing, pairing up like this?"

"Step Five."

I waited for her to explain. When she didn't, I prompted her. "Step Five?"

She shifted her chair to face me like the other pairs of witches were doing. "Admit to another witch the wrongs we've committed against humans."

Wrongs we've committed against humans. Dirty demons,

this could get ugly. "Like a confession?"

She nodded at my quick study. "Right. The first step is to admit you have a problem. Then you take a moral inventory and then you unburden yourself to another. It's redeeming."

Making a quick mental list of the wrongs I'd committed that fell in that category, I knew it could be a long evening. "Wiccans only perform white magic, Liddy. All that *harm none* stuff. How many wrongs could you have committed?"

She dropped her gaze and started worrying the cuticles on her fingers. She'd bitten her nails to the quicks. Or maybe they were chewed up from the white light zigging and zagging between the tips. "You'd be surprised at the defects in my character."

Defects? Using my natural-born empathic skills, I opened a small fissure and probed her. Lots of angst, but I couldn't find any black energy. I leaned in, patted her leg and gave her a wink. "You can always claim the Devil made you do it."

My stab at humor garnered me her serious wide eyes and a shake of her head. "It wasn't the Devil. My family made me do it."

Another display of crackles stood her curls on end. Yep, families could do that to you. Considering my only living relatives were Emilia and our neurotic grandmother who'd holed herself up in a nunnery in Romania, I felt an instant kinship with Liddy. "Mine's less than stellar too. Don't sweat it."

"Your family, are they...you know...in the occult like you?"

"I have a sister who just went to the dark side." I did my best Darth Vader breathing-through-a-mask imitation, but Liddy looked confused. I waved it off. "Emilia's the reason I'm here, trying to go good again."

"Why would you want to worship Satan in the first place?"

The question of the ages. I thought about Lucifer—his dark, brooding eyes, his skillful lips, his talented fingers. A shudder ran down my spine. The bad boy in him called to me, even here, sitting with Liddy and her poor battered fingernails and fried hair. "It's hard to explain. Luc—that's what he likes to be called—is sort of the, uh, ultimate seducer. Pretty damn hard to resist."

Liddy's eyebrows drew together as if she didn't get it. Again,

227

I wondered how many defects she could have. I tried an example. "You know in high school how all the girls moon over the hunky quarterback, but, in the heart of the night, yearn for the bad-ass biker boy?"

She tilted her head to one side and stared at me, thinking hard. "You mean like Dean Winchester in *Supernatural?*"

Holey jeans and cocky attitude. "Exactly. You watch that show?"

Her eyebrows drew tighter. "Once. It was too scary for me, but I liked Sam the best."

"Ah, the wounded-soul, reluctant-hero type." I placed my hand over my heart and sighed deeply. "Hard to resist those, too." Especially when seducing them was *so* entertaining.

A heavy energy settled over us. The witches on either side of our chairs had picked up on the thread of our conversation and were openly staring.

Liddy didn't seem to notice. "But Satan hurts people. You don't seem very mean."

Again, the image of Lucifer rose in my mind, his lips curving up in a dangerous, seductive smile. Remembering the dark magic we'd performed together sent a tiny tingling through my veins. Like a trained dog, my thighs tightened in response. I coughed, tried to clear the image of Lucifer's head between my legs, and squirmed. "The magic I did was for personal gain." Deeply, *deeply* personal. I fanned myself with my hand. "I never hurt anyone but myself." And, come to Momma, bad-ass biker boy, I wanted to do it all over again.

Except, probably at that very moment, Luc was making Emilia's thighs squeeze the same way. My heart jerked inside my chest.

Liddy bit at a non-existent fingernail. "I hate my sister," she said. Every body part I could see crackled. "I want to do her harm."

The out-of-the-blue confession mirrored mine so perfectly, I sat back hard in my chair. It squeaked backwards on the linoleum floor. "Really. That's...um...interesting."

She slapped her hand over her mouth, her eyes bugging out behind the lenses. Her curls did the hula on top of her head. "Oh, my, God, I can't believe I said that out loud."

Me either, but, hey, a girl's gotta confess what a girl's gotta confess, and Liddy obviously needed to get some of that crappy energy out of her system. "Your secret's safe with me." At her continued look of abject horror, I reached over and patted her knee again. "It's okay, Liddy. We've all been there, wrestling with that blood-is-thicker-than-water stuff. It's good to get it off your chest. The redemption thing, you know?"

"You." The Witches Anonymous president, Marcia Something-Or-Other, rose from her chair to my left. She pointed a finger at me. "You made her say that."

What? "What?"

Another woman stood and glared at me. "Liddy would never say something like that. She wouldn't hurt a fly."

"It's you," Marcia said, hands on hips. "You brought out the evil in her."

"I...uh..." I looked at Liddy's scared expression and the crazy lightning bolts flashing around her. "...did not."

Did I?

Had I somehow inadvertently transferred my feelings toward Emilia on Liddy? I pushed back my chair and stood as Marcia and several of the others gathered around my new friend in a protective, human shield. Marcia shook her finger at me again. "If this is your idea of a joke, it's not funny."

The rest of the women moved forward and joined the protective ranks. Once again I was staring down a dozen angry Wiccans. Their energy glowed red. Strike two. One more and I was out. *Harm none,* I chanted in my head in case any of them were mind readers. "Look..." I raised my hands and turned them face out to reinforce my innocence, "...I didn't do anything to Liddy. We were just following your Step Five and she sort of had a personal epiphany about her family. That's all."

Liddy's head popped up over Marcia's shoulder. Her eyes were still bugged out, but lit with something new. Something happy. "She's *right*. I had an *epiphany*." Her voice was almost giddy. Her head bobbed up and down, her now-relaxed curls jiggling with wild abandon.

Marcia glowered at me, but spoke to her. "Shut up, Liddy. You did not have an epiphany."

"Yes, I did. I did," she insisted. "I know what's wrong with me now and how I can make amends." She turned a glassy-eyed smile on me. "And I owe it all to my new friend, Amy."

Marcia's mulish face continued to stare me down as Liddy tried to convince the rest of the witches that she'd just had some kind of spiritual awakening.

After a minute, the women moved off in small groups to gather around a table set up with punch and cookies. Several threw me curious looks over their shoulders. Others still regarded me with disdain. The energy level was now a burnt orange.

Marcia crossed her arms over her chest and narrowed her eyes at me. "Watch your step, Atwood."

Her tone thoroughly pissed me off. Or maybe it was just her pompous attitude. I clenched my hand around the Dove in order to keep from reaching for her neck. Giving her the sweetest smile I could generate, I channeled mock innocence. "Would that be Step Nine or Step Thirteen, Marcia?"

Chapter Two:
Did I Scare You?

As the nice witches filed by me on the sidewalk, some of them sending me more looks of open curiosity, I slunk into the shadows and pulled the Dove from my pocket. Satisfaction was sweet. My first Witches Anonymous meeting was over and I'd survived. More than survived, I'd actually made a new friend. It was like running on a treadmill. Getting on was the hard part, but once finished, I felt renewed. Invigorated, even. Ready for anything the universe could throw at me. Or at least Marcia.

Setting the dark chocolate square on my tongue, I sighed and closed my eyes. Heaven. Pure heaven. I leaned my back against the old brick building and savored the chocolate, fantasizing about the dimpled guy who would soon be taking me for ice cream. *I could get used to this kind of life...*

A hot wind blew across my chest and a deep, seductive voice whispered in my ear, "Amy?"

Goosebumps ran over my skin. I jumped and choked on my chocolate, my eyes flying open to find the Devil standing in front of me. Tall, dark and sexy as hell, he was nevertheless too handsome for his own good. No visible horns or claws, but an insatiable hunger for all things denied him.

Placing one hand on the wall behind me, he leaned in closer and pinned me to the spot with his body. The streetlight's glow did nothing to soften the blue glints in his raven-black hair. As he smiled down at me, his white teeth gleamed in the shadows of his face. "Did I scare you?"

Straightening my jacket, I swallowed the last of the

chocolate and itched to throw a curse at him. It wouldn't do any good, but it would make me feel better. "Of course not," I lied. "What are you doing here?"

"Precisely what I was going to ask you. Witches Anonymous, my dear?" His gaze traveled over my body and certain parts tingled in response. "You must be joking."

I cleared my throat and told my parts to knock it off. "It's no joke. You and I are done. I never want anything to do with you again."

He laughed under his breath and one long finger reached out to stroke my cheek. I flinched at the feel of the scorching heat of his touch. "You've gone too far to walk away from me."

"Get off me and you'll see me walk away with no trouble at all."

Luc parted his lips to say something or possibly laugh at my threat, but a man's voice interrupted him. "Hey, there you are."

Luc drew back and dropped his arm, taking his luscious heat with him.

My knight in shining leather once again came to my rescue. Adam, the streetlight illuminating his face, hooked his thumbs in his belt loops and narrowed his eyes at Lucifer. "Is there a problem?"

Waving a hand in the air in dismissal, I smiled so hard my cheeks hurt. "No problem." I skirted around the demon who owned my soul, and hooked my arm through Foster's. "Let's go."

Lucifer spoke a low warning. "*Amy.*"

The tone of his voice was hard to ignore. I pulled Adam away from the building, heading toward the parking lot where a bunch of other men were talking alongside their Harleys.

I felt the shadow of Lucifer's hand on the back of my neck, ready to snatch me back. Shrugging it off, I kept walking. He wouldn't do anything in front of all these humans. "See this?" I called to him over my shoulder without meeting his eyes. "This is me walking away. We're done. Finished. The End."

A bullet of heat shot through my heart—Luc's nonverbal answer.

Heart pounding, I scanned the motorcycles and gripped Adam's arm tighter. "Where's your bike?"

"Over here." He pointed to a big, black Dodge truck.

"That's not a bike."

He shrugged, pulling out a key fob and hitting the automatic door locks. "Bike's in the shop." Motioning with his head, he asked, "What's his deal?"

"Ex-boyfriend. Thinks he still owns me."

"Ah."

The truck sat high on oversized tires. Adam gave me a hand up. I bounced in, wondering if I was really going through with this. I didn't know this guy from Adam, even if he *was* Adam. He could be a jerk, a serial killer, a Britney fan. And me, Miss Reformed Witch, without my powers.

But as I slid across the seat, I saw Lucifer still standing in the shadows of the building, a faint but distinctive red glow illuminating his body. He was pissed.

Feeling the first flush of revenge, I smiled to myself. *Point to the witch.*

We pulled out of the parking lot, and a sudden weight tugged at the pocket of my jacket. Sticking my hand inside, I found not one, but a dozen Dove chocolate squares.

All of them glowing red.

Chapter Three:
Sin City

My first instinct was to throw the glowing candy out the window. Knowing Lucifer the way I did, I figured the chocolates were hexed and some innocent kid or unsuspecting mutt would end up with the Devil in them. So, I kept them in my jacket, silently begging them to disappear, since I couldn't vanish them myself.

"Your pocket's glowing." The dashboard light showed a hint of curious amusement on Adam's face.

"Uh," I stuttered, searching my brain for an explanation. "Hand warmer. One of those little packs you break and it gives you heat. These cold nights, you know..." I bobbed my head, "...a girl's got to keep her hands warm."

He turned his gaze back to the road, smirking. "It's fifty degrees outside."

The chocolate continued to glow. If I didn't do something soon, it would melt in my pocket and ruin the leather. "I'm very sensitive to cool air."

A two-way radio on the seat between us buzzed, and a woman's voice spoke in an urgent manner. "Unit Seven, this is dispatch. House fire reported at 66 Wingate Drive..."

"Hang on." Before the dispatcher finished with the details, Adam did a U-turn in the street and reached behind his seat to grab a strobe light. Shoving it through the open window, he set the flasher on top of the truck. Then he picked up the radio, confirmed he was en route, and put the gas pedal to the floor. "Sorry," he said. "Davy's out sick with a virus and I'm on call."

"You're a fireman?"

"Captain. Tonight was supposed to be my night off."

There was no time for more questions. He wove in and out of traffic, ran stop signs and answered a continuing stream of information coming over his radio. I admired his ability to multitask so effectively.

I also admired the fact he knew how to put out fires. A skill like that could come in handy for someone who messed around with Satan.

Arriving on the scene, I shifted my eyes between the orange and red flames bursting from the downstairs window to Adam, who was pulling up his fire-retardant pants. "Rain check on the ice cream?" he said, setting a hat on his head and grabbing his turnout coat from behind the seat of the extended cab. His crew was just beginning to shower the house with water.

"Sure." Watching the fire eat the water, I wondered how I'd get home to my apartment. I'd walked to the meeting and there was no cab service in Eden, unless you counted Denny's Bar, which ran a van for the town drunks to keep them off the streets and encourage the average drinkers to indulge, guilt and designated driver free.

A family of four stood outside, shook up but unhurt. The little girl cried against her mother's leg. Her fear and pain rippled through the air as the flames rose and fell in the house. Mesmerized by the fire, I continued to watch the scene with a group of other gawkers as the firefighters moved in sync with Foster's directions. He seemed to think one step ahead of the fire, and within minutes, he had it contained. The little girl's crying had stopped in the arms of her mother.

I could still feel the heat coming from the house on my face when the air behind me spiked in temperature as well. The candy in my pocket glowed brighter. "You always did love fire," Lucifer said, running his fingers down my back.

Even in the midst of the oven-like air around me, I shivered under my coat, arching away from him. Keeping my eyes on the house, I hissed, "What are you doing here?"

His breath, hot as acid, touched the back of my neck. "Thought you might need a ride home."

I turned to look him in the eyes, a thought dawning on me.

"You did this. You started the fire, didn't you?"

A casual shrug confirmed my suspicions. "Job security for your new boyfriend."

"He's not my..." I stopped, remembering that I was using Adam to make Lucifer jealous. I wanted to give the Devil a taste of his own medicine. "Are you going to burn down a house every time I go out with him?"

Luc grinned, dark and wicked. "I'll do whatever it takes. You should know that."

Boy, did I. "I took an oath not to use my powers anymore. I'm of no use to you. You want to fool around with Emilia? Be my guest. Lure her in. Turn her evil. I'm not your playmate anymore. Do you understand?"

The grin fell off his face. "Oath or no oath, you'll do my bidding, witch."

If I could have vanquished him, I would have. But even in my days of evil witchery, my powers weren't strong enough to vanquish the Devil. We stared at each other as the crowd around us began dispersing. A tingling heat flared between my legs.

A voice came from far away, snapping me out of the trance. "Amy? You still here?"

I whirled around to see Adam standing behind me. The fire was out and the firefighters were rolling up hoses and patting each other on the back.

Relieved once again to find Adam rescuing me from Luc, I smiled up at him. "I wanted to watch you in action. That was amazing how you guys put the fire out so fast. You're a talented guy."

He grinned, a small, embarrassed grin. Then he fixed his gaze on a spot over my shoulder. The wall of heat at my back flared higher. "Funny how we keep running into each other." He held out a hand to Lucifer. It was still grimy with ash and soot. "Adam Foster."

The corner of Luc's mouth curved up with malicious intent. "Luc." He gripped Adam's hand. "Smith."

The handshake lasted a few seconds too long. Even through the soot on Adam's hand, I saw his knuckles turn white.

"Well." I grabbed Adam's coat sleeve and tugged him away from Lucifer. "You must need to get back to the station and do...um...captain things."

Adam pulled his gaze from Luc's and looked down at me. "I'll take you home first. That is..." He shifted his feet and took off his hat. "If you want me to."

"I'd love you to," I gushed with a touch too much enthusiasm. As Adam turned to head back to his truck, I looked Lucifer in the eye. "Stop following me, and stop setting fires." I emptied my pocket of chocolates and shoved them at him. "We're done. Finished. Over."

The curve of his mouth sharpened, and for one brief heartbeat, a flame sparked in his eyes. "We're not over until I say we're over." He let the chocolates fall to the ground. "Witch."

"You live above Evie's Ice Cream?" Adam pulled into a vacant parking spot in front of my building.

He smelled like smoke and had soot smeared on his cheek. "Yes," I said, breathing deeply and fighting to keep my hand from wiping off the soot. "I actually own the ice cream parlor."

The look on his face would have lit up Manhattan for a week. "No way."

My night manager, Keisha, eyed us through the window as she locked up the front doors. I willed her to be on her way and saw her raise one eyebrow in challenge as she felt my mental hands shooing her toward the back room. Her fists went to her hips and she returned her own mental hand slap before turning to go. She was more of a sister to me than my flesh-and-blood one. "It's been in my family for generations. The first Evie was my great-great-grandmother's grandmother."

"I love your ice cream. It's the best I've ever had." He held up three fingers. "Honest."

The boy-scout gesture tugged at my heart. I laughed at his kidlike exuberance. "What's your favorite flavor?"

"Sin City Chocolate. I like those little pieces of dark chocolate mixed in with the vanilla ice cream."

A man after my own heart. "Would you like to come in and

have a dip?"

I could see it in his face, he was tempted. Really tempted. For more than just ice cream. "I would, but I have to get back to the station and fill out the paperwork on tonight's fire." He sniffed at his shirt. "Besides, I stink."

I was more than a little disappointed. I'd obviously misread the look in his eyes; the heat coming off him was from the fire, nothing more. What was that guy always saying on TV about guys being into you? If they made an excuse, even a legitimate one, not to come inside your place, they *weren't that into you.* "I understand. Another time, maybe?"

"How 'bout breakfast tomorrow?"

Not that into me, huh? My confidence rebounded. "I'd love to."

"I'll pick you up at eight."

I opened the truck door. "Excellent."

Avoiding Keisha, I went up the outside stairs to my apartment. Smelling like smoke myself, I showered, fed my cats, Cain and Abel, and snuggled down in bed to dream about my new firefighting friend.

This thing with Adam was going to work out perfectly.

I woke from dreaming about Adam in his fire suit to the feel of a hot body next to mine. A body too big to be one of my cats, and much too hard. And then there was the hand cupping my breast through my Snoopy sleep shirt.

Frantically, I tried to clear the cobwebs out of my brain and get my bearings. Had Adam accepted my offer last night? Had we enjoyed more than a scoop of ice cream?

An image of him waving goodbye to me from his truck surfaced, and with it, a chill spread down my spine. With sudden clarity I knew who was sleeping in my bed. I jerked away from Lucifer, tumbling to the floor in my haste.

I have only one vice in life—lust. I lust for sinful men, dark chocolate and designer shoes. For ten years, Lucifer satisfied all my desires and then satisfied them some more.

The embodiment of lust, he made me choose bad over good, dark over light, hell over heaven. I simply couldn't resist his wicked ways. Until he slept with Emilia, that is. Just thinking about him touching her, kissing her, the same way he'd touched and kissed me made me shake with disgust. Betrayal was one thing. Betrayal with my sister...well, that was more hell than I bargained for.

He rose up and peered at me over the side of the bed, his hair mussed and his eyes full of enchanting lust. "Good morning, Amy. Dream of me?"

Chapter Four:
Bed Buddies

Since I no longer had protection spells keeping my apartment off limits to demons and other magical creatures, it was no surprise Luc had wandered in.

"What the hell are you doing?" I shouted at him, even though I knew exactly what the hell he was doing. He'd been seducing me for years. I was familiar with his guerilla sex tactics.

He ran a hand through his shoulder-length, blue-black hair, mussing it into an even sexier look. "Thought you might be lonely since your boyfriend left you high and dry."

"He did not..." I broke off, knowing it was useless to explain anything to him. Pushing myself off the floor, I grabbed my robe and shoved my arms into the sleeves, pulling the belt tight. "Get out."

Luc threw the covers back and walked buck naked across the floor toward me. "I made your favorite breakfast."

On cue, the tantalizing smell of French toast wafted by me. Breakfast. Adam was picking me up for breakfast.

I glanced at the clock. The blue numbers read seven-forty. Crap. I had twenty minutes to shower, make up my face and do my hair, not to mention kick a naked man out of my apartment. A naked, *supernatural* demon-man.

Who was not so surprisingly well endowed.

Taking a deep breath, I racked my brain for a non-supernatural way to take care of him *and* me. "I'm getting in the shower. When I get out, in like two minutes, you'd better be gone. Understand?"

He scratched the stubble on his chin. His eyes glowed with lust. "I could scrub your back. Massage your scalp while I wash it with that new herbal shampoo you just bought."

How did he know about my new shampoo? Obviously he'd been snooping while I wasn't home. "You have to leave. Now."

"How about a pedicure? Or a bubble bath instead of a shower? Remember the bubbles I produced for you last time?" He advanced on me with each suggestion and I shook my head as I stepped backwards. The heat pouring off him made me want to shed my robe and the thought of those crazy, pheromone-laced bubbles made sweat trickle between my breasts.

Sticking my hand out to stop his advances, I hit his sculpted chest. Energy zigzagged through my fingers and up my arm. "Stop it."

But he didn't stop. He pried my hand off his chest and kissed the tips of my fingers. Panicking, I jerked my hand away and ran for the bathroom. Throwing the door shut and twisting the lock, I leaned against the solid wood door and prayed. *Uh, God? Are you there? Your old arch enemy is at it again. I could some help here, your Godship. A little strength to resist the Devil?*

"Amy," Luc murmured to me through the door. "Come back to bed. Your breakfast is getting cold."

I shook my head adamantly, even though he couldn't see me. "No."

The door warmed under my hands. "I brought your favorite boysenberry syrup."

Oh, curses. Every cell in my body tingled. Boysenberry syrup and the Devil. What woman could resist such temptation? *Come on, God. Cut me some slack here.*

"There's fresh whipped cream." His sexy smooth voice singsonged through the door. "You know what I want to do with that."

In the mirror over the sink I could see my flushed face. My robe had fallen open and my nipples were rock hard under my sleep shirt. *Mercy*, my brain screamed. *Can you hear me, God? I'm crying*, mercy.

Lucifer chuckled low in his throat, as if he were listening to my pleading cries for help. His heat rushed over me like the wind and it was all I could do to form a coherent thought. I was almost ready to untwist the lock when I heard Emilia's voice in my head.

"You're pathetic."

It wasn't in my head, though. Emilia was on the other side of the door with Luc. Apparently my lack of a protection charm left me open to her as well. Wonderful.

The door's warmth faded and the fire burning my skin evaporated.

"Em." Luc's voice held a hint of embarrassment. "What are you doing here?"

Casting a glance up at the ceiling, I rolled my eyes. *You sent my sister? That's the best you could do?*

Turning on the cold water tap, I shed my clothes and jumped into the shower. As the last of Lucifer's heat evaporated from my skin, I forced myself to ignore the yelling outside the door and the sound of crashing breakfast plates in the other room.

Chapter Five:
Welcome to Temptation

Adam took me to Eden's arboretum for breakfast. Breathing in the fresh air and soaking up the beautiful scenery, I imagined the landscape was, in many ways, like the original Garden. Leaves on the trees were edged with red and yellow. Birds sang and dipped under the soft blue sky.

The morning's earlier fiasco with Luc and Em seemed like a distant memory as the sun soaked into my clothes, warming them.

From a white bakery bag, Adam handed me a cherry turnover and a foam cup filled with espresso. His own bag contained a chocolate-covered donut and a carton of white milk.

As we sat on a bench, mainlining sugar and watching a pair of swans glide around the edge of the arboretum's small, man-made pond, Adam's leg leaned against mine with easy familiarity. "I figured you for a steak-and-eggs-breakfast kind of guy," I said, licking cherry filling off my finger.

A mischievous look passed over his face. "And I figured you for something lighter, but no less satisfying. Hence, a sweet pastry and strong coffee for a most interesting woman."

Heat rose in my cheeks and I enjoyed it, sipping my espresso to hide my smile. "How did you know I love cherry turnovers?"

He swung his gaze around to look at me. It bounced off my hair, down to my eyes, and came to rest on my mouth. "You just seemed like a cherry-turnover kind of gal. Pretty and delicate on the outside, and full of rich, delicious filling on the inside."

Certain parts of my body tingled in response to his obvious flirting. When was the last time a guy used a food metaphor to describe me? When was the last time a guy actually stopped to think about what I might like, for that matter? I couldn't keep the grin off my face. Breaking off a corner of the turnover, I held it out to him. "Wanna bite?"

My heart galloped at the sudden heat in his eyes. His answer was to lean forward and take the piece of turnover out of my fingers with his mouth. Warm lips closed over the tips of my fingers and my breath caught at the cool electricity sliding up my arm and into my chest.

His gaze stayed locked on mine as he chewed and swallowed. "Yum."

Exactly what *I* was thinking.

I was suddenly hungry for more than breakfast. Maybe my libido was still in overdrive from Luc's unexpected and unwelcome visit. Or maybe the new, improved Amy was also horny. Dropping my shaking fingers to the turnover, I jerked my eyes away from Adam's so I wouldn't jump him right there in the arboretum.

"How about we catch a movie tonight?" he asked around a bite of his own breakfast.

I nodded without thinking and then remembered my WA meeting. "Darn, I can't. I have another meeting tonight." And the way things were going with both Lucifer and Adam, I needed the reinforcement of Witches Anonymous to keep me on the straight and spell-free path I'd chosen.

"What kind of meetings are they?"

"Um," I stammered, searching my brain for a plausible, non-magic type of meeting. I couldn't claim AA or any other substance-abuse group without throwing water on the fire we were building between us. I needed to shine a nice light on myself, keep Adam's interest piqued. He needed to think I was a good person. "It's for Halloween. A bunch of downtown business owners are working with the Chamber of Commerce to sponsor a trick-or-treat festival this year."

"Cool." He finished off his donut. "I hadn't heard about that."

"Oh, it's top secret. We haven't actually decided on anything yet, so we're keeping it under wraps. A few of the women in the group are..." Marcia's hard-set face popped into my mind and I had to temper the word that popped into my mouth, "...challenging."

Nodding his understanding, he sipped his coffee. "Know-it-alls, huh? Bossy?"

"You can say that again." I wiped my mouth with a napkin. "It's their way or the highway. I'll probably just end up doing something on my own at the ice cream shop, but I should still go to the meeting tonight and see what they're going to do."

He shifted, making a small production out of cleaning up our wrappers and napkins and crumpling the paper bag. Before I knew it, his full leg was up against mine. He stretched his arms over his head and one came down on the back of the bench around my shoulders. "Maybe I could help you out."

Of course he could. He had no idea how many ways he could help me. "That would be nice of you. I could show you how to make ice cream witches and spiders and such."

His head bobbed once. "I love Halloween."

"Me, too."

We sat in silence for a few minutes, watching the swans. A light fall breeze played with the tree leaves hanging over our heads. Discreetly, I snuggled closer to him, enjoying the warmth his body generated.

"Tonight, after your meeting..." his thumb rubbed the side of my shoulder, "...I'd like to turn in my rain check on the Sin City."

My body hummed with sugar, caffeine and Adam. I was nearly purring with contentment. If things continued at this pace, I'd be spoon-feeding him decadent ice cream before midnight. "We're open until ten," I said, giddy with the prospect. "I'll be home from my meeting by nine-thirty."

The swans eyed us as they swept by. I could almost feel Adam's heartbeat against my other arm. He turned his face so his lips were next to my ear. "I'll be there at nine-thirty-one."

Goose bumps rose all over my skin. "Oh...ah..." I stammered. "Good."

His lips dropped to my earlobe and then made their way south, their touch so soft and gentle I squeezed my thighs together and clenched the tops of them with my fingers. "Very...very good."

Adam sunk his hand into my hair at the back of my neck. He tipped my head a fraction to the side and lightly ran his lips back up to my ear. Nibbling my earlobe, he massaged the back of my neck with his strong hands. "Yum," he whispered in my ear. "I just discovered my new favorite breakfast."

Yum, my mind echoed. *Me, too.*

Chapter Six:
The Devil Wears Armani

Just so you know...the Devil does not wear Prada.

For business, he wears an Armani suit The Donald would kill for. Otherwise, he's like any other mortal guy...comfort above all else.

When he entered the ice cream shop at six-thirty that night, he wore his usual casual attire—faded Levi's, a rich, chocolate-colored leather jacket, and calfskin cowboy boots.

At the sound of the bell tinkling above the door, Keisha looked up from scooping a double dip of Bubble Gum ice cream for a four-year-old. At the sight of Lucifer standing there in all his raw maleness, her mouth dropped open like a nutcracker's.

Handing my customer—the child's father—his banana-split mixer, I snapped my dishtowel at Keisha to bring her back from fantasyland before I went to deal with Marlboro Man.

"What do you want?" I pulled him toward a corner booth, away from my customers.

His voice dripped innuendo. "What do I always want from you, Amy?"

Sex in a public place. An ego stroke. Free ice cream. The same thing all men, mortal or supernatural, seemed to want from me. "One chocolate shake, coming up."

Marching back to the counter, I bit the inside of my cheek to keep from mumbling curses. Mechanically, I went through the motions of preparing a shake for him, reminding myself I'd feel more in control after my Witches Anonymous meeting and an ice cream treat with Adam.

Keisha shut the cash register and sidled up to me. She worked at drying her already dry hands on her apron. Her multiple silver bangles jingled softly against each other. "What's he doing here? I thought you gave him his walking papers."

Digging deep in the bucket for a scoop of ice cream, I released it into the cup in my hand. "He was in the mood for a chocolate shake."

Keisha made a sound in the back of her throat that suggested she knew I was lying. "I know what he's in the mood for and it ain't chocolate. He's bad news," she conceded, eyeballing him. "But, damn, he is a fine-looking man."

"He's a demon."

"Aren't they all?"

Adam's face flashed in front of my eyes. "No, they're not." I pointed the ice cream scoop in Luc's direction. "But he is. King of the demons, right there."

Keisha twirled her stack of bangles and waggled her eyebrows at me. "Fun to play with, though. You have to admit."

Rolling my eyes, I stuffed the cup under the mixer and tuned out any further comments. After the shake was finished, I set it on the table in front of Luc and held out my hand. "Five dollars and fifty cents."

He shifted to pull a stack of bills from his back pocket. "Prices have gone up, I see."

"You get what you pay for." I took the dollar bills and used them to point at the shake. "I made it with premium ingredients."

His eyes narrowed with a hint of suspicion. Using the plastic spoon, he scooped up a bite. Then another. "Not bad. How come you're being nice to me?"

"Yelling at you to go away doesn't work. I'm trying nice instead. You hate nice. Is it working?"

His lips pulled down in one corner. "Oddly enough, nice is a turn-on coming from you."

I gritted my teeth to hold in the retort pushing against my lips. "You. Are. Un-*believable*."

The corner of his lips turned up. He continued to spoon ice

cream into his mouth. "You're going out with Adam tonight, aren't you?"

Again, I bit the inside of my cheek. He was keeping tabs on me. Being the Devil, he knew a lot of things I didn't want him to. Rotten, dirty demon.

Ignoring the set of my closed lips, he sunk his spoon back into the shake. "He's going to invite you to a Halloween party Saturday night at the fire station. Say no. You can't go. You're busy."

I worked at unclenching my teeth so I could speak. "I am *not* busy."

A wicked expression I knew only too well lit up his entire face. "I've got something for you to do, my dear witch. A whole lot of somethings. Keep you busy the whole night."

"No. Way. You can't stop me from going to a party with Adam if I want to go, and, newsflash, I want to go."

"You don't want to go. Trust me, Amy."

Trust the Devil. Sure. That had gotten me far. Still, I was curious to find out what he knew that I didn't. "And why don't I want to go?"

Luc licked his spoon and I heard Keisha moan under her breath behind the counter. I shot her a look of pure disgust and she shrugged her shoulders in an *I-can't-help-it* gesture.

He tipped his spoon at her before returning his gaze to mine. "The explanation is beyond what you can comprehend. Let's just say, if you attend that party with Adam, you could change the history of the world."

I slid into the booth opposite him, unable to ignore such an opening. "The history of the world? That's overdoing it a bit, isn't it? Even for you?"

He coughed as if something were caught in his throat. "Overdoing what?"

"This is obviously another of your ploys to keep me from seeing Adam. Admit it, you're jealous."

Setting the spoon down, Luc cleared his throat. "I need some water."

Knowing what was about to happen, I gladly went to the sink and filled a plastic, disposable cup with water.

"Put ice in it," he croaked from across the room.

My customers and Keisha stared at him, gawking. Returning to the seat across from him, I smugly noted his red face. He gulped the water, but I knew it would do nothing to soothe his throat. Another coughing fit followed, just as I expected.

"What did you put in that shake?" he choked out when he finally got his breath back.

"Organic ice cream," I said, smiling. "Natural, pure, and good for you. Well, maybe not *you* per se, since you hate anything pure and good."

His face hardened. He raised a finger and pointed it at me. "You'll regret this."

"Why? Is it going to *change the history of the world*?" I mimicked his finger-pointing. "Personally, Luc, I think that might be a good thing. I'm not too impressed with this version, since you're in it bothering me."

He grabbed my wrist and pulled me out of my seat and toward him so we were nose to nose over the table. "You'll never get away from me, Amy. Deal with it. You belong in my world, not Adam's."

The bell above the door tinkled and in walked my sister. "Well, well," she said to Lucifer, planting her hands on her white, Versace-clad, Wiccan hips. "I should have known I'd find you here. Running back to the Wicked Witch of the West yet again. What is it with you and her?"

Like she was Glinda. My customers switched their gawking to her, their eyes dilated, their ice creams melting. Pulling my wrist from Luc's grip, I rose from my seat and faced Emilia. "I'm not wicked anymore, sis. That's your department, now, remember? You wanted to play with fire, and now you've got it. He's all yours. Please, take him home and keep him there."

Emilia's pale lips curved in a rueful smile. "He *is* mine, Amy, and don't you forget it."

Lucifer stood up, eyes blazing. "I'm not some dog that you own," he yelled, or tried to yell. His voice came out squeaky, like a pubescent boy's. Emilia frowned at him. Rubbing his throat, he shot daggers at me again. "I want you to stay away from that freak Adam, do you hear me?"

He grabbed Emilia's arm above the elbow and ushered her out the door. As the bell's tinkle faded away, I smiled to myself. "And people in hell want ice water."

Chapter Seven:
Orlando and Marshmallows

Streetlamps flickered on as I walked to my WA meeting. A sickle moon was barely visible overhead. The buzz of cricket song rose and fell around me and I kicked at the leaves blowing past my feet in a kid's game to keep my mind off my ex and my sister. I kept one eye out for Luc, my nerves jumping at every moving shadow, but no demon emerged from the dry leaves swirling in the alleys or the darkened doorways. Having readied myself for what seemed like his inevitable appearance, I was almost disappointed when he didn't show up.

I was even more disappointed when Emilia did.

"Amy," she said, materializing from behind an oak tree. I flinched, my hand flying to my heart. She didn't seem to notice. "Stop seducing Lucifer."

Dropping my hand, I let out the breath stuck in my throat and started walking again. "Come off it, Emilia. You know I'm not the one doing the seducing. Like I told you earlier today, you wanted to play with fire. Now you're playing with fire."

She fell into step with me, her high-heeled Gucci boots clacking on the sidewalk. The Dark Side was obviously working for her in the fashion arena. She'd never cared about designer labels before. "If you really want to be free of him, let me bind your powers."

I stopped in mid-step. "You think I'd let you—a witch who blows up her kitchen making a simple love potion—bind my powers?"

Annoyance flashed across her features before she shut it

down. Then she turned on her charm. What charm she had, anyway. "Why put yourself through these stupid Witches Anonymous meetings? Let me help you. Once I bind your powers, Lucifer won't want anything to do with you. Solves both our problems."

Fudge sauce could have dripped from her smile. Shaking my head in disbelief, I continued on my way. "In your dreams."

She stayed put, but her eyes bore into my back. Her normal voice trembled with a guttural sound. "You always were a spoiled-rotten, holy terror of a bitch."

So much for charm. And what was with the eerie octave of her voice?

Ignoring the shiver that went through my bones, I stopped. We'd had this fight one too many times growing up...I knew exactly where to sprinkle a dose of salt. The sisterhood of the magic witches. "And you always were an overachieving, first-born, bossy prude."

As if unseen hands were attacking me, the leaves at my feet sprang up and whirled around my legs like a cyclone. Her anger slammed against me as if she were physically pushing me. I tripped, but caught myself before totally losing my balance. Good thing I'd worn my Pumas instead of my Choos.

Straightening upright, I saw Liddy across the street by the building's entrance. A small calico cat wove its body through her legs in a figure eight. Her hair was pulled back in a ponytail and she waved a little-girl-type wave. I waved back, keeping my hand lowered so Emilia didn't see it. No way did I want Em to set her sights on my new friend. She, too, knew where to sprinkle the devastating sisterly salt.

"Look." I turned to face her, trying to block Liddy from her view. Under the streetlamp, her skin appeared ashen and pale, but her eyes were clear and intense. Feverish-looking. Unblinking. Demonic.

I hesitated just a second, letting that sink in. Emilia had been acting out of character ever since Luc seduced her. Like she was possessed. Sleeping with the Devil could do funny things to a person, especially when the person had once been all goodness and light. Maybe Emilia had gotten more from her demon lover than a bonus orgasm.

That idea would have to be explored later. "Why don't you pop over to my apartment and clean up the mess you made this morning, Emilia, and we'll talk about binding my powers when I get home from the meeting?"

The demon in her flashed like heat lightning and I took a step back as another shiver ran through me. Yep, she was definitely possessed. By what, I wasn't sure.

She saw my fear, or maybe smelled it. Her nostrils flared. "What, you didn't clean it up yet? Oh, that's right." She snapped her fingers. "You aren't acting like a witch anymore. No housekeeping charms. Poor Amy. She has to clean the toilet just like a human."

She was right. I'd cleaned up the broken plates and the cats ate the French toast scattered on the floor, but there was so much damage, I'd been overwhelmed with the amount of cleaning, which was why I was trying to bribe my sister into doing it for me. One wave of her perfectly manicured hand and all would be repaired. "You can bind my powers if you clean up the apartment. And while you're at it, scrub the toilet as long as you're there," I added. "Deal?"

Emilia hesitated for a minute, tapping her booted toes on the sidewalk. The demon receded a bit and my sister returned. "You trust me alone in your apartment?"

I did a mental inventory of potentially embarrassing items my snoopy sister might uncover. There was the erotica between the mattresses of my bed and the poster of a half-naked Orlando Bloom hanging on the inside of my bathroom medicine cabinet. An assortment of Luc's S&M products tucked into the closet in the spare bedroom and my *Partridge Family* DVD collection stuffed behind my *Buffy* one.

The only thing that truly worried me was my spell book. Full of intensely potent black magic, if that fell into Emilia's hands, she could hurt herself. Plus, she'd know all the hexes I'd developed to please Luc. Why should she get the credit, and pleasure, for my work?

"He-lllooo." Liddy was crossing the street, grinning at me and doing that wave thing at Emilia. I didn't have time to worry about protecting my sister from herself, nor was I sure I really wanted to. Not at the expense of Liddy's good nature. "Sure,

Em. Go for it." I waved my hands in a shooing motion. "I mean it. Go. We'll bind my powers later."

"Bind your powers?" Liddy skipped up beside me. "You don't have to do that, Amy. We renounce our powers once we've completed all Thirteen Steps."

"Is that so?" Emilia's lips stretched wide across her professionally whitened teeth. "Are you in Witches Anonymous too?"

Liddy nodded. "Amy and I are partners."

Emilia's gaze left Liddy's face and flashed on mine before returning to my friend. "Really? You and Amy? Partners?" Again, her gaze cruised to my face with smug attention. "Something in your closet you want to tell me about, Amy?"

The cat had followed Liddy across the street and now slid against my leg, purring. I took Liddy's elbow and pulled her a step back from Emilia. "My closet is full of interesting things you'll never know about." Spinning Liddy back toward the street, I gave her a little push. "Nice seeing you, sis, but we gotta go. Meeting's about to start. We'll talk later, 'kay?"

Dragging my friend away from Emilia, cool tendrils of magic, like Emilia's fingernails, raked my back. "Oh, Amy?"

Caught in the spider's web, I stopped and looked over my shoulder at my sister in her misleading, white haute couture.

The grin was still wide. "Why don't you bring your *partner* home with you after the meeting? I'll make a fire in the fire pit on your roof, and the two of you can fill me in on your relationship."

"Ooo," Liddy said, her head bobbing up and down at Emilia. "That would be great! We could roast marshmallows and give each other manicures. I just got this new nail polish, TinkerBell Tan, that dries in like five seconds."

"Marshmallows." Emilia's eyes blazed feverishly again. "Of course. What else would we roast?"

The cat's back arched and it hissed at her. Mentally, I did the same. "Later, Emilia."

As Liddy and I crossed the street, I heard the spider laugh under her breath. "Oh, yes, Amy. Later."

My apartment was still a disaster when I got home from the meeting. "Hello?" I called out, praying earnestly that Emilia had found something better to entertain herself with.

I needn't have worried. Sensing something was off even though I couldn't feel her anywhere inside my home, I stumbled into my bedroom. The closet door was open and all my shoes were scattered helter-skelter on the floor like a hobgoblin had gone Taz on them. The bitch went through my shoe collection. Why would she do that? What was she looking for?

The clicking of her high heels echoed in my mind. Her feet were at least two sizes bigger than mine. Surely she wouldn't steal my shoes.

Eyeing the pile of discarded pairs, I searched for my favorite Dolce and Gabbanas. The black ones with the studs and ribbons. The ones Emilia had repeatedly asked to borrow back in the summer. Back when she was planning to seduce Lucifer away from me. She was such a copycat.

"I don't believe it." Cain and Abel had crawled out from under my bed and were now sitting on top of it. "She stole my favorite pair of shoes."

The cats lowered their eyelids to half-mast in what I took to be sympathy. "Curse you, Emilia," I said, looking up at the ceiling. "I hope you get bunions the size of Simon Cowell's ego."

Curses. I slapped my hand over my mouth. *I had just cursed.* Leave it to my sister to push my buttons and get me to fail at my oath. Rubbing my forehead to stave off a headache, I chastised myself and re-swore my oath. No magic of any kind!

Curses...curses...

Oh, hell in a handbag. Kicking shoes out of the way, I shuffled purses, shoe boxes and jewelry aside to reach the secret hiding place in the back of my closet. Sure enough, my sister, the bloodhound, had discovered the very thing I didn't want her to get her hands on. Besides the D&Gs.

She'd stolen my spell book.

I could easily envision Emilia sitting in her favorite recliner with a glass of wine and a pad of sticky notes, marking all the spells she wanted to try, giggling like a possessed woman.

How long before she found the best spell of all?

I flopped on my bed between the cats, and pulled my pillow over my face.

The Atomic Sister Slave spell was one of my favorites, even though I'd never used it. Keisha had added the touch of voodoo to up the potency. That's why we'd named it Atomic. Just having the wicked incantation gave me the feeling of superiority to Emilia. No matter how she taunted me, no matter how many of my boyfriends she stole, I always knew that one verse of the wicked spell and she'd be my slave. Power, my friends. Deep, satisfying power.

But now that power was in her hands. The moment she found that spell, my freedom would be over. I'd be begging her to let me be her slave. I'd offer to handwash her delicates, polish her pentacles and tell her how beautiful she was.

Yeesh. So not going there.

Fear is an energizing emotion. I bolted off the bed, rummaged through my closet again and finally found what I was looking for—my power crystals, karma circle necklace, and several gremlin statues I'd used as domain guardians years before. In the deep recesses of the far corner, I came across a Do Not Disturb sign that read Go Away instead. *What the hell.* I pulled that out too.

When my doorbell rang ten minutes later, I had the crystals washed and set in the four points around my apartment and one in my pocket, the necklace dangling from my neck and the gremlins in place over every entrance. Busybodies, unwanted visitors and evil sisters beware. It wasn't magic; magic was a slippery slope, which was why I had sworn it off lock, stock, and devil. The warding of my apartment and myself was preventative self-care.

Throwing the door open, I found Adam leaning against the frame with a sly smile on his face. His arms bulged under the sleeves of his gray T-shirt and his jeans sported a silver belt buckle with the Chinese ideogram *Fu*.

Good Fortune. Yes-sir-ree. Good fortune was exactly what I needed.

As I shut the door behind me, I hung the Go Away sign on the doorknob as a finishing touch.

Chapter Eight:
Fake Snakes

Since my apartment was such a disaster, I'd decided to entertain Adam on the roof of my building. I avoided lighting a fire in the fire pit, lest it act as a beacon to any supernatural sources out and about. Instead, Adam and I laid low, staring at the stars and eating spoonfuls of Sin City Chocolate from a bucket he had toted up to the roof in a classic fireman's hold.

"The guys at the station are throwing a Halloween party Saturday night," he said, twirling the spoon between his fingers and kicking back on the lounge chair next to mine. "A costume party. I thought maybe, if you wanted to, we could go together." He snuck a look at me. "As a couple."

Pausing my spoon halfway to my mouth, I thought of Lucifer and his warning. There was no way I was letting him scare me off my growing relationship with Adam. Besides, I needed something to take my mind off Emilia and Lucifer and my rotten track record with men. Having grown up in Eden, most of the male population knew about my love life—a lot of them had helped me earn my ribbons before I got desperate enough to hook up with Lucifer. I had finally run out of available, worthwhile men. Next stop was online dating. Yeesh.

But then there was Adam. "I *love* costume parties." I finished licking the ice cream off my spoon. "Especially Halloween ones. What famous couple should we go as?"

"I was thinking..." He checked out the stars before glancing back at me. "Adam and Eve. You know, since I'm Adam and your great-great-however many greats-grandmother was Evie, and we do live in Eden..."

I let him trail off, watching his sudden shyness as he searched my face in earnest for a response. He was so darn cute, I could have kissed him.

Having never done cute before, I found it charming. And sexy as hell. "And what, dear Adam, will we wear?" I teased. "Fig leaves?"

He chuckled. "We never wore fig leaves." Pulling up short, the smile fell from his face. "I mean, um, never mind. Fig-leaf costumes will work, or we can pretend it's after The Fall and wear animal skins. Fakes, of course," he added.

"Of course," I said, conjuring up images of the two of us. Mostly naked images. Heat rose in my face and I glanced at the moon to make sure it hadn't suddenly grown full. Nope, it was still the quarter moon I'd noticed earlier. After clearing my throat a touch too loudly, I swallowed another spoonful of ice cream. "And we need a serpent—fake, of course—and an apple."

Tossing his spoon into the bucket, Adam pulled me beside him on the lounge chair and wrapped an arm around my shoulders. His earlier hesitation evaporated and he brought his lips to mine in a slow, soft, brush of skin to skin. There was nothing demanding, just inviting.

Welcoming the feel of him, I returned his kiss. His lips were cool from the ice cream and he smelled like chocolate. As we did a slow perusal of each other's lips, the initial coolness of his turned hot. Taking my cue from him, I chased his tongue with mine, advancing and retreating. One of his hands gripped the back of my neck and the game of cat and mouse ended.

My stomach fluttered like a manic butterfly and my thighs tensed with lust. I held him by the shoulders and pushed the length of my body against his. He broke the kiss, out of breath and staring at my lips. "You are going to make one hell of an Eve, Amy."

If he only knew. I teased his lips again with mine, enjoying their soft, inviting pressure. "And change the history of the world while I'm at it."

Pulling his head back an inch, he peered into my eyes. "Huh?"

I waved the spoon, still in my hand, in dismissal. "Never

mind." Cuddling into his chest, I let myself once again enjoy the mental image of him in nothing but a fig leaf. "You are going to make one heck of an Adam, Adam."

We giggled together, coconspirators.

Chapter Nine:
Sin in the City

Adam's hand stroked my back, sending feathery shivers up and down my spine. His heart drummed a soft rhythm against my chest as I lay my head on his shoulder. Breathing deeply, I inhaled the masculine smell of his neck and knew he wanted more than a lip-melting kiss, but was too much of a gentleman to go for it. Our first date and all.

I, however, had no reservations about plunging in hook, line and firefighter. Forget revenge on Lucifer. I wanted Adam, and I wanted him on the rooftop with the whole town of Eden spread out below us.

Just as I puckered my lips to kiss his neck, he sighed. "I know what you're thinking."

I froze. What, now he could read my mind too? "You know what I'm thinking?"

"Yeah. We just met and here I am all over you. Moving kind of fast, huh?"

His hand was actually moving with exquisite slowness. I wanted to arch my back into it. "No, not at all," I purred into his neck.

"It's been a while for me." He tipped his head to look at the sky again and brought my hand with the spoon to his mouth. Peeling the spoon out of my curled fingers, he tossed it in the ice cream bucket and kissed my palm. "Maybe too long." His tongue danced on my palm and I sucked in my breath. "I can't stop thinking about you. Wanting to touch you."

Damn. I kissed his neck, felt the texture of his skin, and

scooted my body so I lay completely on top of him. "Sounds good to me."

His eyes reflected the baby moon as he gazed up at me, heat and lust burning in them. Gentleman or not, he was still a man, and in my experience, men would believe anything you told them if it meant they'd get laid. "Really?"

Lucky for me, I didn't need to lie. I nodded, licking my lips and pressing my hips down, just a little. Just to tease him again. I wanted to know how much it took for Adam to lock his cute, shy hero self in the closet and let the bad boy come out to play.

The lust in his eyes flared brighter and his hands went to my hips. "I like you, Ames. I like you a lot, but if you're looking for a rebound boyfriend, that's not what I'm into."

My heart squeezed at his sincerity and his new nickname for me, and I realized how tired I was of pushy, demanding men. I liked nice. I liked charming. I liked Adam. A lot.

If I were a decent woman, I would have crawled off him and sent him on his way. He deserved someone nice and normal like him. A woman who was stable and had morals.

But even though I'd given up my witchy lifestyle, I wasn't a masochist. I'd dumped that gig along with Lucifer. Caressing the side of his face with my palm, I smiled into Adam's eyes and once again told the truth. "I'm not on the rebound or looking for a short-term fling. I'd like a meaningful relationship, and I'd like it to be with you."

He scanned my face. "You're sure?"

For the first time since I'd sworn that stupid oath to be good, I really *was* sure about something. He felt solid underneath me and I liked solid. I placed my hand over his heart. "Yes."

His eyes darkened in response with a look I knew to be very, very sinful.

Before I could dip my head for another kiss, he wound his hand in my hair and pulled my face down. There was nothing shy about Adam's lips as he took mine this time and I laughed softly into his mouth.

Bye bye, charming hero. Hello, bad boy.

Chapter Ten:
The Fall

Saturday night, Adam rode up on his Harley, took one look at me standing on the sidewalk in my Eve costume, and nearly crashed the bike into a parked car. "Damn," he said, staring at my fig leaves. Or possibly lack thereof. "You look…"

"Stunning?" I flipped my long hair, decorated with baby's breath, over one shoulder. "Even better than the original?"

"Oh, yeah. Much better than the original." His eyes roamed downward. "You're all but naked, Ames."

Unfolding the trench coat I carried, I slipped it on and tied the belt around my waist. I was certainly less naked than I could have been had Keisha not raided the neighborhood florist for artificial ivy branches and daisies. We'd sewn pieces of each, along with the baby's breath, to the bodysuit in creative ways, and Keisha had braided sections of my hair with the leftovers. I now looked more like a kinky version of Mother Nature than the Mother of Humankind, but at least my butt was covered. The single fig leaf the suit had come with in that area wasn't big enough to cover an ant's butt, much less mine.

"Where's your costume?" I said, carefully fitting a helmet over my tresses.

"Hard to look manly on the Harley in a fig leaf, not to mention, it's uncomfortable. I'll change when we get back to the station."

I eased onto the bike behind him and relished running my hands around to his stomach. Hard and compact, every muscle moved in unison under my fingers as he gunned the bike and we took off for the party.

The Eden firehouse was hopping when we arrived. Romeo and Juliet stood on the sidewalk talking to Marilyn and Joe. Butch and Sundance practiced their gun-drawing skills out front while balancing cups of punch. Music from inside thumped and vibrated into the parking lot.

One side of the station had been converted into a dance floor. Cobwebs and tombstones decorated every corner. The punch on the far table was blood red. As Adam led me through the partygoers, he stopped several times to introduce me to his fellow firefighters. They were so distracted by my natural assets wrapped in ivy and dotted with daisies, most had trouble following a real conversation. Normally, I would have flirted with every man there, but for some reason, I blushed and hung on Adam's arm instead.

Upstairs, while he changed into his matching costume in his office, I roamed the floor. I wandered through the sleeping area and toyed with the idea of sliding down the fire pole. Being a total klutz and wearing a bodysuit covered with flora seemed like enough reason to nix that idea. No sense in embarrassing myself in front of Bill and Hillary. One never knew when a Cabinet position might open up for a reformed witch.

Leaving the sleeping area behind, I walked down a short, dark hall, past Adam's office. There were restrooms on one side, and a storage room and water fountain on the other. At the end, flashes of light danced and flickered in bursts from another glass-fronted office. Since the light couldn't be coming from the party below, I figured the intermittent bursts were from a light bulb about to burn out.

As I came to a stop outside the office, I did a double take. On the other side of the glass, Lucifer fought with another man—a winged, luminescent creature who traded blows with my ex like a prize fighter. Every punch, every kick set off an explosion of light.

My breath stuck in my throat, I watched, mesmerized, as the two of them ducked, swiveled and flew into the air in an ongoing attempt to pulverize the other. Neither seemed to be winning or losing.

As though he felt my gaze on him, the angel stopped in

mid-swing and pivoted his head. Our eyes met and a chill ran like water down my spine. The skin over his angled cheekbones bunched as he smiled, but there was no kindness in the gesture. The blood in my veins froze.

Lucifer followed the angel's gaze and his eyes went wide with alarm when he saw me. Even my formfitting bodysuit did not distract him. He moved as if to leave the office and the angel's hand shot out, gripping him by the neck. Lucifer's mouth formed a word. "Run!"

Instinct swept through me, making me stumble backwards. As I turned to run, my foot caught on a chair sitting against the wall. I tripped and, falling, cracked the side of my head against the water cooler.

Pain, sharp and brutal, ripped across the back of my eyes and everything went black.

A voice cut through the fog in my head. "Amy Evelyn Atwell, I command you to open your eyes."

I blinked a couple of times, trying to obey the voice, even though I didn't want to. A dull throb beat above my right ear and it intensified when I looked at the incandescent glow coming from the angel's face. Another blink and, narrowing my eyes, I could take him in. Long waves of blond hair hung from his head, his features matched the hair, more feminine than masculine in their design. Deep blue eyes that held complete neutrality.

"Where's Adam?" I croaked. "What did you do to Lucifer? If you've hurt either of them, I swear..."

He stroked my forehead with a single, long finger. "They are at the firehouse. Unharmed."

Knocking his hand away, I eased myself into a sitting position, my gaze drawn to the sight before me—mountains in the distance dressed in clouds, a valley cradling a clear stream, trees full of birds, their songs echoing softly in the clear air. There were animals everywhere, roaming and grazing in complete harmony. My pulse jumped and I rubbed my head. "And where are *we*?"

The angel surveyed the beautiful garden before him. "Do you not recognize this place?"

Oh, God.

Literally.

"I'm *dead*?" I started to shake uncontrollably. "This is heaven?"

The angel scoffed and reached down to take my hand. "I'm Gabriel, and this—" he motioned at our surroundings, "—is Eden."

I expected his touch to be warm, but it was neither warm nor cold. The sensation was more like spiders crawling under my skin. Jerking my hand away, I struggled to stand and keep my balance. "This doesn't look like Eden," I said, hugging my body and crushing baby's breath in the process. "Where are the houses? The arboretum? My ice cream shop?"

"You, Amy, are at the crossroads of good and evil. This is Genesis."

"Oh," I said, sure I had totally lost my mind. "*That* Eden." My laugh sounded tight, incredulous. No surprise since I was freaking out inside. "Sure it is. I knew that."

Gabriel's gaze lingered on a giraffe stripping leaves from a tree. "Adam has been sent back to Earth for a second chance at resisting temptation. He's picked you from the entire human race to face the test with him." His eyes dropped to my face, challenge in the blue orbs. "You must be wiser and stronger than the original Eve and resist Satan, or humanity will once again be lost to sin and death in the fires of hell."

Right. *Someone knock me on the head again so I can get back to reality.* Scanning the area for anything that might look like reality, I freaked out an ounce more when absolutely nothing resembled my Eden. This had to be a trick. "That's a good one." Nervousness made my laugh sound like Alvin the Chipmunk's. "You and Adam's friends are punking me, right?"

Gabriel cut his eyes to me. "Punking you?"

"Yeah, you know, pulling a fast one on me." I pivoted around. "Where's the camera?"

"There is no camera. Nothing high-tech, in fact, at all."

"Of course there is." My voice sounded shrill. "This is just an illusion. A good one, too, but I'd like to get back to the party now."

Gabriel stood silently, sizing me up. His wings fluttered a micron and a wave of impatient energy washed over me.

I met his challenging stare and pushed it back at him. "Tell me this is an illusion."

"This is not an illusion, Amy. This is Eden."

I scanned the beautiful landscape again. I was standing in the original Eden with God's right-hand angel. I bit the inside of my cheek. Apparently, I should have listened to Luc and his prophecy.

Hell and damnation, I hate it when he's right.

"Just in case this is real," I said, deciding to reason with the angel. "I have to tell you, I'm not the best candidate for the job. Lucifer—Satan—and I have a history, in case you didn't know."

Gabriel's sigh was whisper-soft. "Satan claims you're quite good at resisting him."

Okay, there *was* that. "Here's the thing, see. Even though I took an oath to stop the witchcraft stuff, I'm still under contract with him. I sold my soul a long time ago. There's no way I qualify for this job."

Gabriel's wings fluttered again and I realized that was where he held his emotions. Wisps of irritation mixed with his impatient energy, but he also liked to reason. "Perhaps you should view this as redemption for you, too."

Redemption. At that moment, I wasn't sure I wanted redemption if I had to spend eternity with good ol' Gabe staring me down with his cold blue eyes and fluttering his wings at me. "I would really like to go back to the fire station now."

Another ripple of his wings. If possible, his eyes grew even harder. "Help Adam, Amy. Whatever Satan offers you, remember it is a trick. God's depending on you to save humanity. I'm depending on you." He spread his wings and took my hand in a strong grip. "Oh, and by the way, you have three days."

I opened my eyes to see Adam's furrowed brow and concerned eyes hanging over me. "Amy, what happened? Are you all right?"

He helped me to sit up, and though the pounding in my head intensified, so did my relief. I was back in the dark hallway of the fire station. Chuckling with giddiness, I grabbed his arm as a new stab of pain split my skull. I careened to the side.

Adam's grasp tightened on my arm. "Whoa, there."

I rubbed the sore spot on the side of my head. "I fell and knocked myself out."

Adam's gentle fingers probed the spot and images of Eden—the original Eden—flashed through my mind. My stomach tensed. "And then I dreamed I was in The Garden of Eden."

His fingers stopped moving, and he blinked at me. "Let's get an ice bag on that bump."

Twenty minutes later, an EMT at the party declared me healthy, but suggested I go to the hospital. I refused and Adam took me home, offering to stay with me in case I did have a concussion. Totally tired out and needing the feel of his solidness beside me, I agreed.

Inside my apartment, he babied me, bringing me a cup of chamomile tea and helping me remove the flowers from my hair before easing me into bed. He was still wearing his fig-leaf costume and I took a moment to admire it before I closed my eyes. "You look good enough to sin for," I teased. "Sorry I ruined our night together."

His hand caressed my cheek. "Nothing's ruined. We have plenty of time."

Gabriel's voice echoed in my head. *You have three days.*

A tremor of dread ran through me. "What's three days from now?"

"Three days?" He thought for a second. "Halloween."

Of course. The test would come on All Hallow's Eve. My weak spot. I'd been dreading it, along with my fellow Witches Anonymous compatriots, all week. We'd already made a pact to spend the night watching Drew Barrymore films at Marcia's place just to keep our minds occupied and our wands unused.

A tiny noise sounded from the kitchen table. "My beeper," Adam said, hurrying out of the bedroom. He came back with a sheepish look on his face. "It's a code-red fire in the industrial strip outside of town. I have to go, but I can't leave you. You might have a concussion."

"Go," I said, waving him off. "I'll call Keisha to come stay with me. She's only two blocks away."

"You're sure?"

"I'm sure."

He brushed my forehead with his lips and handed me my cell phone. "Don't do anything but rest. I'll be back as soon as I can."

The moment I heard the rumble of his motorcycle outside, hot air rushed over me on the bed like an invisible blanket. Lucifer stood in the shadowed corner.

"Please tell me you didn't start that fire," I said on a moan.

His face was grim. More grim than usual. "I didn't start any fires. Now, tell me what happened."

I was too tired to pretend I didn't know what he was talking about. "Your angel buddy took me to Eden. The original version. He told me I could help Adam with a do-over. Save humanity from sin and all that."

I waited for Luc to laugh. To tell me I hallucinated the whole thing. "Gabriel is a skilled liar."

Closing my eyes, I wished the whole night would go away. Except, maybe, for Adam and his fig leaf. "Gabriel's an angel. A messenger of God. He can't lie."

"He's an angel with free will. Like me. Lying comes quite easy for the right reasons."

I slanted my eyes open a micron to look at him. "You're not an angel anymore. God kicked you out, remember?"

"Because I wanted to be a god. Gabriel's not so different."

Something small and petty burst in my chest. "Right, he wants to be a god, too, since it turned out so well for you."

Lucifer moved toward the bed, his arms crossed over his chest, one finger stroking his goatee. "Did he tell you what would happen if you succeeded in rescuing Adam from temptation this time around?"

"I told you. He said I could save humanity. Wipe out sin."

"Did you agree to do it?"

"It's a no-brainer. Why wouldn't I do it?"

"Everyone on the earth at this moment was born in sin." Luc paced to my closet and back. "What do you think happens to them when you restore Paradise, where sin no longer exists?"

My brain spun in foggy circles as I tried to follow his train of thought. "I don't know. What happens to them?"

"They cease to exist. Poof." He snapped his fingers. "You, little Amy Atwood, will be responsible for eliminating the entire human population. Except Adam, of course."

Everyone? Poof? I swallowed hard. "God wouldn't do that."

Luc held up a finger to make a point. "Did you speak to God?"

"No." I sighed. "Only Gabriel."

"Don't you think God would speak to you directly about something so...damnable?"

Narrowing my eyes at him, I tried to unwind the tangled ball of thoughts making my head hurt again. "I think you're the one trying to trick me." I rubbed my forehead, hoping to ease the pain. "If sin ceases to exist, then so do you."

Lucifer walked into my kitchen and I heard the rustle of a bag. I knew that sound. My mouth watered. He returned and sat on the edge of the bed, holding out three squares of Dove chocolates. "I may be a fallen angel, but I'm still an angel, Amy. If Gabriel succeeds in creating a new Eden using you and Adam, he becomes the god of it, but I will never cease to exist." He unwrapped one of the chocolates and held it in front of my nose. "And I will never stop tempting you to come back to me."

I wanted to ignore the chocolate as much as the Devil's words, but I found myself leaning forward to take both.

"Why?" I said around the smooth chocolate melting in my mouth a moment later. "Why am I so important to you?"

He smiled, but it was full of sadness. "Because, Amy..." One finger touched the bump on the side of my head. The pain vanished as if it had never been. "I love you."

Chapter Eleven:
Confession

Sunday morning, I sat at in my office and stared at the gremlin on my desktop. He smiled at me with jagged teeth and a lolling tongue and I was sure if I looked at myself in the mirror, I'd see his twin. My head seemed to weigh a hundred pounds and my mouth was dry as sin. Every noise, from trucks on the street outside rumbling by to the freezer motors in the ice cream parlor kicking on, made my stomach clench. I'd slept fitfully and woke to the worst non-alcohol-induced hangover of my life.

Keisha bustled into the office around nine, her hair wrapped in a psychedelic-colored cloth that doubled as a sarong. To save my eyesight, I focused on the gremlin instead. Keisha clucked at me. "What's the matter with you? Too much par-*tay* last night? You look like you saw a ghost."

"Close. I saw an angel."

She snorted under her breath. "Oh, sweetie, I know Adam must seem like an angel compared to Lucifer, but he's still just a man."

Or not. I dropped my head into my hands. I wasn't sure Emilia was just a witch either, but was she being possessed by one of Lucifer's minions or Gabriel's? Why would Gabriel want to possess Emilia? Was that even possible? "What do you know about demon possession?"

Keisha's eyebrows had this way of pulling down in the center and rising at the tips when she was aggravated or confused. "Demon? You just said Adam was an angel."

"I think Emilia's possessed."

"She is sleeping with the Devil, in case you've forgotten."

"She stole my favorite pair of Dolce and Gabbanas."

Keisha leaned on the back of the chair across from my desk. "Amy, even I would do anything to get my hands on your D&Gs. That's *ob*session, not *po*session."

"The shoe thing is definitely Emilia being Emilia, but she shows classic symptoms of possession. Her voice, her eyes." Goosebumps rose on my skin. "She wanted to roast my new friend Liddy in my fire pit Thursday night."

Keisha shrugged. "Not to be rude, but blood sacrifices are not out of character for Emilia, even when she's a good witch. She's threatened to disembowel you more than a few times." She winked at me. "Now tell me all about the costume party and Adam the Angel."

"Keisha, Emilia stole my spell book."

Sliding around the chair, she dropped down in it, her eyebrows now up under her bangs. "You let her have the Atomic Sister Slave hex?"

"I didn't let her *have* it. She stole it."

"I thought you kept your spell book in a safe..." Her eyebrows crashed back down. "Wait a minute. Since when is Emilia and her antics more important to you than your sex life? You did spend last night with Adam, right?"

I laid my head down on my desk. "Sort of. Our evening got interrupted."

"Let me guess, Lucifer."

"Try Gabriel."

Her hesitation lasted only a second. "As in *the* Gabriel, Angel of God?"

I made a small nod with my head.

"OMG. You met Gabriel? I can't believe it! Is he fine?"

Lifting my head, I squinted at her and her rainbow head. "*Is he fine?* What kind of question is that? Do you think about anything besides *your* sex life?"

She ignored my jab. "Well, is he?"

I laid my head back down and closed my eyes.

"He's...different."

"Different? What's that supposed to mean? Different how?"

Finding the right adjective to describe the angel was hard. "Weird. Icky. Repulsive."

She gasped. "No!"

"Yes."

Silence fell as Keisha digested my news. "So why was he at the costume party?"

"For me."

"Seriously?" She snorted softly again. "Man, you get all the good ones, you know that?"

"That's the thing," I said, lifting my head. "I'm not sure Gabriel is good."

"Come again?"

I massaged my temples and closed my eyes. "Long story."

Pushing herself out of the chair, Keisha left the office, shaking her head and muttering under her breath. Five minutes later, she returned with two cappuccino milkshakes. She plunked one down in front of me and dropped back into her chair. "Okay, spill it. All of it."

Sitting back in my chair, I sipped the cold milkshake and told her about my visit to Eden and Gabriel's missive. When I was done, she was staring, openmouthed, at my gremlin. "Your life is never dull."

"Tell me about it. I can't decide what's worse—a demon-possessed sister with a slave hex hanging over my head or an angel of God dumping the future of good and evil in my lap."

"This is bad. Really bad." Keisha shook her head in a slow arc. "What are you going to do?"

Taking a long pull on my straw, I swallowed the cool, coffee-flavored ice cream and met her eyes. "It gets worse."

All the muscles in her face tightened in fear. "Worse?"

"Lucifer told me he loves me."

Her eyes lit up, her face muscles relaxed and she smiled. "I knew it. That man is fine, no matter what you say."

"He is not *fine*. He's the Devil."

Chuckling under her breath, she stood and shuffled to the

door. "Don't you just love a happily-ever-after ending?"

"Happily ever after?" I slammed my milkshake down on the desk. "Do you understand what I'm dealing with here? I could snap my fingers and you could die. I could wake up tomorrow and have to clean dog poo off my sister's shoes—*my* shoes—and tell her she's prettier than Gwyneth Paltrow. Come on! My life *sucks*."

Keisha and her psychedelic hair shook with laughter in the doorway. "Love conquers all." She raised her milkshake cup to me and winked again before disappearing.

"That's it?" I yelled at her. "That's the best advice you've got? Love conquers all?" Growling in frustration, I kicked the side of the desk. "Just so you know, I'm hiding your romance novels!"

In the parlor, I heard her humming some silly love song. Gripping the arms of my chair, I spoke to the gremlin, still grinning widemouthedly at me. "Love conquers all. Bet you didn't know that." I gave a derisive grunt under my breath and rocked the chair back and forth with manic speed, staring at the ugly, unlovable talisman. "If that's true, Gremmie, you and I both are in big, big trouble."

Chapter Twelve:
Redemption

Eight p.m. All Hallow's Eve... Desperate, I stood in front of the Witches Anonymous group asking for their advice since Keisha's had been so lacking. The tick of the clock on the wall made my pulse race—I didn't know in what form temptation would appear or what I would do when it did. All I knew was I was running out of time.

"If I don't keep Adam from giving into temptation, he loses his chance to redeem himself," I told the witches. "If I do keep him from sinning, everyone ceases to exist. Poof." I used Lucifer's finger snap to emphasize my point. "Gone. Except Adam. And me."

"That is so cooool," Liddy said from the front row. Her eyes were twice their normal size, framed by her long curls.

"On top of that, I think my sister is possessed by something. Not Lucifer, but something evil nevertheless. I looked up demon possession on the Internet and she definitely shows symptoms. Anyone know a good exorcist?"

Liddy raised her hand in the air like a student trying to get the teacher's attention. "There's a priest at Immaculate Conception who does them."

"They say he's really good," a gal in the back piped up. "And he's cute too."

Behind Liddy, Marcia exchanged an eye roll with the woman next to her. "That's quite a dilemma, Amy. Good luck with that." She stood, rubbing her hands in anticipation as she beamed at the group. "Who's ready for our Drew marathon?

Everybody to my house!"

A handful of women rose from their chairs, grabbed their coats and started for the door.

"But, what should I do about Adam?" I raised my voice above the noise of scraping chairs. "Don't you have any suggestions for that?"

Liddy, still seated, raised her hand again, but before I could call on her, commotion erupted in the back.

The door swung open with a bang and Emilia blocked the exit. "I have a suggestion," my Sister Dearest said. She was dressed in a black velvet gown, cape, and matching hat. Her eyes were solid black. *Supernatural,* here we come. "Redeem yourself and go to heaven so I can be rid of you."

Silence bloomed in the room as every head turned to look at me. Liddy dropped her hand and her jaw. At the same time, her hair tensed.

Emilia was scary on normal day. Throw in demon possession and she was downright terrifying. Her angry energy poured and crashed in waves through the room, making the chairs spin.

"Good to see you, too, sis," I said, masking the groan in my head. "What brings you here tonight? Don't you have a house to haunt or a zombie to raise from the dead?"

"He kicked me out," she snarled from between red-stained lips. I prayed the color came from Lancôme.

The women closest to Emilia took several steps back, their gazes now ping-ponging between us. "He kicked everybody out. Said he doesn't want any witch but you."

I didn't have to ask who *he* was. While I'd been sincerely trying to ditch Luc for a couple of weeks now, the idea that he was pining for me to such a degree made me smile inside. "I made it very clear to Lucifer that I wasn't going back to my old ways, Emilia. You know that."

She took a step forward, her cape flowing around her, and the women moved backward in unison. "The only way he'll get over you is if you're gone." Her voice rang with that eerie baritone echo. "Either redeem the world with Adam, or I'll resort to desperate measures."

It was obvious she hadn't found the Atomic Sister Slave spell yet, or desperate measures wouldn't be necessary. A spark of hope bloomed in my chest. There was still time to steal my spell book back. Unless, of course, she killed me in the next few minutes.

"If she redeems the world from sin," Liddy said, her face a mirror of complex thought. "You'll cease to exist, too. You do understand that, right?"

Emilia's black eyes narrowed at the ex-Wiccan. "I'm a servant to the Devil. My soul is guaranteed to survive."

Liddy chewed a cuticle and looked at me. A tiny bolt of energy shot from her finger and ricocheted into her hair. "Is that true? What about *our* souls? Will they cease to exist like our bodies?"

The technicalities were beyond my comprehension. "I don't know for sure, but my guess is, if everyone born in sin ceases to exist, it doesn't mean they die, it means they cease to exist, souls and all."

Marcia pushed her way through the group of women, coming to a stop in front of me. "You are really something." She shook her head in disbelief. "You have to be the center of attention at every meeting, don't you, Amy?"

In the middle of my demonic-sister showdown and the clock tick-tocking away on the wall behind me, our lovely WA president wanted to pick a fight. "I'm dealing with your future here, Marcia, as well as everyone else's. If I screw this up, you all pay the price."

"There'd be no pain," Liddy said in a dreamy voice. Her hand dropped back into her lap, but her hair still stood at attention. "No accidents, no sadness, no lonely nights waiting for the phone to ring. Sounds wonderful."

Having given it a lot of thought, I had to add, "But all of the things people have created in this world will also disappear, Liddy. There'll be no Beethoven's 5th or Springsteen's 'Born to Run'. No Emily Dickinson or Edgar Allen Poe. No Egyptian pyramids or Taj Mahal. No Orlando Bloom." I paused to emphasize my next sentence. "No chocolate."

Several of the women sucked in their breath. "No chocolate?" one of them echoed.

I nodded, my taste buds crying too.

Marcia turned on her and the others. "Are you listening to her? She's Satan's ex-girlfriend? Her sister's possessed? She's dating Adam, the original man? You can't possibly believe this insane story."

"Oh, it's not insane," Emilia said. Her red lips tilted in a ruthless smile. "It's absolutely true. While Amy has always believed the world revolves around her, this time, it actually does."

"Look," I said to all of them. "I'm not making this up. Everything I've told you is true and if I don't figure out what to do, we're all in trouble."

Emilia reached out and slammed the door shut. A new and powerful wave of energy zoomed around the room. "Too late. You and your group of freaky friends are already in trouble."

A creepy, crawly feeling raced up the back of my neck. "What are you doing, Em?"

She snapped her fingers. "Poof."

With a wave of her hand, she raised a protective bubble around herself. I saw her lips move in a silent chant through her wicked smile. The next moment, I smelled smoke.

"Emilia." The voice in my head was screaming to get everyone out. "Stop it. Whatever you're doing, don't take it out on the others. It's me you're mad at."

Outside the room, a fire alarm came to life. "So fight me," she taunted. "And save them."

Brushing by her bubble of protection, I grasped the doorknob and twisted it. Locked. Conveying calm I didn't feel, I herded the women to the far corner. "She's just trying to scare us," I told them, trying to sound believable. "Stick together, and stay down on the floor. I'll take care of her."

Liddy grabbed my arm. White-hot electricity zinged over my skin. "She's possessed, Amy. How are you going to handle her without using any spells or enchantments?"

Good question. Gray smoke seeped under the door. Taking off my jacket, I ran to the door and jammed it in the crack at the bottom. Then I looked around for a fire extinguisher. Nada. No extinguisher.

Break a window, I thought, and jump.

Nope, no windows either.

She could have wiped us out with one flick of her hand. Torturing us—me—was more fun. As smoke began seeping right through the walls, I returned to my WA compatriots and demonstrated what I wanted them to do. "Cover your mouths with your shirts. Breathe through the fabric."

A few exchanged worried looks. Taking out my cell phone, I called Adam. He answered, out of breath. Sirens blared in the background. "Can't talk now, Amy. There's a fire downtown in the Golden Building."

"I know," I shouted over the background noise. "I'm in the building with my group. We were having our meeting and all of sudden a fire broke out."

His concern touched me through the night air. "Damn. How bad is it?"

"Bad." My eyes watered from the smoke and I used my shirt to wipe the tears off my cheeks. "We can't get out of the room. We're locked in."

"Locked in? How did that happen?"

"Uh, I don't know." I shot a look at Emilia. Her red lips moved in her ghost-white face. "I guess the doorknob got jammed somehow."

"Stay as close to the floor as you can. I'm only two blocks away. I'll be right there."

Something in me refused to lie on the floor with the others and wait. This time, I had to do the rescuing. After all, Emilia was *my* sister, possessed or not.

Handing my phone to Liddy, I gathered up momentum and charged Em's bubble. Upon impact, I bounced back like a rubber ball, landing hard on my butt. "Ouch," I yelped, rolling ass-over-broomstick backwards.

She clapped her hands in mock applause. "Oh, that was funny. Do it again!"

Like Liddy said, without my powers, I couldn't hope to stop her. The fear in my stomach turned to self-righteous conviction. In my mind, the words of a spell formed. I didn't try to stop them.

Before the first line of the spell could leave my lips, however, Gabriel appeared in the bubble behind Emilia. She didn't seem to notice, she was so focused on doing me in.

Satan appears in many forms, his cool, firm voice chided me.

Emilia was Satan, I'd give him that, but she wasn't *the* Satan. Still, if this was the test, using my witchcraft would kill Adam's chance at redemption. I racked my brain for another way.

My eyes continued to pour tears and my throat felt like it was stuffed with Brillo pads. "You set the other fires, didn't you?" I yelled at her. Distraction had worked on her before.

She pointed her pale, well-manicured index finger at me. "You slept with Lucifer even after you told me it was over between the two of you."

The wail of fire engine sirens outside overrode the smoke detector's blaring ring. Another minute and I'd have help. "Technically, he showed up in my bed, but nothing happened. I was sleeping." I coughed and croaked out the rest. "I just woke up and he was there."

Reasoning with Emilia was like reasoning with Paris Hilton. "You lured him there," she yelled at me. "I know it's your fault."

Coughing hard again, I pulled my shirt over my mouth to filter some of the smoke before I continued. "Emilia, if you kill my body, my soul will still spend eternity with Lucifer. Neither one of us wants that."

Gabriel, watching the exchange, nodded his head, an almost-smile on his lips. Suddenly, I was sure he was behind my sister's over-the-top craziness.

Emilia's forehead creased as if my logic rang true to her. "I never thought of that."

At that moment, an axe hit the door from the outside, wood splintering in every direction. Emilia screamed, Gabriel rippled his wings and I dropped to my knees in relief. Adam to the rescue. My hero.

The moment he came through the door in full protective gear, Emilia waved her hands and I heard the sharp crack of wood splintering. A ceiling beam overhead wobbled. "No," I yelled, powerless to stop it from falling.

Adam's gaze locked on mine a second before the beam hit him, knocking him to the ground. His ax slammed into the floor, and his helmet skidded behind a chair. The oxygen mask on his face slipped sideways.

Scrambling on hands and knees, I reached for him. "Adam." He was out cold. I shook him hard. "Adam!"

Flames licked the now-open doorway. Pushing at the heavy beam, I tried to free him. I yelled at the women behind me to help. Liddy and several others broke from the group.

Dodging the flames and coughing our lungs up, we heaved the heavy beam off Adam and pulled him away from the door.

Unfortunately, that was our only way out. A wall of fire leapt from floor to ceiling, blocking our escape as completely as the locked door had done. No other firefighter appeared.

I had no choice. I could not let Adam and the WA women die because of my jealous sister, redemption or no redemption.

Time running out, I cradled Adam's head in my lap, restoring the ring of the oxygen mask over his mouth and nose. The floor, ceiling and walls were cracking and popping in the blistering heat.

"I'm sorry," I said in his ear over the roar of noise. "I can't save humanity or change the balance of good and evil. The only thing I can do, at this moment, is save you."

Laying his head back down on the floor, I rose, coughing, and faced Emilia in her bubble. Calling all my particles into the center of my body, I raised a hand and spoke. "Flames extinguish, stop this game..."

Emilia's frown deepened. Gabriel extended his wings, his face turned to stone.

Ignoring both of them, I raised my voice. "Free Adam from all blame, and return the deceptive angel of God..."

Before I could complete the spell, Gabriel flew at me. The sight of him, wings fully extended and a look of utter hate on his face, made me jump back. I tried to duck, but he was too fast. He picked me up by the neck with one hand and slammed me against the wall. Heat seared through my jacket and into to my skin. I smelled my hair burning.

His grip was so tight on my neck, I couldn't swallow. His

eyes, a golden brown a moment before, now burned a deep red. There was no air in my lungs, but I forced the words to my lips, whispering, "...back to the realm from whence he came."

Gabriel disappeared in a flash of white light. I fell to the floor in a heap and lay there, every bone in my body mush. The room was deathly quiet.

No smoke. No flames. Just blessed peace.

And then, out of nowhere, a lone person began to clap.

I sucked fresh air into my lungs. Raising my head an inch, I saw Lucifer sitting on the refreshment table. He smiled at me, his hands continuing to clap at my performance. Emilia had disappeared. With Gabriel? I wasn't sure. The fire was out. The members of Witches Anonymous sat on the floor hugging each other, still stunned by their recent brush with death, a demented angel, and my ruthless, possessed sister.

"Is it over?" I asked Luc, my voice raw.

He slid off the table and helped me into a sitting position. "It's over."

Using his fingers, he touched my neck at the base of my throat. A sensation like ice cream running over my vocal chords repaired the damage done by the smoke. "For now," he added.

For now? Forcing the implications of that statement to the back of my mind, I pulled away from him and crawled over to Adam. He wasn't breathing and I couldn't find his pulse. His heart had stopped. "Liddy," I yelled, waving her over. "Come here."

Positioning her hands over Adam's heart, I said to her, "Think of your family, Liddy, and the rotten things they've done to you. They're just like my sister. They push all your buttons and turn you into a bad person, no matter how hard you try to be good."

Liddy's brows drew together and electricity crackled in the air. Sparks jumped in her hair and ran down both arms to her fingers. Adam's body jerked. When I touched his neck to feel for a pulse, he blinked his eyes open.

"What happened?" he asked through the oxygen mask.

Removing it from his face, I sighed, feeling like a total loser, but happy that Adam was okay. "I blew it. I used my powers to stop the fire instead of resisting temptation."

He blinked again and frowned. "Your powers?"

"I'm a witch, Adam. And not a good one. I work for Lucifer. Luc." I pointed with my thumb over my shoulder at the Devil. "I wanted to be a good person, a normal person, really I did. That's why I came to these meetings, Witches Anonymous. I even swore an oath not to use my powers, but I blew it tonight. I broke my oath. I cast a spell."

"You're a Devil-worshipping witch and you swore an oath to God?"

"To myself."

"Oh."

"She saved your life and ours," Liddy said, smoothing back her hair. She stood and brushed dirt off her pants, examined her calm fingers. "If that's not good, I don't know what is."

Lucifer moved beside me and stared down at Adam. "She also saved your chance at redemption."

Adam glared up at him. "You again?"

"The proper response would be, 'thank you, Amy'." Lucifer crouched over Adam. "You see, my dear boy, in her spell, Amy protected you. You still have your chance at redemption. She sent Gabriel back to heaven, so you're on your own now, though. The future is up to you."

"It is?" Adam and I said in unison.

A cacophony of noise erupted behind us as several firefighters came busting in through the charred door. "Captain? Are you all right?"

Adam sat up, rubbed a hand over his face and through his soot-filled hair. "What took you guys so long?"

"It was weird, Cap," a beefy guy answered. "There was like Plexiglas or something across the threshold out there. After you went in, none of us could get through it. We kept bouncing off."

I exchanged a knowing look with Adam and realized Lucifer had disappeared. The pockets of my jean jacket suddenly felt like I had a couple of watermelons in them. A pleasant yellow glow radiated from both sides. Reaching inside, one hand found foil-wrapped squares, the other touched the edges of a small book. I pulled the book out enough to see the worn black cover.

My spell book.

Adam rose to his feet and motioned at the others. "Get these ladies out of here."

"Right away, Cap."

As my fellow WA members filed out, I shoved the spell book back in my pocket and stood with Adam, helping support him. Some of the gals, like Liddy, embraced me in a hug. A few patted my arm. Marcia stopped beside me, looked down at the floor, and sighed. "I guess I owe you an apology. I thought you were—" she hesitated, looking for the right word, "—in serious need of a psychiatrist."

We were even then, since I thought she was in serious need of Valium. "No hard feelings."

She lifted her gaze to mine. "That other guy who was here?"

"Yeah?"

"Was that..." She blushed. "Was that really Satan?"

"Yes, Marcia, that was him. He prefers to be called Luc."

"Luc, right. Do you think he might, you know, speak to our group sometime?"

Another woman seduced by a wicked man in faded Levi's. "I'll ask next time I run into him."

She giggled all the way out of the room.

"Amy." Adam took his arm from around my shoulders. "I'm not sure I understand what happened here."

"The short version?" Slipping my hand into his, I pulled him toward the door, wanting to get the heck out of there and go home. I needed a shower, ice cream and a full night of sleep. "I stopped my evil sister from killing innocent people. I vanquished an angel, who wanted to be a god, back to heaven. And I improved my status in the Witches Anonymous group significantly. After tonight, I'll be able to unseat Marcia as president next month when we have elections."

"You're sticking with Witches Anonymous even though you broke your oath?"

I shrugged one shoulder. "Everyone falls off the wagon once in awhile. Besides, even though I did use my supernatural powers tonight, I did it for good. I think I'm getting the hang of being human."

"What about, you know, Lucifer?"

I felt the weight of Dove chocolates and my spell book in my jacket pockets. "I'm sure he'll be around, but I think I can handle him. Right now, he very much wants to stay on my good side."

Adam's lips quirked. "And the long version about tonight?"

"Oh, that." Squeezing his arm, I hoped he'd understand my philosophical rant. "You see, free will begets self-responsibility. You can't force someone else to be responsible for your decisions, even if the destiny of humanity rests on your shoulders." I sensed he understood what I was getting at, so I took a breath and plunged on. "You take the credit and the blame, one-hundred percent, for your choices. No passing the buck. Or the forbidden fruit, for that matter. Eve sinned and so did you. You can't blame her for tempting you to eat the apple or ask me to save you from eating it again."

A chuckle resounded low and soft and sexy in his throat. "Sounds like you have a lot of ideas on the subject. I think I'd like to hear more."

Lust crackled in the air between us. I raised one eyebrow. "How much time do you have?"

He pulled me close and brushed his lips over mine. My heart did a little dip and soft warmth spread through my chest. "Possibly eternity, but at least all night."

Tendrils of anticipation ran up my spine. "Ice cream on the rooftop?"

His fingers touched the back of my neck. "Sin City Chocolate?"

My legs went weak. "Of course."

What else would a wicked witch serve an innocent man?

About the Author

To learn more about Misty Evans, please visit www.readmistyevans.com. Send an email to Misty at misty@readmistyevans.com or join her Yahoo! group to join in the fun with other readers as well as Misty!

http://groups.yahoo.com/group/MistyEvansSuspense.

Look for these titles by
Misty Evans

Now Available:

Super Agent Series
Operation Sheba (Book 1)
I'd Rather Be In Paris (Book 2)

LaVergne, TN USA
29 November 2009
165467LV00005B/67/P